CHRIS HEFFERNAN

DELIRIA

ODYSSEY
BOOKS

Published by Odyssey Books in 2015
ISBN 978-1-922200-24-2

www.odysseybooks.com.au

A Cataloguing-in-Publication entry is available from the National Library of Australia

ISBN: 978-1-922200-24-2 (pbk)
ISBN: 978-1-922200-25-9 (ebook)

Cover design by Elijah Toten
Cover photo by iStock

DELIRIA

Bellevue Heights, Kev and Doug

All right, let's begin. Let's begin with the city of Adelaide. Festival City, cosmopolitan yet *bijou*. Twenty-minute city. City of Churches, City of Restaurants. Oh planned city, Vision of Light. But I'm sorry. It's not exactly as the city fathers' press kit would have you think.

Adelaide is composed of suburbs with a thumbnail CBD. You have suburbs where everyone is seventy years old. Suburbs where everyone is on the dole. Suburbs where everyone has a dismantled car, like an exploded assembly diagram, on the front lawn. Suburbs where guys go out on the weekend and shoot the heads off rabbits. Greek suburbs, Italian suburbs, Pommy suburbs. Suburbs of cheap post-war housing. Suburbs where the houses look like they're built from a kit, up on stilts. Suburbs where the kids hang around shopping malls; suburbs where they spend their leisure hours in supervised study.

On the hill above Flinders University is a suburb named Bellevue Heights, where I am minding a house found through the student accommodation service for thirty dollars a week. I met the owners only once: English migrants who had sold up their child-size dwelling in a northern industrial city, and who had since then been living in the middle of a Hans Heysen painting. Out through the picture window, the back yard slopes down to a genuine creek, a million years old, with real erosion, revealing many strata of clay and sandstone. The recent, human addition is a little wooden bridge. The back yard is about half an acre. In any other city in the world, they'd have to be rich to live like this. The wife's framed retirement certificate on the lounge room wall, however, confessed her to be a former telephone operator for a fertiliser company. The husband had also occupied a clerical position. Voicing concern over the contents of their 'liquor' cabinet, they gazed searchingly up at me. Both of them were about five feet tall: the winning combo of shitty genes and post-war nutrition. In the cabinet was a bottle of Blue Nun, about nine years old, its label partly eaten by mice, and a bottle of strawberry liqueur, encrusted with evaporated sugar solution. I assured them I'd behave responsibly. In fact, that's what I said: 'I assure you I'll behave responsibly.' How impressed they were! What vowels! What enunciation! They had escaped from class-ridden England, and come to a country where the classless society is bragged about in badly written newspapers, but they were still impressed by things like vowels and consonants. Chirpingly they pronounced my suitability.

I don't mean I'm upper-middle class or anything in the English sense, God no. It's just that I've re-invented my voice, adopting what linguists term 'educated Australian' as opposed to broad Aussie. Why, it might be asked? Why am I not content to speak in the accent of my own family? Well, after all, I've invented a new voice twice. I speak French and Thai. I've just been given the Banque du Sud-Pacifique Prize for French, presented by the French cultural attaché. There's another reason why I don't speak broad Aussie. It is the accent of the bullies in the school playground, of sports heroes with limited intellect, of petrolheads.

I'm doing French honours, having given away my military aspirations after a preliminary interview. I had considered myself as a potential soldier-poet, a kind of Guillaume d'Aquitaine of the late twentieth century. It had not occurred to me that Guillaume, my model, my namesake, and a complete military bungler, got all his men killed outside Jerusalem some time in the twelfth century. Still, the army needs all sorts of people, and there might well have been a place for me. *We definitely need people who can speak Indonesian.* What about people who can speak twelfth-century Provençal? But the better I got at Indonesian, the less I respected the Indonesians. How could a civilisation get by without finite verbs? I suffer from that learner's enigma: I enjoy learning languages, but I don't enjoy being able to speak them and read them when the native speakers' minds say nothing to me. Out went the pages of crap Indonesian poetry. In came the pages of Guillaume d'Aquitaine, Jaufre Rudel and Sunthorn Phu. They are splayed on the kitchen table, with my huge dictionaries, my vocabulary books and my Thai videos. They speak to me.

Having acquired the house from the generous industrial northerners, I don't really want to share it with the relics of their taste: their bad art and their insulting decorations. For instance, looking down from the dining room wall is the portrait of an idealised four-year-old of indeterminate gender, globular tears collecting on the lower eyelids. Accompanying this is a science-fiction poster in which a growling, magnificently breasted woman, hips blended into the haunches of a tiger, would seem to be at my disposal sexually. Plaster sheep and shepherdesses form the salt and pepper collection. On top of the fridge, in a goldfish bowl, is a collection of matchbooks and soap briquettes from American hotels. So the science-fiction poster is taken down, leaving its white shadow on the wall. My classical CDs replace the soft-pop party collection. The World War Two fighter-aircraft pictures? They can stay. I quite like Spitfires and Messerschmitts. In the toilet, however, I discover a series of framed cartoons depicting unlikely accidents happening to women's breasts. Into the spare room they go. There's an ashtray in the form of a set of buttocks. Spare room. Anything else? Well, swinging from a nail on the back of the kitchen door, which opens onto a Federation slate balcony, is a mag wheels calendar, boasting twelve girls reclining over twelve sets of mag wheels. That's the first thing a woman thinks when she sees a set of mag wheels, isn't it? How she would go about reclining over them. Do people actually like this stuff? Spare room.

Shirted and out the front door, after ladling out the dried Frusties for the sumo-cat, I empty a kilogram of junk mail from the letterbox, which takes the format of a miniature house on a length of hairpin-bent upright chain, welded stiff. The letterbox is almost immediately topped up with crash-repair and water-bed-emporium brochures by an old bloke wheeling a bicycle. Sole user of the footpath other than him, I pass through the suburb of Bellevue, past the inscrutable curtained windows, closed doors and abandoned front lawns, and take a succession of buses to another suburb, Glenelg, where my father and brother still live.

The details of the suburb are more noticeable to me because of my absence. Take these three-bedroomed, single-standing houses. They all possess well-behaved front lawns, and concrete driveways containing two cars, under each of which is placed a rectangular aluminium drip tray. Some driveways show imaginative variation: the central divide may be filled with gravel, red bark or rounded beach stones. The front fences are invariably composed of three or four courses of brickwork backed by a row of shrubs. The footpaths have nature strips, brushed and groomed, barbered with lawnmowers on Sundays, with trees planted at measured distances. The asphalt of the original footpaths has been replaced by pretty, interlocking pink bricks. They're very user-friendly footpaths. No one uses them.

The houses are all identical in the most important aspect, that of size. They are vast. In France they would be extravagant; in Thailand the driveways would be clogged with imported European cars. But here it's just ordinary. Everyone lives like this; the generous space in which to flower just comes in the package of being Australian. Sadly, this great wealth isn't recognised; the space embarrasses us. Everyone's been awarded this wonderful prize of a big house on a quarter-acre block without having the first idea of what to do with it. The front yard intimidates. No one wants to be seen alone there; they want to stay inside. The only reason they occupy the front yard is to get from the front door to their personal vehicle and drive out. When someone does occupy the front yard, it's often a sign that something's wrong: the little girl playing with dandelions that have sprung up in the lawn, who hasn't yet learned that she shouldn't be there; the man in the middle stages of Alzheimer's disease clutching the front fence, welcoming the junk-mail delivery. See this guy up ahead, for example, leaning through the bars of his own gate, the uncombed white hair a definite warning sign.

Doug, on the other hand, is the only bloke I've ever seen who regularly appears in the front yard without being insane. See him lug that mower across the lawn on a Sunday morning; see him eagerly joining the rituals of milk and newspaper collection. He loves that front yard; he can't stand that null space. He's always transplanting bulbs, or digging a hole for a fishpond, or pouring boiling water down a trapdoor spider's nest. Armed with a cardboard carton and a gardening fork, a folded-up newspaper under his knees, he spears weeds and shakes the dirt off the taproot. While these days it's an exceptional human being whose interests, fully laid out, can occupy even a two-room apartment, Doug's interest *is* space, or more specifically land. It was for him that the quarter-acre block was drawn up, in those heady days of the nineteenth century when it was supposed that we would all grow our own vegetables. The quarter-acre was to have been lovingly arranged into plots of asparagus, maize, climbing beans and parsnips, and we were supposed to have the time to tend them, as well as a few chooks and a cow.

Doug, my dad (I've never met anyone else called Douglas: his name, like the word *chooks*, has left the language poorer by its absence), is seventy. On his retirement and Mum's death, which were almost simultaneous, he turned up the whole back lawn, hammered tomato stakes into the ground, and powdered the resulting tomato plants with dust to kill mites and the notorious red spider. Climbing beans sprang up the trellis, tendrils grasped. What to do with all that space? he seemed to ask. So now our backyard is atypical but exemplary. No wasted space here: all is used.

I reach our front fence: three courses of brickwork backed by a row of unidentified shrubs. Like all suburban fences, it is entirely symbolic, a request for security rather than actual protection. A piece of string would as effectively serve to keep out the bad guys. We depend on people being honest and on the cops being effective. It's crazy, I agree. TVs, video cameras, Gameboys, music systems and assorted high-value electronic gadgets continually walk out the window when people are at church, but no one takes the logical step of erecting a four-metre brick wall with broken beer bottles cemented to the top. Wouldn't be Australian, would it?

The sunlight has shrunk my pupils. Australian sunlight: after walking inside, there's always that twenty seconds of adjustment to the interior gloom. I can just make out a metre-high stack of old newspapers against a chest of drawers in the hallway. At the moment of recognition, the whole edifice begins a smooth and irreversible acceleration sideways.

'That you, Will?'

I step over the thatch of world news going back years to discover Doug, curved over the bathroom sink, peeling off a layer of dried shaving soap. The yellow razor jerks and stops, then gets up the courage for another tiny dash. These bumps and jerks are painfully reiterated. At his age, it's like ripping masking tape off your face. The stroke doesn't help, either. Oh, did I neglect to mention he's had a stroke? When I said there was nothing wrong with him, I meant relative to the man leaning through the bars of the gate. Now Doug's head rotates and the face appears, the flesh slopping to one side.

'Dad.'

He consults the mirror and continues shaving. Under the white singlet lies the ruin of his musculature, everything hanging in folds, a drapery.

'I seem to have had a bit of an accident with the newspapers.'

'What's that?'

'The papers.'

'What papers?'

'The papers. The big … by the door.' The razor stops. The

carved face and cannonball skull are directed at me again. 'Do you know what you're talking about?' he says.

I notice a fateful addition to the bathroom wall: a safety rail. Its staunch chrome hugs the wall. I bet he never uses it.

'I see the OT's been around.'

'I got to show you these great tomatoes.'

'Great. So did you get any red spider?'

'Took care of them okay.'

The valiant Doug, lying in wait for his red spiders, toting a watering can full of Dieldrin, leaves only the burst globes of their bodies as his wrath rains down upon them.

'Actually, I've noticed some aphids on the rose bushes up at Bellevue. I wonder if you could recommend …?'

'*Aphis*?'

'Of course. The Latin plural.'

'Aphis,' he repeats, with a sibilance on that final 's'.

Shaving done, the disposable razor clatters into the sink, throwing a gob of lather and whiskers onto the mirror. A grin of pain wraps Doug's lips around his face. He steadies himself on the sink, widening the fissure between the sink and the wall until it is supported entirely by its plumbing.

'Yeah, they're all clustered around the base of the thing … what's it called?'

'The bole.'

'They're all clustered around the bole.'

He shudders out of the bathroom. The maker's label and interior seams beneath his chin confirm that he's got his singlet on inside out and back to front. A John Wayne cowboy walk commences, as if his leg joints were fused.

On the floor, the cat is clawing apart the newsprint.

'What's all these papers?' It is difficult to convey the exact tone of Doug's bewilderment. Let's just note that for Doug, 'papers' forms a true rhyme with 'aphis'. He's lost his hard 's'; now everything has that kettle-like sibilance.

'Let's get rid of them, shall we? Let's give them to Meals on Wheels or something.'

I begin stacking the newspapers on the front verandah. The dust, long accumulated, is released, squirting with liquid density. The no. 2 shirt is soon striped with it. Meanwhile Doug is dressing, requiring no assistance, he claims.

Outside Kev's door are the polished boots of the Army Reserve. My practical brother, 'doing something for himself'. On his wall, the sister of the Bellevue owners' science-fiction poster girl lies naked on a hillside, smiling in invitation at a hugely endowed stamping unicorn. Kev is centred in a bean bag focused on a TV game show. When he stands up, my eyes just meet his chin. He's definitely from Doug's side of the family. We shake hands powerfully, the muscles in his forearms almost bucking, as in a Michelangelo cartoon.

'What you been doing?' Kev opens.

'Nothing much. Studying.'

A conversation ensues, average length of utterance about two words. If I'm stuck, I can always ask him about his car. Kev is not monosyllabic, oh no. He speaks a fluent industrial pidgin, consisting largely of concrete nouns. He can speak to me for five minutes about his car, while I'm nodding and trying to imagine what all these car parts are. Modified exhausts. Ceramic headers. Fats. Injectors. Cams. Nitrous. Fuel-system upgrades. Computer-enhanced RAM air intake. Eventually I'll ask some question like, 'What does a carburettor actually *do*?'

'Are you getting any work?' I ask. Kev is a subcontractor for building sites.

'Couple of new subdivisions. Golden Grove. Noarlunga.'

'Quite a drive from here.'

'I'm outta here at six.'

'What time you get back?' I'm slipping into the grammar of rural Australian.

'Seven. Fuck of a long way to Golden Grove.'

Kev's conversation is sturdy, conceptually solid, like a piece of four-by-two. The downside is that our conversations die after seven exchanges, unless we're shooting rabbits or stripping down his crossbow. Here we go again:

'Go on any camps?'

'Yeah. Woodside.'

'How was it?'

'Good.'

I'm grateful for the TV show: it fills the gaps. What did people fill the gaps with before TV?

'Immaculate fete's on tomorrow,' I open.

'Yeah.'

There is no further attempt, by either of us, to build a conversation around a convent school fete. On the TV, someone is screaming. He has won a set of garden furniture.

'How's Doug?'

'On the way out.'

Doug reappears in the kitchen. After a struggle of perhaps fifteen minutes, he is now partially dressed in pyjama bottoms and dressing gown. Having thus readied himself for a full day's retirement, he is muttering a series of numbers. 'Two five four … six eight?'

'Two five four six eight five two,' shouts Kev.

'Two five four six eight five two,' repeats Doug.

'What's that?' I ask, not conversation building.

'Number of the bookie.'

'Jesus.'

We hear Doug's hesitant, too-loud phone voice. 'Silver Streak, two dollars fifty to win? Our Jack, four dollars fifty, win and place? Beg your pardon? Oh, I thought this was the …'

Immaculate

Immaculate College: bun-oven of teen pregnancy and pregnant nuns, fountain of sacked physical education instructors, bounteous supplier of Catholic centrefolds. The institution slides past the window of the bus, the handsome stone walls topped with ornamental yet purposeful spikes. On the wall is sprayed, in large white capitals, a girl's name and her preferred sexual act. Yes, it is a convent school.

Quite a lot going on, for Adelaide: the pink-stoned footpath is for once not bare, but directs a current of humans, who proceed obediently through the college gates. It's a measure of the smallness of this town, or should I say capital city, that a minor profit-raising activity at a Catholic school—with a few stalls, a dozen minibikes, a chocolate wheel, a barbecue, a lucky dip, a fortune-telling tent and a shooting gallery—attracts hundreds of people. They're all crammed onto the basketball court in a density which recalls a Bangkok market. We see the long trestle tables staffed by mum-and-dad volunteers, with leather sporrans of change sitting on the slopes of their bellies. Everything for sale is donated by parents of the convent girls, and like most things that people donate, it's valueless. What would intelligent people give to a convent fete? Old lawnmowers, soup ladles, used books. But sometimes, what's valueless to them is of value to me. I'm talking about English Classics. To get to these commodities, I have to shoulder my way through a bunch of students who are actually bargaining over the price of an aluminium colander. I witness triumph and despair at the chocolate wheel, as a fully grown man is handed a teddy bear. I have to get past the flipping slabs of potato and the seared meat of the chops and sausages stall, and, final hazard, I dodge a huge spider of flame after a generous lollop of methylated spirits has landed in the centre of a barbecue. After these trials, I reach my goal: the bookstall. It has already been plundered: all that's left is a few bales of romances and a Graham Greene, which I already have. My goal recedes.

One other person is at the bookstall, half-recognised from behind. I get an impression of busy female movement, seen somewhere before. Yes, unless I'm about to make a fairly mild social error, this is Deliria. She used to play with Kev.

'Sorry, is that Deliria?'

The woman turns around. 'William. Haven't seen you in ages.'

This is where I reach the limits of language, alarmingly quickly. It's just not possible to describe the physical shock occasioned by Deliria's beauty. You fall back on crap like, 'Into the room walked the most beautiful girl he had ever seen'—which is true enough, but it doesn't *tell* you anything, it doesn't *say* anything. Why don't I just state her height: 178 cm. The top of my head is about level with her nose.

We're making conversation in front of the pillaged bookstall. She, in fact, is the pillager: her shoulder bag contains kilograms of Dickens, Trollope, Jane Austen, Fielding, Smollett and Swift. I wish I'd come an hour earlier.

'So, the bard of Glenelg meets the maid of Immaculate,' she continues. Like her utterance, which is jaunty, thought-up and a bit effortful, she is fantastically overdressed for a school fete. The effect is one of vintage clothing, the nineteen-twenties. A scarf, wound twice around her neck, touches the asphalt of the basketball court on both sides. I can't even name the material: it's shiny and has several types of thread.

Now I suppose I should come up with one of those What-Do-You-Say-After-You-Say-Hello bits of dialogue. Directing the conversation the way you want it to go without forcing yourself on the other person. Being assertive without being domineering. Using body language, human transactional analysis, human management skills; communicating what you want to communicate and not what you don't want to communicate. I'm Okay, You're Okay, Winning Friends, Influencing People. But why bother? When she was twelve years old, I saved her life from a swarm of bees.

'How's your mum and dad?' I start.

'Mum's ironing and listening to the early Baroque. Dad's commuting on the tram, frittering away his existence.'

'Adult life. The World. Work.'

'How's the faithful Kev?'

'Muscular. Inarticulate.'

'Doug?'

'Getting worse and worse.'

'Old age is a terrible thing.' Deliria is eighteen. She is also the possessor of that most valuable accessory: youngish parents. Doug, when he can remember anything, can clearly remember the Great Depression. Louise, Deliria's mum, can barely remember the Beatles. Gary, her dad, was a lieutenant in Vietnam: last year he strongly advised me against the army.

We talk about pranks, to which she is addicted. When she gets going, her pranks have this over-the-topness; they are all just that little bit further than I would be prepared to go. Take this, for instance: a boy kept pulling her hair on the bus. Next day, she poured over his head an entire milk-cartonful of blood.

I can't top this. Instead, I offer that I once rode a bike through the nun's courtyard here, at midnight, naked. This is simply not true, or rather, it's a re-invention of the truth, combining two separate incidents. I'm trying to hint at myself as a sexual object. It doesn't work. She is amused, but the concept of my nakedness in the Immaculate courtyard at midnight provokes not arousal, but a subversive delight, as if I'd mentioned that I'd burgled the school and stolen some of their science equipment. She views my nakedness, in other words, as I would view Kev's.

As I narrate this increasingly embarrassing tale, I can't maintain eye contact, and it's not just because of the subject matter. She's got these fathomless, mineral-green eyes, the particular shade so pure that it challenges the laws of nature. At an intersection, she could cause a serious traffic accident. Probably has …

Time to say something about my appearance, which is getting relevant in the presence of so much beauty. I'm just a guy. I'm five-foot-six. My hair's going, a 'thinness problem', as I refer to it in the presence of my hairdresser. I have very nice cheekbones. My profile, however, is weak, my nose and jaw insignificant. The body: nothing special, but no defects. An okay-looking guy, shall we say. An interesting guy.

So here's this interesting guy sitting with a major-league beauty. She may not be falling into bed with me, but she's talking to me.

Deliria, let it be made clear, is anti-Australian. For a whole fifteen minutes, she gives me a critique of this fete: look at these dads with the Aussie triangle of open-shirted sunburn, the chest hair like teased cotton wool, the yellowed incisors; these barbecues with bucketfuls of onion rings hissing to ashes on the cast iron, steaks that look like the detached soles of shoes, yolks of eggs blurring into the whites, ice-cream tins of today's takings dappled with egg yolk and tomato sauce.

'Look at that ice-cream tin, Will. Doesn't it tell you everything? Doesn't it just sum up Australia? "Chop and two sausages thanks, mate." "Okay mate." "Thanks mate." "Beauty mate."'

I agree to some extent. In what other country in the world do you call complete strangers of the same sex 'mate'? What gives rise to this speech phenomenon? Is it perhaps the long and venerable history of Australian homosexuality? Probably not. I call Kev 'mate', and I don't think either of us is gay. But I'd agree with her assessment of the food. Just watch those sausages burst. The material on the hotplate looks like footage from a war documentary.

We're in broad agreement about everything. We perceive more or less the same problems with Australian society, we read more or less the same books, we have more or less the same feelings about classical music; everything about us is more or less the same, except the one thing. Occasionally I drive out into the mallee with Kev and blow the heads off rabbits. She doesn't.

The 216 bus drops us at Bellevue Heights: yes, I've got her back to my place, the success so easy that it isn't even a success. Things just aren't heading that way. We are becoming—oh God—*mates*. Clearly, I'm not masculine enough; I'm not threatening enough.

She turns out to be a boozer. At the drive-in bottle shop, which we enter tragically on foot, she purchases a four-litre cask of Australian white wine. Did I know, she remarks, that just a few years ago it would have been called *Moselle*, which is a *vin* délimité de qualité supérieure?

No, I didn't. I pursue the topic. A lot of countries impertinently steal alcohol brand names. There's a Thai whisky called 'West End, The Spirit of London', a city where it is unknown. There's a Japanese whisky-producing town that is trying to get itself renamed 'Scotland'. There's …

She's listening. It's the Australian hunger in her, the longing for something *else*.

The key speaks with authority in the lock. I'm compelled to explain the tastelessness of the Bellevue interior. Although pulling down the posters was easy enough, I had to draw the line at ripping up the carpet. Deliria doesn't mind. Instead, at the sideboard, she arranges the shepherds, cattle, sheep, anthropomorphic dogs and grinning toads into a diorama. A growl from the kitchen challenges her presence: the sumo-cat, its tail upright and snaking, profligate with fur, is spraying the refrigerator with piss. I scoop him up, kick open the back door and throw him off the balcony. Don't worry, it's not that high.

'What's this? What's this?' She is leaning over my work table. Her scarf caresses the pages of Guillaume d'Aquitaine and Jaufre Rudel, the medieval French troubadours; and Sunthorn Phu and Sri Praj, the Thai court poets of the early Bangkok era. Reading these blokes takes up a good six hours of each of my weekdays.

There are three common responses to this discovery. *Why would you want to study French?* elicits an urgent desire to get away. Please, never ask me this question in a moving vehicle. *Say something in Thai* is fair enough. I'd probably do the same if I met someone who spoke Mongol. *That must be amazing to speak a foreign language, to experience someone else's language and culture* is touching, and very Australian, but off the mark. It's not amazing. It's a lot of work. It's like shoving six telephone directories in your head.

Deliria out-responds all previous discoverers. 'You *scholar*, you. William, you've really changed.' I've risen in her estimation from a kangaroo-murdering monolingual to a trilingual version. This transformation forms the subject matter of the next few hours' chat. Deliria's school French. Twelfth-century French. Provençal. Its derivation from Latin. The Indo-European languages. Proto-Indo-European. The magnitude of what I've accomplished with Thai newspapers, tape drills, videos of TV soaps sent from Thailand, ten-kilogram dictionaries, talking to myself in Thai, hanging out at the Thai restaurant on Jetty Road talking with the kitchen hands.

'You really must get out of Australia and go to these places, William.'

Time for the sorry revelation: I have never been out of Australia. I hope I haven't misled you too much, what with the fete reminding me of a Bangkok market and my knowing references to Asian whiskies. My embarrassment grows in yearly increments, with the accumulated weight of my non-going, my twenties threatening to be spent in this vale of tears.

Having said that, I'm far from angst-ridden as Deliria proposes a toast to Courtly Love. Now the tradition of Courtly Love, as exemplified by Guillaume d'Aquitaine and Jaufre Rudel, my heroes, will be familiar to you, though you probably won't have read Provençal. It has reached us through an unfortunate trickle-down effect, an historical accident, a cultural death by misadventure. I'm talking about the development of recording technology and mass distribution. Yes, these days it's 'Everything I do, I do it for you.' The hideous Bryan Adams is the late twenti-eth-century's representative of the tradition of Courtly Love.

I'm squirting the non-*Moselle* out of the cask into two non-wine glasses. To Courtly Love we toast. We're out on the balcony now; she's moderately close to me on the garden seat. Her right-angled arm is white; down her forearm rolls a single drop of transparent wine. This is what happens in Courtly Love. You examine the beloved, noticing how white her arms are, and funnily enough, the landscape often reflects your feelings, as now: the suburbs appear as a phosphorescent spillage from hills to sea, the headlights of cars skittering like microbes in suspension. The alternative proposition, where it's pissing down with rain and her arms are like a construction worker's, just never seems to come up.

A critique of her family follows. At her breakfast table, she comments, the *Business Review Weekly* is recited like prayer, perhaps as a veiled reproach to her enrolment in first-year Music. Her dad checks her geopolitical knowledge: who's the President of China? What countries border Switzerland? What's GATT stand for? She can never answer. She's one of those people, highly intelligent but geographically naive, who's not sure whether Libya is 'quite near' Egypt or if there are 'countries like Algeria' between them. Having said that, she knows the names of places if they have appeared in novels. 'We must get to Paris one of these days,' she says. 'What about meeting for a coffee on the Boulevard Saint-Michel in a year's time to the minute?'

'You're on.'

Her departure, which I wouldn't mind postponing for the rest of her life, is occasioned by the following micro-accident: she picks up the volume of Jaufre Rudel and the cover detaches easily, noiselessly, like a dead butterfly's wing. Of course, I couldn't give a fuck, but something seems to chime in her mind. She'd better go. She has to get up early.

Next morning, the four-litre cask is impossibly light. I'm down in the Hans Heysen landscape painting, at a decidedly imported orange tree. In the tree's upper branches, one of the owners' wrought iron garden seats sways meditatively. I swear I have no idea how it got there. Picking up the oranges, I soon reach forty-seven, forty-eight, forty-nine. After a dangerously oily English breakfast, topped with orange juice, I'm at the letterbox, confronted with a rolled-up gutter press tabloid. The owners forgot to cancel their subscription, or perhaps they felt I'd like to supplement my intake of Thai, French, Provençal and English literature with sensational human interest stories and soft porn. I unroll the newspaper. *Spina Bifida Twins!* it shrieks. The stretched capitals occupy the top half of the front page. Jesus, can't you leave people to their grief? Or did you just pay the poor bastards? On page three I find an attractive topless girl, who has just destroyed her considerable potential for a modelling career by appearing in this piece of shit. On page five I find a pornographic confessional segment which will do for my prose translation assignment. 'She gave herself fully.' How to conjure up the heavy-breathing closeness of this adverbial? *Elle s'est donnée entièrement* just doesn't do it. In between bouts of cask-induced vomiting, I ponder the difference between *fully* and *entièrement*. Will Deliria give herself *fully* or *entièrement*? Probably just not have sex with me.

The 'pathetic fallacy', a term originally used by Ruskin (another one of those blokes I've never actually read), is the fallacy that nature shares and to some extent co-expresses our emotions. So you get paintings where everyone's happy and lo! the sun is shining. Or else everyone's looking pretty grim and, yes, the weather's lousy too. A thunderstorm is rage, a rainbow reconciliation. I suppose it's bad art. But what's bad in art is often great in life. This morning, let me tell you, the landscape is informed of my love. The sun is shining. Birds sing in the trees. At Glenelg Beach, we hear the tearing open of Coke cans—ah, sweet music. The air is heavy with UV cream; frankincense and myrrh could not be more pleasurable to my nostrils. The sea is just fizzing with life. Small fish zap in the shallows. The majesty of St Vincent's Gulf. 'Isn't this wonderful?' I say to a piece of kelp, to a sea grape. Some fat guy bomb-dives off the jetty. Aren't people wonderful? Isn't Deliria wonderful? I'm scrubbed by sand, rolled over in the froth. I go for a walk up the jetty, seeing pensioners with their writhing bucketfuls of garfish and whiting. Is it possible they don't share my exultation?

It's supposed to be chemicals, a release of dopamine, natural heroin. It's called *joie*.

Joie

A bus ride at eleven am in Adelaide is like a vision of death. The seats are spotted with the very old. These are people who can no longer drive a car, people who can't concentrate hard enough, who can't turn the steering wheel far enough, who can't slam on the brakes quickly enough, but who can still get on the right bus, produce the right coins and sit still long enough to get to their destination, if they can remember it. Our culture produces terms like 'grey power' to soothe us, and true enough, they are soothing terms. That's what they're for, to soothe. They're certainly not to *describe*. I can barely skim a newspaper without being slammed by 'the powerful pensioner vote'. I can't pass a magazine rack without receiving the info that sex after fifty can be *better*, or, a scarily common variant, sex can be better *after* fifty. Well, I can't wait. And after sixty, I suppose coke, smack and speed are left far behind. 'Fifty isn't old these days,' I keep hearing, the opinion often enough supported by statistics of nineteenth-century lifespans. But I'm sorry, age isn't quite as relative as they would have you think. There's an upper limit. I'm twenty-two, and it doesn't matter if I feel sixteen, which I often do. I'm still twenty-two.

The country is getting very old. I like old people, but the presence of a large proportion of them, say, twenty percent of the population of Australia, does something to the young. It makes them think they're younger than they are. The Australian adolescence must be the most protracted in the world. You get guys, twenty-nine years old, with half-completed bachelor's degrees, still thinking about putting a band together, or travelling around Australia in a van. Talk about throwing away your twenties.

There follows my arrival at the family house. I'm home, recognised and validated by the cat. Doug, though not insane, is in the front yard. His cardboard box is loading up on weeds. The fork in his right hand is deft, surgical, easing out those complete tap roots to the last hair before posing the fork, while fingers shake off the nutritious dirt from the root system and fling the contemptible weed into the box. Doug's left arm, which would considerably help him in this task, has been blessed with hemiplegia: dormant, forearm at forty-five degrees, fist clenched, drawn back as if to deliver a punch.

I don't know if you know much about strokes, or if you've ever had one, but if I were compiling a list of evidence against the existence of God, I would start with strokes. Doug's got right-sided brain damage, which fucks up the left side of his body, and fucks up his visuo-spatial skills a lot, but leaves him with the ability to speak. Very often he doesn't know where he is. 'I'm *here*, aren't I?' he'll ask me. Or, alternatively, 'I'm *there*, aren't I? Am I *there*?' This is not confusion, which we all know about (the woman with Alzheimer's not recognising her own kitchen, forgetting how to turn on the light switch, forgetting her address and telephone number). No, this is one of the more subtle pranks played on the species. Doug can see the kitchen perfectly well, but he doesn't know whether his body is in it or not. He can be sitting at the table, on one of the kitchen chairs; he can look down and see himself sitting on the chair, and can put his hands on the kitchen table, yet needs to ask: 'I'm on the chair, aren't I?' And now, on the front lawn, if I were to ask the cruel question, 'Dad, where are you?', you'd see the wheels turning, the collection of evidence ... *Okay, I got the fork in me hand ... cardboard box ... grass ... weeds and that ... must be on the front lawn.*

Without halting the rhythm of his weed-upheaval, he indicates a brown glass bottle, whose depiction of a poisoned, gasping aphid on the label confirms it to be the long sought-after aphis killer. 'Now don't you make it too strong,' he warns. 'Bloody stuff'll kill you.' I heft the brown bottle. 'Make sure you wash your hands afterwards. Bloody stuff'll kill you.'

'Yes, Dad, thanks a lot, this is exactly what I need. Get rid of those *aphis* once and for all.'

There are, of course, no aphids at Bellevue Heights, nor any rosebushes. I just find it so difficult to talk to him that I bring up the *idée fixe* of gardening, just get gardening into the conversation as soon as possible. I wonder if he knows.

'So, how's the old French going?'

The leap of discourse is stunning; this is possibly the third time he has ever mentioned what I do.

'Pretty good,' I say. 'I've just been awarded the Banque Nationale prize.'

'Must be doing something right, then.'

'Certainly looks like it.'

'Kev's been pulling apart his car again,' Doug continues, as if Kev's car and the French prize were thematically linked.

'Has he?'

'Yep. Walked into the garage, nearly donged me bloody head on it. Hanging from the roof on a chain.'

'What, he's winched it out of the ...' The car vocabulary eludes me. The engine block? The housing?

'Better watch your head if you go into the garage.'

'Will do.'

Ever vigilant, Doug spots a luckless caterpillar, which he bisects. 'Little bastard.'

'What kind of car is it?'

Moving his gaze from the still-trembling halves of the caterpillar, he directs at me its full force, complete with the yellowed irises, the matted capillaries and the fused eyebrows. It is the classic eye contact, as practised by people in bad fiction, in Thai soap operas, in Californian self-improvement books; but in Life, only by babies, the insane, the dishonest, the newly in-love, the elderly confused, and Doug. It is very disturbing.

I leave him on the front lawn.

Christ, I should take him down to the pub or something. I should take him for a drive. I should cut his toenails.

Clouds of meat smoke issue from the kitchen, where Kev is cooking his 'tea', in his classic rural Aussie. It's a simple, horrible process.

'You ever thought about getting an exhaust fan?'

Kev laughs. Somewhere within him lurks an awareness of what he is doing, an appreciation of the absurd.

'Doug says he nearly had a mid-air collision with the engine of your car.'

The sun-blanched eyebrows signal total incomprehension, as if I'd just shown off in Thai. I mean, 'mid-air collision' is a grammatical metaphor, but surely you get the idea?

'The engine. Of your car. In the garage.'

'That's six months ago.'

'Jesus.'

The promising topic of Doug's short-term memory is abandoned as Kev's 'tea' lands on his plate. Now, with the Courtly Lover's verbal urgency, I'm just about to mention the beloved's name. But when I view the half loaf of wholemeal, the bottle of tomato sauce, the tub of margarine, together with their attendant war footage, and hear the screeching of Kev's steak knife and audible chewing, talking about Deliria seems inappropriate.

'So how's the car?'

Deliria and I are a most fluent conversational team. We're really cerebral; we really work it, and on this plateau we pause, panting with intellectual fatigue. Our conversation exhibits the verbal brilliance you associate with well-written TV drama or a Tom Stoppard play—a kind of jousting in which we oppose each other but nothing is seriously meant. It doesn't even matter who's taking which side; *William said, Deliria said* is superfluous. I quote the following:

'What do you think of films like *The Exorcist*?'

'Well, I think you have to be Catholic to really enjoy it.'

'You mean it relies too heavily on religious awareness?'

'Well, either you're frightened of the idea of someone speaking English backwards, or you're not.'

'I'm not.'

We converse. We also play at being a couple, in some ways. She's around at Bellevue pretty much every day—as I said, no problems about getting her back to my place. Pottering about the stove, I do a good spaghetti marinara which she compliments; her kitchen skills are *absolument nul*. Like an intrigued Aztec, she puzzles for many happy hours over an electric can opener. She's more comfortable with my books, which she understands fine, the interior pages of the Grevisse seeming to have a reassuring smell of paper, of trust. Does she *trust* books? And the volumes of Thai. To me, in a way, they're just info. They could be on my hard drive. They have no animus in themselves. But she is sniffing the binding, her nostrils dilate, her shoulders heave.

There's another way that we play at being a couple. I'm trying to pretend that I've grown used to the physical shock of her beauty. Her mineral-green eyes—after weeks, I can actually hold their gaze for at least two seconds.

Of course, there are some things you just can't get used to. Her hair, for instance. She's so bountifully endowed in this department. It tumbles down in a hundred different shades of blonde, right down over her breasts (which I hope to get to later). It's wild, undisciplined hair. It rushes down, threateningly, as if a city's reservoir has been bombed, and the whole water supply has been unleashed upon its unsuspecting suburbs.

And there's one thing I'll *never* get used to. I mean, there are blinding smiles, wall-of-teeth smiles. These days we see healthy African colour-contrast smiles, but nothing I've ever seen comes close to hers. The lips stretch wide, elastically, opening up the whole bottom of her face, and all her magical dentition is on display, shining like city lights, with the white fluorescence of her incisors, her canines, her molars; and if you're lucky, you can see both rows at the same time. Christ, you could signal a plane with that smile. You could signal astronauts. You could signal God.

She tells my fortune as we sit on the balcony, the brisk breeze whipping her skirt. I note the interested but impersonal contact of her palm-reading finger. Whereas other women might use it as an excuse to hold hands—it is a favourite gambit, along the lines of 'would you like a neck massage?'—she is diligently mapping out health lines, heart lines, life lines. Apparently, I will be going to a small building in North Adelaide where uniformed women will gently tend me. A hair-loss clinic.

'Thanks a lot, bitch.'

The uncourtly reply generates unhoped-for praise of my cheekbones. She would die for my cheekbones, she affirms, and my long eyelashes and perfect eyebrows.

'You should try to make more of your face, cherub, maybe get rid of the hair altogether, go designer-bald and wear huge gold earrings and sunglasses. Allow people to concentrate on what you've got, not on what you haven't got.'

This is excellent advice, sure, but from a *woman*?

So we are fast developing into that most fascinating and unstable pairing where opposite sexes are concerned: the best of friends.

Perhaps she shares a problem that is common to many startlingly beautiful women: a horror of her own body, of *always* being desired, of always *merely* being desired. A staunch reader of women's magazines, I am told by them that many extremely beautiful women are—in their heartless wording—'non-orgasmic'. Strangely, the topic of orgasm is often raised, by Deliria, as metaphor. One day I was talking about a piece of music that Kev hates because I play it all the time—Bach's Partita No. 2 in D minor, Heifetz playing. If you like virtuostic solo violin for half an hour or so, it's great; if you're Kev, it's shit. Trying to *explain* that it's great is a waste of time.

'Yes,' she agreed. 'It's like trying to explain an orgasm to someone who's never had one.'

Interesting metaphor. *I* wouldn't have thought of it. Or more likely, I would have thought of it, but I wouldn't have used it with her.

I've noticed something about Deliria which, if I were her mum, I'd be very worried about. She doesn't seem to know how much of her body she's displaying. If you're a woman, or for that matter a man, you should have some idea. I wouldn't expect a man with a big dick, subject to frequent erections, to go about wearing tight-fitting running shorts unless he wants people to notice. With women wearing skirts a lot of the time, you'd expect them to be even more aware. You see them constantly adjusting their skirts, smoothing down the hems so they reach the knee. They are wary of breezes, sudden gusts that can get under the hem and lift it up. Most women wouldn't go out in a light skirt on a windy day. Deliria, however ... Is it all a big tease, or is it really unconscious?

I'd say it's unconscious. She'll be lying on the bed, scribbling notes to me in one of our favourite games—collaborative free verse—with the crotch of her knickers completely exposed, to the point where I can make out, but try to avoid looking at, a small tear in the seam of the pantihose that sheathes them. Or she'll wear these big men's shirts, unbuttoned halfway to the waist. Sitting next to her at the Bellevue lunch table, industriously blending the mayonnaise into the coleslaw, I view a perfect breast, in its entirety.

Well, I've devoted so much time to her eyes, her hair and her brilliant double-rowed smile, that if I don't describe her breast I'm gonna kill myself; so here goes. In an era when the 'perfect breast' is thought by many to resemble a paint tin with a bullet super-glued to the top, Deliria's breast is like the sail of a yacht pulling slowly out of Glenelg Marina into St Vincent's Gulf, when the wind is blowing at half-speed and the guys can't quite go parachute surfing. Over the imagined ribcage, her skin starts to fill out, from slightly below her collarbone. It cruises into the front of her shirt, just a few inches. Then, after the low island of her nipple, it starts to move back in on her heart, overshooting it a bit, but recovering itself and turning back—as if, after a leisurely Sunday race, when no one particularly wants to win, it wins.

Our *relationship*—yuck—consists of magnificently unrolling streamers of conversation, taking place in locations around the city of Adelaide. At Bellevue, for instance, where we spend a lot of time conversing; at the Adelaide Uni bar, where we meet for conversation; and in Rundle Mall, where we converse. What about at her place? No, she doesn't want me around there just yet. Wouldn't want her mum and dad getting the wrong idea—the clearest signal yet that she's not interested in *that*. This is really perverse: I see Gary on the Glenelg tram all the time, not that we're great mates or anything, but we did once have a real conversation about Vietnam.

My transformation, since the Army Careers fiasco, is astonishing to her. At our last pre-Immaculate fete encounter, when she was fourteen, post-bees, I had plastic bags of dead rabbits in the freezer. I had a triple-two, a twenty-two and an over-and-under shotgun in the garage. I regularly spotlit and shot the macropod symbol of Australia—that's right, the one chatting up the emu on our coat of arms. I was aware of the world in a kind of job-seeking sense; Angola figured prominently in my small talk. Well read? Yes, certainly. I bought *Guns and Ammunition*, *Soldier of Fortune*, SAS paperbacks and *Survival Under Fire*.

Now I'm a trilingual, a pacifist who is also an excellent shot, a devotee of Thai Court poetry and twelfth-century French Courtly Love. Deliria is trying to work me out, as I in turn am trying to work her out.

Chivalry

I wake up from a night terror with my fist nearly broken. I've been frantically punching the wall. My dreams possess this narrative edge, this full-colour intensity, like the best computer game you've ever seen. I take the practical step of moving the bed away from the wall with my undamaged hand. I consider the possibility of the night terror happening if I ever get to sleep with Deliria.

Daylight clarifies. In daylight most things are explicable, and in the face of the explicable I am brave enough. Take this, for example. When Deliria was twelve, she was in my backyard for some reason, possibly in the final stages of putting aside her childhood friendship with Kev. A swarm of bees landed on her, and I knew she was allergic to bee-stings. I ran through the swarm, the bees bouncing off my face, a couple of them bouncing off my eyeballs. I hoisted her on my shoulder (Christ, she was heavy), got stung about twenty times myself, dumped her in the bath, removed quite a bit of her clothing (you don't spend a lot of time asking permission when you know someone's going to die in the next thirty seconds), pulled out the stings with Kev's electronics tweezers, emptied boxes and boxes of bi-carb soda over her, and turned her on her side so she wouldn't inhale the bath water and drown. I called an ambulance, screaming the details. Deliria stopped breathing. I gave her mouth-to-mouth. Her hair, all mixed up with bi-carb soda, was plastered all over her face, which was starting to swell up like a football being inflated. Everything I'd ever learned in the Boy Scouts and the Learn to Swim Campaign was brought into play. I breathed straight through her hair, filling up those lungs. Then Deliria's heart stopped. I gave her cardiac compression, just like in the movies. When her heart restarted and there was the tremendous suck of her starting to breathe again, the ambulance arrived, whooping along the street. Paramedics were sprinting around the place with a stretcher, lots of equipment with dials on it, a defibrillator, oxygen tanks … it was like a reality TV show in that bathroom.

As you can see, when things get frantic I seem to be okay. The paramedic had said, 'Good job, mate. What you did saved her life.' It's when things aren't frantic that I seem to falter. Behaviour in a life-threatening situation is not exactly daily life. Choosing a career is. Getting out into the world is.

I'm released from these depressing thoughts by activity. I transfer the junk mail from the letterbox to the adjacent garbage bin. The letterbox may as well *be* the garbage bin. Hey, wait: I retrieve a postcard from the owners, with a Paris stamp.

'Paris is very nice.'

In these rapturous terms they treat the great city. I reflect that they have been kind: I mean, what am I paying for this place? A whirl of vacuuming follows, through the four main bedrooms, living room and dining room. There remains the bathroom, where the first brave legions of mould are establishing a beachhead. I eliminate them with Rid-Mould, whose highly toxic fumes (I have not read the label) cause me to stumble from the shower alcove out into the passage, numb, my nervous system plundered, the horizon seesawing.

In the words of a seventeenth-century opera, I make a *décision irréversible:* I will mow the front lawn. I journey down to the back shed, there to encounter the lawnmower. Girding my loins—how exactly do you gird a pair of jeans?—I boldly open the shed door.

The lawnmower is parked in front of a squad of petrol drums. A glance inside the petrol tank verifies its emptiness. The drums, though, are full. I try to pick one up by the handle. It's like some torturer's wire noose biting into my hand. Embracing the drum with both arms meeting around the back, I waltz it off the pallet.

The cap grimly defends the contents. Fortunately, an adjustable wrench is available among the hanging tools. With its aid, the cap is off, winding irretrievably under the bench. I hoist the drum, tilting its huge inertia sideways, and the liquid comes lolloping out, drenching the lawnmower and surrounding floor, while perhaps a teaspoonful enters the petrol tank. I sit forlorn. What would Guillaume d'Aquitaine do, confronted with a recalcitrant lawnmower? What would Jaufre Rudel do? What would Sunthorn Phu do? What would Kev do?

'Yeah, you gotta get a siphon,' he explains. I have telephoned him on his building site. He has trudged across a hundred metres of drainage trenches to answer the phone.

'Thanks a lot, mate.'

'No worries, that's okay.'

Shortly afterwards, my mouth sluiced with lawnmower fuel, I'm spitting furiously into the back lawn.

You should be introduced to my Uni milieu, about which I've been silent. First there's Prosse, head of French, supervising me in Provençal. I meet him in the corridors of the French Department, where he says, in front of about five other people:

'William, your essay is quite brilliant. *Tout à fait brillante.*'

Does he know what he's talking about? He appears to know nothing about the real world. Coming from me, that's really saying something. At that award lunch, with him and the French Department and Consulate staff, and, most unpromisingly at first, a completely Australian guy from the Banque Nationale, I remarked that the Australian dollar was so low, I would have to save one fifth as much again as I would have the previous year, in order to get an air ticket.

Prosse's response: 'It will soon be back up again. These things, you know. Up and down.'

'Ah, I wouldn't agree with you there, I'm afraid,' said the banker.

That's Prosse. No fucking idea. The helicopter-blade moustache, the bad tie, the Proust on Glenelg Beach, the wall of slightly out-dated texts.

Next, there's the students themselves, almost entirely female, languages long having been felt to be the domain of women. Men are better with *things*, women are better with *languages*. Possibly true around the globe, but in Adelaide, French is the women's dodge subject, the subject they do when they're not doing a subject. Hear their awe when I speak. *Wow, he can really speak it.* Listen to them try to string together a few words. It's *je ... je ... je ...* Jésu-Christ.

But I envy them in one respect. They know what they're doing. They'll get a degree and perhaps join the public service: the Australian Taxation Office, Centrelink, the Department of Foreign Affairs and Trade. Prosse says I should be trying to get an assistantship in a French school. He goes to some lengths to obtain documents and applications, which he waves at me. Meanwhile I am locked into the troubadours, the code of Courtly Love, the worship of the beloved object, high deeds and chivalry. I find myself on the 216, thinking: what would be the chivalrous response to such an action? For example, someone insults Deliria, questions her virtue, etc. To every action a chivalrous or unchivalrous response. I long for a code of behaviour. I can't accept the Church anymore, not since Mum's brutal exit. I'm not cut out for the army. Are there any spare codes of behaviour around, other than the Seven Characteristics of Highly Successful CEOs?

I watch the French majors as they come down the library steps, still maintaining their high-school groups. They will go into the cafeteria, and play tennis to work off their lunch. On the courts their legs are cruelly tanned. They will swing and twist those attractive upper bodies; they will tauten their bodies and spring, executing serves of good standard. Their game of tennis will be followed by a refreshing shower. On Friday nights, a net-ball-induced sleep; on Saturday nights, a single Mexican beer. How I envy them, how I envy the way they feel the usual things. They would never feel, for example, a tremendous compulsion to change their nationality. Everyone here knows what they're doing, they know what they are. I don't know what I'm doing. I'm the only one that doesn't know what I'm doing.

An *Australian* wanting to change his nationality? Are you kidding? William, you must be mad. Christ, think of the free healthcare. And have you ever thought about how many people want to *be* Australian, who can't? Have you ever seen, let me hazard an example, the queue at Australia House in London? Besides, if you change it, you can *never get it back.* I refer you to the Department of Foreign Affairs and Trade's charming booklet: *Advice to Australians who are Thinking of Becoming Citizens of Other Countries: Fuck You.* They're very romantic about it really: 'we're building a new country' and all that crap. Oh, the family picnics, the quarter-acre blocks, the absence of hand grenades. It's a wonderful thing to have, this Australian nationality, except that it stops you working in Europe.

I *nearly* changed it. Imagine, reader, if you can, William, a few weeks ago, being drawn inexorably towards the Consulat de France, all the way from Adelaide Uni bar through Victoria Square, along footpaths lined with sleeping drunks, to elegant Hutt Street.

'*J'ai envie d'appliquer, par naturalisation, pour la nationalité Française,*' I said to the same guy who had given me the Banque Nationale du Sud-Pacifique award. It would be difficult to say what he was most surprised about: a) to see me again so soon, b) to see me drunk in his office, or c) to see a holder of one of the most desirable nationalities in the world offering to exchange it for his own. We had a conversation in which I tried to persuade him to give me the form.

'Are you under thirty?'

'I'm twenty-two.'

'Then there would also be the matter of military service.'

'Military service?'

'One year's military service.'

'May I have a copy of the form?'

Shopping

In those days, the poet usually started with a description of the beloved's lips (coral), eyes (like the sun), or hair (radiant, golden). Skin like unto the lily; the roses in her cheeks. This quite workable formula derived from the sartorial habits of the twelfth century, because the poet could only see her from the neck up. Back then, the rest, including her mind, and her private behaviour, was merely speculation, and however entertaining that speculation might have been, you couldn't have built up a tradition on speculation. So you started from the face, or facial region shall we say, and moved downwards to the breasts, which started appearing in the sixteenth century. They were usually, as you would expect, white (as snow). You catalogued the bits that you could see. If there were any bad bits (moustache, cold sore, irritating facial tic), you had to be a gentleman about this. You left them out. In this, you did pretty much as you did in Life; try marriage, for example, without leaving things out. The recent observation (late twentieth century) is that we shouldn't be concentrating on the woman's appearance so much, that a woman shouldn't be defined by, or imprisoned in, her appearance. I couldn't agree more, sisters. But it's so difficult to write lyric poetry about anything else. In deference to the twentieth century, I'm going to start with Deliria's legs.

They cut the air like shears. They measure one metre, more than half her height. No, I didn't get a tape measure. She did. The beloved's legs, descending from an accordion-pleated skirt (see how my sartorial vocabulary has shot up? I, who could not even identify the material lamé), terminate in designer ankles and size-six feet, which fit neatly into shoes of loud green suede. She swanks across North Terrace to greet me, famous-name shopping bag brushing against her knee. Again, she's fantastically overdressed. She appears to be studying for a degree in shopping. Every time we meet, she is wearing a different, never-to-be-repeated set of clothes. This time it's not the eccentric 1920s vintage style, but ultra-modern job interview gear—that is, job interview gear for the fashion editorship of *Elle*. I, whom fortune of such triumph bars, have worn the same T-shirt, jeans and bomber jacket every time we've met. In fact it was she who identified it as a bomber jacket.

'The bomber jacket has to go.'

A new chunk of vocabulary chalked up.

Our conversation—time to give you an extended sample—has started to aspire to the condition of a Criticism of Life, in the Matthew Arnold sense, not that it actually rhymes or anything, but it does have a kind of metre. Consider the following exchanges:

'Clothes mean something,' she says. 'They define you to some extent. They certainly affect your mood. Ask any woman.'

'You look like shit, you feel like shit?'

'Exactly, *chéri*.'

'Careful. You wouldn't call me "baby" in English.'

'The cloak of a foreign language, baby.'

'So, you mean you would never wear jeans and a T-shirt?'

'Only if I were strolling along the beach.'

'I seldom wear anything else.'

'I don't think I've ever heard anyone say "seldom" before.'

'It's a perfectly good modal adjunct. People should use it more.'

'You say "thus" a lot, too. Could you imagine Kev using a word like 'thus'?'

No doubt you get the idea. Anyway, let's join me and Deliria on our discursive walk through Rundle Mall, where the urban landscape glows with love: pathetic fallacy again. The most banal item, say, a plastic cup crushed on a seat, somehow acquires a benevolent tone, as do the signs for fast film development, the overpriced fruit from a stall, the sparrows jabbing their heads into a cream bun. Let choirs of shop assistants sing from the windows of Myer and Tremaine; let skateboarding teens flip their boards and fly; let pizza-shop staff strew our path with leaflets. Transformed by my love, the whole mall becomes a literary object. This drug is called *joie*.

We're in a bookshop. While she hovers at a shelf of children's books, I haunt the Penguin Classics. The world's learning is spread before me in a single bookcase. If you knew just one shelf of this, really well, you could … you could start on the next shelf, I suppose. Von Clausewitz. *On War*. 'War is a continuation of politics by different means.' I toy with the resonant phrase. Politics is a continuation of sex by different means. Sexual politics is a continuation of war by different means. I consider buying the Von Clausewitz. Books are so damned expensive, though, in Australia. Pick it up and look at the back cover. Yep, can't afford it. Here's a nice one: *Oliver Twist*. Can't afford this one either. Take, for example, this entertaining ramble: *Humphrey Clinker*. Can't afford it. My stack of bought books wouldn't fill a single row. Yes, that's right, I usually resort to piracy, photocopying the whole library book after hours in the French Department, which for purposes of fair dealing is a bit naughty. Yes, it's me against whom the Intellectual Property Commission rages. I'm a literary pirate, or let's say privateer.

I wait outside the shop for her, facing my elongated reflection in two stainless-steel spheres, one atop the other, a wonderful pop-art feature of the mall—cost millions, worth zero. Deliria is taking rather a long time. A woman's privilege, I reflect. Some things never change. The man has to wait for the woman to come out of the shop. This has been going on for thousands of years.

After no more than twenty minutes, my image in the stainless-steel balls is joined by Deliria's. 'Well, shall we go?' she enquires.

Her hair is quite literally bouncing. She looks like a shampoo ad. '*Hey, women with a lot of money, our product can make your hair look like this. Of course it can.'* But there's another aspect to this hair. It's dangerous. It should be listed under 'dangerous'. It's like a waterfall that you're not just observing, but being swept over.

'Got you a present,' she says. I follow her crisp steps, her heels a loud *allegro* on the mall paving.

When we turn the corner into Pulteney, she pops the catch of her handbag. Her white hand dives in and comes up with a Penguin Classic. It is not wrapped. This is the classical Eve + apple gesture. *You should try some, Adam, tastes great, increases your intelligence and everything.* Her blue-nailed thumb sits lightly on the cover of the book, while palm and fingers support it underneath, and her arm is extended towards me.

'You didn't …'

'Of course.' She's doing the direct-gaze thing with her eyes; those mineral-greens, those green traffic lights saying, 'Go with it. Just go with it.'

'Look …'

'You should see your face.'

'We have to return it.'

'Are you nuts?' She's gently chiding me, as if I'd done something wrong and she was the sensible one. In a way she's right: you'd be crazy to return something you'd stolen.

Well, what a marvellous new dimension to her character.

It's all a question of power and restraint, she tells me in the Adelaide Uni bar. She subjects me to a kind of dissertation on the politics of shoplifting, of which the following is the gist.

'The restraint creates the power, don't you see? If the restraint weren't there, the power wouldn't be available. I mean, look at Prohibition. Look at drugs. You think that if drugs were legal, the drug barons would have any power? They'd just be shopkeepers. Look at prostitution. What would a pimp be worth if it were legal? With shoplifting, if everything were free, there'd be no point in it. Also, if *everyone* shoplifted, there'd be no point in it. But if just a few people shoplift they can gain power. Financial advantage over the weaker, law-abiding *citoyens*, baby. Look at the way I dress. Most lawyers couldn't afford to dress the way I do. So I enjoy the advantages of a high income without actually having one.'

'What about the danger?' I say.

'Well, there's a risk. You can't have something for nothing.'

'What about the morality? Or lack thereof.'

I half expect her to come out with some nugget like, 'Morality is a social construct.' Instead, she tells me that it's possible to shoplift morally, never robbing family owned stores, always sticking to huge American-owned chains with shoplifting insurance. The moral shoplifter, no less.

The possibility that she actually *believes* this argument is not very high. No, she's just a naughty eighteen-year-old girl, and this rationalisation forms part of a large body of unserious repartee with which you will be familiar by now. The book, perfect choice incidentally, *Les Liaisons Dangereuses*, lies openly on the bar table, price tag peeled off, the cover vigorously creased to show age, some pages even dappled with beer. 'It's obviously your book,' she says.

Kev is playing a new form of darts. He is the proud owner of a pistol crossbow, an engine of war you've probably seen in anachronistic Camelotian sagas. To his credit, and to my surprise, he is aware that these movies in no way reflect history.

'They didn't have laminated steel back then,' he says disapprovingly, referring to the cold-pressed metal that the arc is made of.

'They didn't say "no way" either.'

A sandbag is propped up against the backyard incinerator, and a series of rough concentric circles is marked out in shoe polish. To the right of the bull's-eye is a cluster of yellow arrows. Kev invites me to try my archery skills. The pistol crossbow, by the way, is a pissy little weapon, highly inaccurate and weak. If someone were pointing one at me, I'd feel reasonably safe. I load the bolt into the groove, stick the butt against my gut, and yank back the string. Click. Sight just under the target. Both eyes wide open, none of this closing-one-eye business. I laugh every time I see a movie sniper carefully closing one eye. Squeeze the trigger. The yellow cylinder joins its compatriots to the right of the bull.

'Throwing to the right, mate,' I conclude.

Kev and I have an unusually long conversation about laminated steel. Its uses, its derivation, its life expectancy. Its percentage composition, its manufacture, its melting point, its springiness, its suitability for making pistol crossbows. What they would have used in Camelot instead of laminated steel. Boy, can Kev and I talk about laminated steel.

'I'm having terrible problems with Deliria.'

'She's fuckin' insane.'

This is Kev's touching assessment of his childhood playmate. Kev has the advantage of clear vision. He doesn't think Deliria is pretty. Not a spunk. The Kev ideal, though he probably wouldn't agree with me, is more matronly, with big tits, height a couple of inches shorter than him ('pashing height', he terms it), a cuddliness, a 'nice personality', a moderate level of education, pliant opinions, and a harsh-but-friendly rural Australian accent, similar to his own. The Kev ideal is nurturing, non-threatening. She is not insane.

Later, we triangulate the dinner table in the places we have occupied since Mum. On the table, Doug's contribution to our diet, a leg of lamb, lies in its sauce.

Around us is the startling disorder of the kitchen. The sideboard is layered with electricity bills, flyers and receipts. From a coffee cup's edge hang the festooned antennae of a poised cockroach. Yet the disorder is a recent accretion. Several layers underneath it, you can see the firm foundation of marriage: the kitchen plan, for instance, is really well thought out. Near the kitchen door, the sideboard precisely balances, with its solidity, the stove and kitchen sink at the far end, the business end. The substantial cupboards house mixing devices, interlocking juicers, vitamisers and graters. Each is dusty. The boys don't know how to use them. Kev can just about manage the sandwich maker, his special grated-cheese sandwiches famed among the radius of his mates.

In case you're wondering how a man with short-term memory loss can cook, Doug can't *really* find his way around the stove, and the preparation of such a dish as a leg of lamb is comically beyond him. His contribution is a supervised one. You can see his bewilderment at every new step. It's a wrenching sight to watch him return to the stove at intervals of a couple of minutes, with evident fresh interest each time, or to watch his meaningless examination of the oven window.

'This is really nice, Dad,' I say. Kev concurs. Doug chews.

'This is really nice,' I say again, after not even very long. The compliment can be safely repeated. To Doug, all information is constantly renewing itself, the slate wiped clean every two minutes.

Doug's table manners deserve comment. Old age can be wonderfully liberating in this respect. All the things that you might do when eating on your own, he does in the presence of others, showing a complete freedom from the social restraints he once enforced on us. Witness his behaviour with this flap of lamb, for instance. Curious to see what the other side looks like, he picks it up with his fingers and holds it up in the air, where it drips, the heavy gravy landing in audible splashes on the polished mahogany of the dinner table.

Have you ever wanted to eat something that you'd dropped on the floor, but been intimidated by the presence of other people? You can look forward to losing those inhibitions with the help of dementia. Ever torn your slice of bread into confetti, just for the hell of it? Emptied the tomato sauce over that perfectly good tablecloth? Blended the dregs of your cup of tea with your mashed potato? Well, one day, you might.

Kev and I watch Doug with intermittent focus. If he does something really dangerous, we'll jump up; if not, the policy is to disregard.

'*Double Blind,* 7.30,' announces Kev. He refers to a TV dating show.

'*Double Blind.*'

'New presenter. Clean cut. No dirty jokes. Crap now. Lost everything,' he continues in his telegraphic style. The strong jaw chomps through Doug's lamb.

'You reckon you could pass the sauce, Dad?' I thus invite Doug to participate.

'This is really good, Dad,' Kev reminds him. It's been at least two minutes.

We hear the muffled clinking, shifting and resettling of Doug's teeth. After a patient thirty seconds or so, Kev's arm unflexes, and the hacked fingers pass me the bottle of tomato sauce.

'Anyway, what sort of problems?' Kev continues our Deliria conversation.

'Oh … communication. Sex-role stereotypes.'

Kev attacks the square footage of his lamb.

'Australian lamb,' comments Doug.

There's always a rush to include Doug, to expand him into coherence.

'Yeah, Australian lamb must be the best in the world, right Dad?' elicits Kev.

'Much better than New Zealand lamb,' I say. 'Have you ever had British lamb?' Kev and I leave the pause open, inviting.

'Nup,' says Doug, after about fifteen seconds.

'Neither have I, actually. Supposed to be really good,' I say, always backing him up, although I must have had British lamb twenty or thirty times.

'This is really good, Dad,' says Kev.

'Yeah, this is great.'

Doug inches the salad bowl towards him. From it he extracts a green lettuce leaf, which he heaps with sugar. He rolls it up like a hill-tribe cigar. There is a horrible athletic crunch.

'How did you go with the mower, anyway?' asks Kev.

At eight pm we shut Doug down for the night. We turn off the gas supply in case he gasses us, and take out the Kitchen Tidy in case he empties it over the kitchen table. Doug is increasingly ambulant around 3 am, a notorious rubbish-categoriser and switcher-on of appliances. At the powerboard, Kev and I discuss pulling out the power fuse but leaving the light fuse in, weighing the possible spoiling of the meat and milk that this would entrain, against the relative safety and peace of mind thereby provided. A roar from the bathroom interrupts us: Doug has put Pine-O-Kleen on his hair.

In the morning I return to Bellevue.

Aphaphirom et Amornvivat

Once upon a time, when Deliria was fifteen, she entered a shoe shop in Melbourne. *Immaculate Chamber Orchestra Hits Swanston Street*. Dressed, as usual, in a Paris afternoon's shopping (stolen), fifteen but already fully formed, like a genius, she was asked by a male cashier if he might look into her handbag. The request was purely routine. The cashier had seen nothing. Can Deliria get out of this one? Can a fish swim?

'You presume I'm a thief?' she accused.

'No, no, it's no reflection whatsoever on you, it's just policy, just a random check,' protested the cashier, instantly stepping into the role she offered him.

'I regard it as an insult,' she said, with the stolen handbag, containing a pair of stolen size sixes, resting against her hip. 'I've a good mind not to shop here again. And you can bet I'll tell all my friends about it.'

Remember, even at fifteen she looked about twenty-five: she could have been the wealthiest trophy bride in Melbourne, with her knowledgeable make-up, her height, her fully developed bone structure. The poor cashier, whose chances of sleeping with Deliria were nil but still determined his whole behaviour towards her, began the usual male apology.

She was lucky, wouldn't you say? She drew from this incident the meaning that best suited her purposes at the time: she could do what she wanted.

'Always be well dressed,' she has advised. 'If people saw you in a thousand-dollar suit, it would never cross their minds that you were simply a very successful shoplifter.'

We conduct a covert war of manipulation. She's trying to get me to go on a shoplifting expedition with her, while I'm trying to get her to do her Music I essay, which is overdue. This is the way it works. She tries to corrupt me; I try to reform her. It's pretty bad, isn't it? It's a classic dysfunctional friendship.

I point out what would happen if she were caught. Just think, she would find it difficult to get certain government jobs. Also, consider the trauma in memory. For years afterwards, it would be a flinch area. Jesus, you get whole episodes of soap operas based on a girl getting caught shoplifting.

Naturally, the advice doesn't work. With a lazy after-lunch grin, she favours me with a demonstration of shoplifting techniques, challenging me to catch her in the act of thieving a hairbrush from the owners' dressing table. She's good at what she does. I never manage to catch her; it's as if the hairbrush is magically inhaled into the shoulder bag, with her stride never interrupted. She's not simply nicking things off shelves, then, like a five-year-old, or a seventy-five-year-old; she's actually put in time, worked out how best to do it. But there are some skills that you wouldn't want to be too good at. If she had put half the amount of time into learning to construct an undergraduate essay as she had into the shoplifting skills, she would now be able to answer this opera question.

It's not what you'd call difficult. 'Discuss the meaning of the term "*illégale*" in *Aphaphirom et Amornvivat*. 1500 words.' This simple task makes her twitch and wriggle with worry. She's lying on the bed, the spine of the libretto whitened with creases, the text growing steadily more obscured by her unsystematic high-lightings. She hasn't written a damn thing.

Her vulnerability gives me the usual hard-on (there's a hint for you, girls: vulnerability. Yes, the V-word gets it up every time). Bending over slightly, to maintain a neutral trouser outline, I have the following conversation:

'What would your strategy be?'

'I don't know. Read the libretto. Write about it. Try to answer the question.'

I try to show how inadequate this is. 'Try it this way. Get a pencil. Put a circle around the word *"illégale"* every time it occurs. I think it comes up about twenty times.'

'How assiduous, William. By the way, nice cock you've got there.' Only joking.

'Then write yourself an index. Act II Scene IV. *"Efforcée à subir des caresses illégales."*'See if you can observe a pattern. Probably has a double meaning or something.'

'Oh William, that's so touching. You're concerned about my essay.'

I give her my desk while I walk, cheap underwear sandpapering my cock, to Blackwood Shopping Town.

You're not familiar with *Apha*? It's an operatic version of one of those seventeenth-century incest plays that were all the rage at the time. The king, a Siamese despot, subjected his eighteen-year-old daughter to *'des caresses illégales'*. Hideous, *non?* But in my view, anyway, in order to understand the play, you have to understand that in those times royal fathers didn't know their daughters that well. They might have had eighty kids by twenty-seven wives. So, after an initial presentation, royal Aphaphirom may never even have *seen* little Amornvivat until she was eighteen years old. That's the palace life for you. My argument to Prosse, a year ago when I studied the thing, was that the king's offence is more of a crime against genetic legislature than simple *'inceste abominable'*.

I hate the plot. The father, King Aphaphirom, is sexually attracted to his daughter. He takes her on a state visit, and gets to know her. Her sexual power is so strong, he confides to us, that he is *compelled* to fuck her. She doesn't tell anyone. Later, she is given in marriage to this prick called Inthusamit, a war hero, and when they go to bed, this veteran of a thousand hymens finds out that she's not a virgin. He complains. The girl goes insane and blabs. Then she commits suicide. Inthusamit kills the king, then commits suicide. Pretty much everyone in the cast commits suicide.

On my return, I'm fully provisioned and detumescent. She's completed the listing; her smile is radiant with accomplishment. She drops the beginnings of the Music I essay and we have an overdressed conversation. Deliria opens.

'So, what about Seven Deadly Sins for this century?'

'Let's see. Poor CD collection. Doesn't include any classical music.'

'Poor host, can't entertain.' And thus we go on to enumerate a list of seven socially crippling evils. Our conversations are always like this, they are never like anything anyone would actually say. Everything is a spill of words, highly articulate, highly worked, full of wit and artifice, but disguising an enormous silence about the most important subjects. What do I know about her? I know she loves Paganini. I know she can do double stops on the violin. I know she is a compulsive shoplifter. But I never know how she feels, for example, about me. So you can look at it two ways. We have brilliant conversations, or, alternatively, all we do is talk. As Kev memorably expresses it (he's heard us, pausing out the front of Doug's, on the phone, etc.), 'It's like, you know. You suck up to her, she sucks up to you. Pathetic.'

He's missing out on the delight of it, somewhere.

What else do I know about her? I know what she looks like. I know all about the tremendous physicality of her presence. If she's in a room, the room has to model itself around her; like the sun, she becomes the centre of whatever space she occupies. Like the sun, too, she has no idea of what she's doing. 'What is heat?' wonders the sun, who feels none. The woman who doesn't know how beautiful she is—this idea has been around for a few hundred years.

By this I don't mean that she has no idea of what she looks like. In fact, she has an excellent idea of what she looks like. I've seen her putting on her make-up in the bathroom, very correct, like a make-up artist, with the blush just under the cheekbones, highlighting. She knows what she looks like. What she has little idea of, and constantly underestimates, is the effect she has on blokes. Has she not read the right magazines? In this wonderfully enlightened society, where it's almost impossible to open a women's magazine without finding instructions on how to bring yourself to orgasm with lightly warmed vegetables, she has grown up sexually ignorant.

By this time you must be aware of the effect she's having on me, all the *joie* that's coming my way. In true courtly tradition, I find myself attempting to write courtly love poetry in a style similar to that of Guillaume d'Aquitaine. But I just don't have the talent. I try to write hymns of praise and I come up with either an enumeration of parts of her body, fawningly described (although 'To Deliria's Collarbone' wasn't *complete* crap), or else a succession of similes. I never really get down to the difficult questions: why anyone would bother to love anyone else, and why a third person, reading about it, would care in the slightest.

The boasted cosmopolitan ambiance of Glenelg is switched off at six o'clock each evening, but the shopfronts remain deceitfully lit. You wouldn't think this was a town of a million people. Where are they? It's more like a town of thirty people. In front of us, the main shopping street, glinting with night tramlines, beautifully paved with those interlocking pink bricks, stretches bleakly to the beach. The sole visible life consists of two dogs. Wait—an event occurs! A bit of an electric spark shoots out from the tram, from the contact point between the power supply roller and the overhead cable, as it starts up in Moseley Square. Another event: the traffic lights change on a two-minute cycle. An electric transformer up on a pole starts buzzing from latent rain.

As Deliria puts it, and on this point we are in complete agreement, it's impossible to grow up in this city. Nothing happens to you. You go to the shop, you buy a pastie. You decide if you want sauce or not. Of these grand events are our lives composed. There are exceptions, however. At an afternoon concert with a minor UK band, the people rise up and trash the police station. The people get upset when the Grand Prix is over: they trash Rundle

Mall. The provincial capital, put momentarily on the map by the arrival of global visitors, is faced with what it is, in itself, and explodes in shame.

'The texture of daily life,' she is saying as we walk through eventless Glenelg. 'It affects people. The suburbs affect people.' I agree, but then again, I'd agree with anything. If she were chalking up the merits of the neo-Stalinist state, I'd agree. I'm like an advertisement for perfume: women, wear this. The white proximity of your neck will exhale a cloud, and the male will swoon and agree, the stuff going directly to his brain.

The suburbs affect people, she explains. People don't really need to be living on quarter-acre blocks. Her hair is shaking rhapsodically. What is it that men have about women's hair? I don't know what it is, but we do have it. Her voice grows dissociated from meaning, becoming just a sound. 'Yes,' I agree. 'Yes. Yes.' The landscape agrees too. The Thai restaurant, the pizza parlour, the police station and the sex shop all benevolently regard us. The tram heaves itself along and clatters past us, blue-sparking. It's certainly a wonderful old tram.

'People on the dole,' she is saying, 'they should all be sent overseas. They could find jobs teaching English or something.'

'Jesus. Whatever you do, don't go into politics.'

'What makes you think I wouldn't be good in politics?'

'They say extremely beautiful women don't do well in management and administrative positions.'

'You think I'm beautiful?'

'Do the US Marines drink beer?'

'I don't know. Do they?'

She knows well enough what she looks like. She knows it like an abstract thing: the distance to the sun, the speed of light.

For some people who live with their parents, food just appears before them. The woven basket is magically full of pears every morning: a full-time Santa Claus must do this. I'm trying to educate Deliria about that condition known as Living Away From Home, by taking her shopping for food. 'How much is chicken a kilo?' I ask. She is comically out in her estimate. It is possible that she has never entered a discount supermarket except as a child with her mum. Her gaze rises up the wall of tins. Tinned bamboo shoots, sambal oelek, Tom Yam Kung. Yes, we're pretty cosmopolitan here in Bellevue Heights. The food I select contrasts favourably with what appears on the dinner table at her home. Chops and two boiled veg. Mince, no herbs. White bread.

We push around one of those steel trolleys with the foldout seat for babies that is never used. In fact, most people in the supermarket are about seventy years old. There hasn't been a toddler in this place for about six months. Blue-rinsed heads are active around the cut-down cardboard carton offering its special on baked beans. Some of the bodies are healthy, still agile; some have diabetic legs, stained with blood under the skin, swollen like pillows.

I'm astonished to see one of these old bags shoplifting tinned food. Yes, this is what it's really like to be old. On a pension, shoplifting peas and corn. With the hopelessness of her technique, when compared with Deliria's, and the terrifying slowness of those movements, she might as well be wearing a bandolier of flashing lights around that floral print housedress and a placard saying, *I am a shoplifter.*

Seeing her, Deliria tells me that shoplifters represent a vast cross-section of Australian society. Every social group is represented. Every race, every creed. Every age group.

'What about gender?' I ask.

'No,' she replies after a few seconds, and I can see she's never thought about this before. 'I'm afraid it's mainly women.'

'Now there's an unwelcome statistic for you.'

Deliria's not shoplifting today. At least, it's safe to assume she isn't, because what she's doing is loudly discussing the ethics of shoplifting—in a supermarket.

'Shoplifting is a completely victimless crime,' she says in a high,

clear voice, ten feet away from a guy whom, without any training in such matters, I immediately identify as a store detective. I
wonder what's happening to the old woman. I wonder what her
getaway speed would be, with those balloon-sized ankles. I wonder how she'd shape up to a police interview.

Deliria continues, with nutty logic, her manifesto. There's no
such thing as guilt, apparently, there's only your capacity to feel it.
Payment itself is a form of theft, she goes on, only it's institution-
alised. It's an historical error. Here is her clinching point:

'See that foam mousse? Four ninety-nine. Do you know how
much it costs to make, can and all?'

'No.'

'Two cents.'

'So what? The price of something is what people will pay for it.'

This is a new concept for her, until she realises she's known it
all along. 'I *don't* pay for it.'

Kev, bursting from his jeans, his top half naked and furred, takes
a parcel of fish fingers from the freezer. He tears off the wrapping
and holds the mass under the hot tap, whereupon the fingers separate and flop into the sink. Kev has a genial indifference to diet. I
open the refrigerator: it's full of bloodied plastic bags.

'Been shooting, I see.'

'Yep. Went up to Stevo's granddad's farm out in the mallee. Got
this incredible rabbit population. Not too many of them left now.'

How varied is the slaughtered animal life that has occupied
our fridge. The usual tenants of the freezer are rabbits. Also frequent are native pigeons (a thousand-dollar fine) and the edible
hindquarters of kangaroos.

Kev and I have a metallic, concrete-noun conversation, studded
with terms. Bolt. Warhead. Haemorrhaging head. Practice head.
Over and Under. Twenty-two. Triple-two. 12-gauge. Revolver
magazine. 10-shot magazine. Bolt action. Semi-auto. Anschutz.
Remington. Walther.

'Triple-two?'

'Twenty-two semi-auto.'

'Twenty-two semi-auto. Anschutz?'

'Walther.'

'Walther twenty-two semi-auto.'

'Yeah.'

Linguistically, like swearing, it is inclusive. It includes me in a group of Kev and me.

'So how's it going with Deliria?'

'I'm really happy, I think it's going really well.'

'It's not, *augh*, platonic, is it?'

'It's certainly not platonic on my part. I don't know about her. Actually, I don't think she's interested in that.'

'She's fuckin' insane.'

There's a rattling of the back door handle and we're joined by Doug, who is clothed in a white singlet and pyjama bottoms. He's holding a cardboard carton with weeds peeping over the rim. A strong earthy smell accompanies. Kev and I watch him in mild alarm as he places the carton on the kitchen table next to the tray of Kev's fish fingers, and just leaves it there. I can see small yellow flowers capping the weeds. A flying ant or moth wrestles itself free and soars to the fluorescent light, where it crawls inside the housing. Doug, his magnificent shoulders just fitting through the half-closed sliding door, disappears into his bedroom.

Blackwood Shopping Town

The shopping mall has stepped neatly into the vacancy left by the church, the weekly visit merely transposed one day to Saturday. The black asphalt of the outdoor carpark becomes dotted with cars, more and more cars, until by mid-afternoon the many colours of car roofs have blended, like dots in a pointillist painting. Colonnades, West Lakes Mall, Westfield, Gilles Plains Shopping Town, Grand Junction Shopping Village, Tea Tree Plaza. The words 'plaza' and 'village' connote two qualities completely absent from these structures: first, grandeur; second, a sense of community, of people knowing each other and taking care of each other. Around the pseudo-Corinthian columns cluster the smoking, ear-ringed, tattooed twelve-year-olds, working their way up to detention centres.

Purportedly, this is a brief detour through Blackwood Shopping Town in the fifteen minutes we have spare before the 216 rolls down the hill. Then there's a small conscience-saving bit of business I have to do: the procurement of Curtius's *Europe and the Latin Middle Ages* from the Barr Smith Library. Following this will come the real thrill of the day, a walk on the banks of the Torrens, the two of us possibly lying down on the grass, Deliria's shoes being removed, her kneecaps getting grass-stained. Now there's an idea for another courtly love poem: 'To Deliria's Kneecap'.

Crystal Galérie, like its redundant acute accent, strives for elegance. Almost everything in the shop is ugly and useless. Shelves are populated with glass fish, shepherds, mermaids, dogs, cats, shrubs, seagulls, anthropomorphic mugs and a globular owl on a branch. Glass may last for 4000 years: imagine the bewilderment of future archaeologists when they dig up this stuff. To Adelaide's credit, the shop is empty. Behind the cash desk the salesgirl, in her casual worker's disinterest, is turning the pages of a magazine about the real lives of actors who appear in soap operas.

From behind me comes a loud clinking. Deliria is bent over her natty Bellissimi shoulder bag, in her hand a very large salt grinder. Something's going technically wrong. The salt grinder will not go into the bag because of the pepper grinder that has already taken up all the available space. The salesgirl has lowered her head beneath the cash desk, and a radio is heard; there's the *fft fft* as she skids over unwanted frequencies, which to some extent distracts from the hair-raising shriek of glass against glass. Push, push against the base of the salt grinder. Glass has never clinked so loudly.

This is nuts. I'm at the cash desk, engaging the salesgirl, blocking her view of Deliria, telling her of my overpowering interest in a glass fish, almost shouting at Deliria, 'Put some money in the parking meter, will you, darling?' She walks out with the bag hanging open and the bottom half of the salt grinder sticking out of it.

I deliver a fluent monologue in praise of the fish. Note the intricate workmanship of the scales, how the spikes on the dorsal fin are so beautifully rendered. Two minutes later, I have bought it. Throwing it in the nearest rubbish bin, I go to the fire exit, where I'm sure Deliria will be. In her hand are two pea-sized balls, which are the rolled-up price tags of the stolen goods. Always remove the price tag, it appears. The salt and pepper grinders are now in a bona-fide shopping bag with the name of a department store on the side.

'Baby, you rose to the occasion magnificently.'

So, welcome to the secret life of Deliria. This is what she does between music lectures. Instead of simply practising her violin, reading her libretto or doing her essay, she skips out into a world of controlled fear, commits simple larceny and gets back to the conservatorium for the five o'clock tutorial.

William, did you really think you would ever get to the Barr Smith? Did you honestly see yourself leafing through the Curtius in the reference library, thence to proceed to the banks of the Torrens, possibly composing verses to the beloved, with the unavoidable and rather mechanical comparison of her eyes to the sun, lips to coral, voice to music and breasts to snow? Did you really think you would be doing that? Because things just aren't going that way. Deliria can't steal just one thing. It's got to be a binge.

At some stage during this retail crawl, we enter a shop specialising in sunglasses. A curtained room at the far end no doubt contains the usual magazine-reading, zero-responsibility parttimer. In seconds, the display wall is harvested, the broken rubber bands dangling from their staples. At the exact moment that I notice the rubber bands are luminous, their clock-hand green a dead giveaway against the black felt of the darkened wall, the attendant blows through the curtains. I get a quick impression of plucked eyebrows, mascara, a beer gut and a five-o'clock shadow. Possibly the most unsuccessful tranny I've ever seen.

'Oh hi. How's it going, love?'

'Fine, baby. William, this is Andrea. Andrea, this is William.'

The calm lunacy of her voice. This is William. Profession: shoplifter by association. Contents of this bag: fifteen pairs of sunglasses that we stole from you, and a salt and pepper grinder set from Crystal Galérie.

Andrea, with over-feminised body language, is inviting her to come back to the holy of holies, to see the *real* stuff, to see the *Paris* stuff. Deliria agrees, of course. She swings the bag. You can just about hear the sunglasses, their earpieces chirping together like the wings of crickets.

There is something almost mentally infirm about this confidence of hers. This is not the confidence that comes with a welllaid plan. This is the confidence of someone in a nightgown strolling across an expressway. Through the curtain and into another chamber of her secret world I follow.

'Try these, William,' says Andrea. 'Try these, Deliria.'

Try these. I recall the broken rubber bands glowing on their staples, hanging in their extravagant moustaches. I recall the Curtius, long-since abandoned. Deliria strikes a model's pose, sunglasses parked on her nose's extremity, fingers laced behind the nape of her neck.

'You look fantastic,' says Andrea, in thrall.

This, then, is the pleasure of theft, is it? Not so much the something for nothing, but to be here with the attendant, whom she knows, chatting and being friendly, getting him in thrall, and knowing that with a single utterance she can replace this pleasant state with her own destruction. The potential to utter her own destruction, and yet holding it back. Thus she measures her control over the world, without really participating in it.

A bit later, we have a conversation in a fire exit:

'Do you think we could possibly go now?'

'What do you think of this pair?'

'They're good. They're all very good. Now what about your tute?'

Her tutorial vanishes. We are almost instantly transported to the lingerie section of a department store in Rundle Mall. The women's change room features the minimum possible screening: the swing doors from a Western saloon. It's a precaution against shoplifting, but it doesn't work. Not with her.

I'm developing my limited dramatic talents to their fullest extent, playing the hapless *mari* stranded amongst women's clothing, his masculinity under considerable threat. I receive a sympathetic grin from the sales assistant. *Lon-je-ray*, she pronounces it, an appalling Anglicisation of a perfectly good French word. I engage her in a kind of banter—'So, do you get many husbands in here?'—to stop her looking at the change-room door where Deliria is, unsurprisingly, stuffing bras and panties into her shoulder bag.

We cut a broad sweep through the CBD. Boutiques flash by. Lorenzo, Nikita, Vincenzo, the CD section of a department store, the stationery section of a department store. She has a thing about calligraphy pens and exercise books. She also has a professional contempt for anti-shoplifting devices. Mirrors? A joke. CCTV? Come *on*. 'Just stand between me and that video camera, will you? That's it.' Our conversations tend to be coded, because whispers carry. *Yes*, I think she would like that. *No*, that wouldn't suit Philippa at all. *Now*, I wonder if that would be right for Jane? *Wait a minute*, she doesn't like jeans. The riotous contents of the shoulder bag grow and grow, what with the resolute non-involvement of the sales assistants, their full concentration given to their eye make-up, to their music-listening devices. We emerge through rubbish-strewn back streets. We emerge through fire exits. Yes, for people who aren't fire prevention officers, we see quite a lot of fire exits.

Back at Bellevue, it's like opening Christmas presents. We've forgotten what we've stolen, each theft so intense that it effaces memory of the one before. She pulls things out of the bag. 'Oh, what's this?' She tots up the value. An exact total is impossible because all the price tags are in little balls floating down storm drains, but she estimates that the useless trinkets have a cost price of around one thousand seven hundred dollars. Not bad for a day's work.

From this pile of goods she takes hold of a cloudy purple dress, or not so much a dress as a breath of gas, and stands, holding the material against her. The rows of buttons on her blouse are clearly visible through it. Well, I say, chaps, I certainly hope she's not going to put this on.

'Does it look good?'

'Yeah. Hey, why don't you go and try it on?'

'Why not?'

Again comes her ready agreement to something with sexual overtones. With me, ready agreement. With another guy, I don't think so. I'm *too* unthreatening, *too* unmasculine.

She returns from the spare room, her bare feet dodging the

spread-out stolen goods. She's not wearing a bra. Apart from this gaseous dress, she's not wearing *anything*, guys.

She stands directly in front of me, one leg straight, one bent, her hands clasped behind her back. Her breasts sail into the front of the dress. Her stomach is a flat plain, with the one small well of her navel. Her hips just keep on filling out and filling out; then, in the equatorial regions—the hot, wet zones—there's a much-worshipped triangle to which I could sing songs of praise.

'Do you like it?'

'Yes.'

'Do you think most men would like it?'

'I think you could rest assured on that one.'

'Good.' And with the air of having satisfied herself about a detail that's been bothering her for some time, she returns to the spare room to change.

What I can't have

In Thailand, people with overseas degrees drink coffee; people without overseas degrees serve coffee. One's future is very clear-cut. At the Thai-Australian Friendship Association, they're all terrified of growing up to serve coffee. To avoid this, they send me, and others like me, a two-weekly package, which I reciprocate with packages of Australian low culture. Thus I receive copies of the tabloid *Thai Nation*, copies of the broadsheet *Matichon*, videos of TV soaps, videos of bad American movies with Thai subtitles, videos of bad American movies dubbed into Thai, interviews taped off the radio, and a tape of Ball, Bean, Beer, Pong, Bonus and Terdsak talking about the events of the week in rapid Thai. You might be able to buy *Thai Court Poetry 1277–1767* in Australia but you could never buy this stuff. I throw myself into it. Memorise, repeat, memorise, repeat. Rote learning may be derided by so-called language teachers but it certainly works. I compile the return package: same kind of stuff. Video of *Neighbours*. Video of a cop show. Documentary on street children. Documentary on smack. Documentary on that peculiarly Australian amusement, random beating-up. Copy of the *Adelaide Times*. Six o'clock news. 5MMM talk show. Junk mail. Tape of me talking about the events of the week in rapid English, shoplifting censored. Do they want a copy of *The Getting of Wisdom*, or perhaps the latest Peter Carey? No, they can get all that at home. You can always get hold of the high culture because that's what we export. It's the low culture that's difficult to get hold of.

I parcel it up and struggle down the hill with it to Flinders, where Prosse is driven to extremes of praise by another of my essays, 'The Representation of Authentic Speech in Modern

French Fiction'. He gives it a ridiculous 95%, and enquires if I've ever thought about taking up an academic career. I have. I'm definitely up to it. However, I've also thought about ending up like Prosse: the man who's always losing his keys, spilling food over himself, tottering through life.

I take the small pleasures that Adelaide so richly supplies. I go to the beach. I play football with Kev. I buy Australian wine by the dozen, smirking when I think of how much it costs in Thailand. I attend the French Club meetings, drinking myself stupid with the medievalists, walking back uphill to Bellevue over the sheep-studded paddock, forcing myself to memorise lists of words when I get home.

To compensate for her strenuous Music I rehearsals, i.e. her absence, Deliria has presented me with, or rather dumped on me, a kitten. It appears to have rickets—those trailing back legs, that sloppy gait. I give it lots of milk with ground-up calcium tablets. I take it to visit Kev and Doug, and it mews plangently on the tram, drawing the attention of the event-starved passengers.

At Glenelg, Doug is working on his insanity: he's almost got it down. He's taken to loitering at the front gate, asking the infrequent pedestrians if they feel like a bit of a chat. Kev tells me he took ten bags of tomatoes down to Jetty Road and tried to sell them on the street, until the police good-humouredly brought him home. He didn't remember the address, but he remembered the sequence of roads and intersections. Sequences of action, such as returning home from Jetty Road, are not easily forgotten. Then again, brushing your teeth is an often-repeated sequence of action, and he's forgotten that. After spending hours in the bathroom, he stumbles into the corridor, his teeth ripe with plaque.

Kev and I practise with his pistol crossbow, and then with his brutal five-hundred-pounder. Like all crossbows, it's a bit inaccurate, except in commando movies, where it knocks the sentry out of that tower every time. It's powerful, though. It's so powerful that the bolt goes through the newly purchased target, through a mature gumtree, and ends up stuck to a depth of twenty centimetres in the neighbours' concrete breezeblock garage, which necessitates a few minutes of fast talking from me and Kev.

Kev keeps inviting me to go shooting rabbits with him. But for some reason I can't. Infected with *joie*, impelled to goodness, I can't shoot those bunnies. The civilising influence of love? The high cost of crossbow bolts? Fish, though, are okay: no brains. I agree to go spearfishing with him, and we manage to get some mullet.

At the moment my *joie* consists of an almost holographic vision of Deliria rotating in front of me in the gaseous dress, asking me, 'Does it look good?' It's a powerful civilising influence. Instead of wanking or shooting rabbits, I find myself composing cloying verses, thus:

> A hair is picked up off the floor and wound
> Finger to finger like a rosary
> But long before her intercession sounds …

And there's at least nine more lines of the stuff. Yes, I quite agree. The poet is clever but superficial, etc. The poet should have a wank. But for documentary purposes, let's examine it. In Line 1, the poet stoops to pick up the beloved's tress from its undignified resting place. That even this small relic should be thus abused! Actually, in the real-life incident it was looped determinedly through one of the eyelets of my shoe, and I just broke it off and threw it in the bin. Wonderful how poetry falsifies. Line 2: identification of the love-object with the Virgin. Line 3: Virgin identification pursued, with associations of her granting him something (e.g. her virginity), or, more subtly, *helping* him in some unexplained way. Is this what I really think about Deliria? No. It's just that I don't have the talent. I can't write lyric poetry; I can't escape from its traditions. I see everything in terms of the *chevalier*, infected with his *joie,* impelled towards chivalrous acts, his heart crammed with *désirs incommunicables* and *inappaisables*, the road between him and his beloved full of *obstacles infranchissables*. 'So, why doesn't he just go and find someone else?' a modern-day reader might ask. I'm asking myself the same question. Deliria's obviously not going to go to bed with me, she's not going to marry me, she's not going to have a kid with me. Why then do I bother? Why do I go to all the trouble? Why don't I just find some nice, 'attractive' girl, like that shop assistant in the lingerie section, with whom I could share so much?

In the tutorial, Prosse explains why I go to all the trouble. Of course, we're not talking about me, we're talking about Guillaume d'Aquitaine.

'You've got to remember,' he says, digging with his long thumbnail at some dried egg yolk that he has discovered on his tie, 'that those fellows were all about eighteen years old. In those days you were dead at twenty-eight. All intensity, no maturity.' He's right. You would never ask yourself questions like, 'Will I still love her in ten years?', 'What will she be like when she's forty?', or 'Do we have enough interests in common to guarantee a mutually satisfying old age?'

When she can get time off from her rehearsals, we go for long walks on the beach, over the whipped froth and piled seaweed. With those long legs of hers, those mighty metres, she can walk from Glenelg to Henley Beach and back. 'Why not combine exercise and conversation, my dear Will?'

She tells me that Immaculate College has always boasted (in addition to its famed and oft-recorded chamber orchestra, and its long roll-call of alumni in the professions of law and medicine) a respectable incidence of student pregnancies. I know I've mentioned this before, but it's both fascinating and appalling to hear how Deliria's Year-12 group was decimated, in the original, Roman sense of the word. Of her cohort, Jane had to put the baby up for adoption, Michaela had to have an abortion, Mary decided to keep the baby, Bridget had to go into a women's shelter, and Sharon tried to conceal that she was pregnant. Plus five makes ten. Deliria joined a coven of virgins.

'So I assume you're still a virgin, then?' I dare surmise.

'That's a very private thing, Will. I don't know that we should be discussing that. Well, actually with *you* it puts a whole different complexion on our—for want of a better word—relationship.'

'You should find some halfway decent lad and at least try it.'

'You're not recommending yourself, are you?'

She's smiling that famous smile. I know it's not on, but I've damaged nothing: her arm even seems to be encircling my waist here.

Back at Bellevue the long-hoped-for escalation doesn't occur. I have dinner with her, I drink some wine with her, I watch a video of *Gone with the Wind* with her, failing to carry her up the stairs. Our walks on the beach continue, during which she starts to demand some fairly empirical descriptions of my own sex life. Well, when you don't have one of your own, the next best thing is other people's. The combination of her bold line of questioning and her complete ignorance leads to what is known as 'discourse breakdown'. She interrupts every description with, 'Couldn't you inject a little romance into it?' I tell her she asked for the facts. Just the facts, ma'am.

'So, do you wank?' she pursues.

'Affirmative.'

'Where?'

'What do you mean *where*? Okay, the bathroom.'

'It conjures up this repulsive picture of mouldy tiles,' she remarks.

Onward, onward with the technical enquiry.

'What about blowjobs? Don't tell me you would actually ask a woman to do that to you?'

'Well, I don't normally "ask" anyone to "do" anything. We just do things.'

She's fascinated by this business of location. 'What's the most exciting place you've ever made love in?' What does she want me to say? What would *you* say? The top of a Ferris wheel? An historical site? What's this thing she's got with *place*? A philosophical discussion ensues, in which I argue that a banal location is rendered special by having love made in it. In this room all kingdoms are, I all princes am, that kind of thing. It doesn't convince her. After one particularly exhausting interrogation—'So, do you eat your own cum?'—she favours me with the most touching reminiscence of buses. *Buses*. Buses I have known. 'We used to stand at the Hail Bus Here sign outside Immaculate, we used to kneel in the road and Salaam the driver: Hail, Oh Bus!'

'Would you say the nuns were important role models for you?' I ask. It's a cheap shot, I know. Who needs William of Glenelg, Psychotherapist? There's enough psychotherapists playing at being psychotherapists.

Buses I have known. Chapter 2: the 216. We bounce towards Bellevue over the potholed roads of Marion Council. Her handbag, like a distended stomach, holds the complete range of Vévey lipstick in its store demonstration case. Deliria is wearing a miniskirt with a zippered flap over the crotch, 'for having sex against walls,' she teases. I'm coming to sartorially resemble Deliria, not that I get around in female attire, but my clothes are starting to reflect a well-offness that I don't have. I'm down to the last twenty dollars of my student allowance and I'm wearing pinstriped banker's trousers, an Italian double-breasted jacket, white shirt and tie. One of the last adventures it's possible to have: wearing inappropriate clothes. Deliria is wearing elbow-length gloves. Who wears elbow-length gloves these days? Look closer: as she peels them off they are loaded with earrings, which rain onto the bus seat. This is getting more and more frightening, my part in it more and more active. This morning, for instance, impatient at seeing her fiddling with the chain that attached the lipstick case to the cashier's desk, I simply unscrewed it with a five-cent piece.

She enquires if I've ever thought about taking up a shoplifting career. I'm definitely up to it, she says. I have this physical decisiveness. It would never have occurred to Deliria, she admits, to unscrew that chain.

The next minute, what with her refusal to ever keep still and the constant folding and unfolding of her legs, and all the pot-holes we're being bounced through, she's hurt her knee. She's also succeeded in jabbing my balls with her stiletto heel. She really shouldn't be wearing this miniskirt, either: she's just displayed her panties to me again.

What's this? One of the earrings has buried its bee-sting in her knee, just under the kneecap. Her finger is enquiring at it, fiddling with it. Clearly my famous physical decisiveness is required here. My arms lock around the back of her warm leg, immobilising that limb. Well, here comes my closest-yet encounter with Deliria's body: I remove the earring with my teeth. Haven't heard the dreaded N-word yet. In fact—wow—I've scored the double-rower. So for a while there, I'm licking happily away at her knee, eventually kissing it, an operation made possible by the complete emptiness of the bus, a frequent condition in Adelaide.

It's such a *living* knee: it's got transparent peach-hairs on it, and there's a tiny horizontal scar: she must have fallen off her bike when she was a kid. I could kiss her knee for decades. I look up at her; those traffic-light greens are telling me, 'Go on. Keep doing it.'

'So tell me, were you aroused?'

'Yes.'

'And would you have been ready to make love, if I had been your lover?'

'Definitely.'

'Such assurance.' She rises from the couch. She puts on Paganini. 'So if I put my foot here,' she says, resting her foot on my trousers' bulging contents, 'I could be in danger?'

'Yes.'

'Is that …?'

'Yes.' I start fiddling with her hand, stroking her forearm, etc.

'No.'

'What?'

'Not me. You.'

I can't believe what I'm seeing. Deliria's white hand, fingers shining with Vaseline, is moving slowly and cautiously up and down my incredulous member. I'm naked on the Bellevue couch, legs spread like a frog's. She's taken off her top ('That should keep you aroused') but kept her bra on. The black of the bra is shocking against her white skin.

'Does that feel good, baby?'

'It feels fantastic.'

The telephone rings. The caller doesn't hang up after the usual six: the demanding, attention-seeking cries will not stop.

'Do you think you should answer the phone?'

'I wouldn't answer the telephone if I were expecting a call from God.'

The telephone keeps ringing. 'Fuck this shit,' I say. I step across the room, erection practically piercing my stomach, kick off the handset, and stamp on the switch hooks.

'Let's keep doing it, William.'

After a few more minutes, my whole body clenches, bending backwards like a pocketknife being opened, and I express my courtly love all over Deliria's bra and shoulder.

'Baby,' she says, looking down at the havoc I've wrought on her talcum-powdered chest, 'I've never seen that before.'

I'm determined not to want what I can't have—*so que no puesc aver.* I like courtly love poetry but I don't want to live it. I can't have her desire, although there's loads of things I *can* have. That's it, William, that's a good little technique for getting through life:

think about what you can have, rather than what you can't have. You can't have her desire, but you can come over her body anytime. Perhaps the very absence of her desire appeals to her sense of the bizarre. I don't mean she's not involved at all. Verbally, she's very involved: I receive a sort of racing commentary. But any involvement of her body is a decision, entirely under her government; it's not *part* of it.

Tell me, is this unusual?

It's been two weeks since the Bellevue-couch episode, during which we've done little else. Even the shoplifting has given way to sexual experimentation. But alarmingly, I've run up against … not exactly a perversion, though some might call it so; I rather think it spices things up a bit. She likes it *al fresco*, especially in buses (Hail, Oh Bus!), on the Glenelg tram, on the beach, in public parks, and on one memorable occasion on a train curling its way up through the Mount Lofty Ranges. A typical Sunday afternoon might find us on the banks of the Torrens, on a picnic rug spread with Blue Castello cheese, Semillon Blanc, pumpernickel bread and at least one dietary recommendation from a women's magazine. 'Tahini—supposed to be really good for you.' Oh, and a jar of Vaseline. Yes, I'm certainly seeing a lot of the Australian landscape, as well as spending large amounts of time on public transport, most of it in a state of great physical urgency.

Since we started 'banging the bishop', in Deliria's archaic phrase, she's begun a cautious involvement of her own body, not precisely as I would like, but impossible to refuse. For instance, she invites me to rub her bum, or her 'bottom': again, her terminology. There's a lot of talking, too, which is distracting. I don't get off on talking. I don't understand phone sex, either. But she wants me to describe her bum. Well, it's very cool and smooth; it's quite big, but very exactly proportioned. It reminds me of a lot of classical paintings and sculptures. In short, she's got quite an ass. 'Yes, but would it be attractive to other men?' she enquires. She's not teasing me here: this is a genuine question. She really doesn't know very much about this, and now she has at her disposal a representative of the other side.

Sometimes her gathering of intelligence leads to unexpected difficulties. She asks me to compare my physical dimensions to those of other men. I mean, how many of you hetero guys out there have actually seen another guy's erect cock? Not a porno star's mighty tool, probably pumped up with drugs, but just Joe Blow's ordinary, common or garden hard-on? Not many of you, I bet. *I* never have. In fact, I'd still be haunted by John Lancer, and all those legendary blokes, if I couldn't rely on the information once gained from a young nurse, that it was the *second*-biggest one she'd ever seen; a phenomenon, she'd told me, which is sometimes noted in guys of small stature, the bishop's size seeming to compensate to some extent for the sheer lack of bone and muscle. So I convey a sanitised version of this to Deliria.

As you may have wondered, I've tried to kiss her. It doesn't work. There's a weird disparity about this, considering that she really likes hugging me. Her arms are twin bands of iron pressing against my back. But the lips won't do it. I'm skidding over them, she's dodging. 'Mm-mm.' A definite negative.

These intensely verbal sessions are followed by recaps, summaries, comparisons. Like some crazed tourist she goes on and on: did you see those beautiful temples, the marvellous cathedrals of desire, the twisting spires of passion? I'm her tourist guide, as it were. I've seen them before. But somehow I'm compelled to tell her, 'I've never done that with anyone else, I'm really astounded.'

And she goes on: 'I feel you've let me into this amazing primitive ritual that no one ever gets to see. I feel so privileged, William.'

'There's a lot to be said for a straight fuck,' I reply.

'Do you have to be so crude?' she says. 'Anyway, Will, that's not what we're doing. That's not us.'

Rain in literature

The function of rain in literature is usually to give that little push to the narrative, to get the heroine all wet so that she contracts pneumonia and dies, to provide the hero with the opportunity of displaying gallantry, e.g. by giving the girl his overcoat, giving her a lift on his horse or in his sports car, or to get the hero and heroine running into that cave *ASAP*, where they end up having sex. So the minute that hailstorm comes over the hill, you can usually look forward to a bit of sex, gallantry or pneumonia. In Literature, that is. In Life, however, you just get wet. So it is that Deliria and I, sprinting through a hailstorm in the city with a too-small umbrella, just get wet.

We've been to the Opera Theatre, where we met some of Deliria's music mates. I was introduced to Theseus, Diz, Joss, and Ebenezer. The name William, fairly unusual in Australia these days, was completely outdone by this wholesale eccentricity. During the interval Deliria stole the umbrella we're currently using.

'Anyone who can afford an umbrella this expensive,' she shouts now through the static of the rain, 'can afford a taxi home.'

'How do you know they can afford the umbrella?' I chirp.

'Oh, I suppose I'm just rationalising the theft of the umbrella.'

The rain maintains its explosive impacts on the road. A hailstone the size of an egg strikes the back of my hand. As if in some high-school physics demonstration, the hailstones hit the surface of the street at forty-five degrees, and bounce upward at just under thirty degrees. It's also extremely cold. The rain hitting the umbrella produces a continuous white noise. Our faces are lashed. Mercifully, the tram stop is soon attained, I'm ladling water off the seat of the shelter, and the nice warm tram is clanking towards us. We're supposed to be visiting Kev and Doug, and I'm remarking that Doug has probably just finished classifying the rubbish and has moved on to his more long-term project of gassing Kev, when I'm aware of her saying words like, 'I want to try something,' or 'Let's try something,' and there's this rush of her proximity, her face approaching mine—hey, this is getting rather close.

With most women, there's that half-second when you know it's going to happen. They lean into you; there's an experienced tilt of the head so your noses won't crash into each other, a moderate parting of the lips, and you can smell shampoo, moisturiser, perfume, toothpaste and food. Most women signal what's going to happen; you always know what's going to happen. With Deliria, you never know what's going to happen.

'I want you to kiss me on my neck, baby.'

I lean into the column of her neck, and my lips can feel her carotid artery pumping; I put my hand on the warm back of her head and scoop up her liquid hair, letting it fall back down in all its wildness. I'm licking her neck, tracing a small circumference with the tip of my tongue; then I suck an inch of skin right into my mouth and let it slide out again.

'Love the audacity, William.'

'Why don't we re-route to Bellevue?' I suggest.

'Did you want to have sex with me?'

'Are you teasing me?'

'Would I?'

In full accord with the Pathetic Fallacy, the street at Bellevue is gleaming under its skin of water. I suppose I must be grinning helplessly. This isn't just any old walk from a bus stop to a house. This one is rendered magical by street-lit asphalt, by the loose sonorities of the footpath, by the cruising snails. The house numbers drift by in their tight curls. At the house we're welcomed by that stiffened chain so gracefully supporting the junk mail box;

we're welcomed by the hummocky bushes, by the sunken lawn. All appears beneficent.

It's over the top, I know, but I can't see it otherwise. The landscape is informed of my love.

Now, in Literature, we don't want a sex scene that'll blow the top of your head off. Why? Because you can't do that any more. Why? Because it's boring. Why? Because these days everyone's had sex. Everyone already knows. It would be like Japanese tourists videoing a steak on a barbecue. In Life, though, a sex scene that'll blow the top of your head off is exactly what you want.

A style has developed: there's a range of permitted caresses, and definite no-nos. But with anything new, I can't anticipate her response. Neither can she, I think. Neither of us knows, at any time, what's going to happen. She'll surprise me: what shocks me doesn't shock her. Conversely, and somewhat annoyingly, what's normal for me is unthinkable for her. It's the normality that shocks her. Falling into this category, I'm learning, is any attempt to remove her clothing. Consider the following terrified exchange:

'You won't get forceful if you see my body?'

'Are you serious?'

'Yes.'

'So you think that because I'm a guy …'

'It's just that. You would be able to, if you wanted to.'

'I thought you were right into danger.'

'If you like I'll strip for you. But I don't want you taking off my clothes.'

Well, who am I to quibble?

She begins to undress. She throws off the 100%-wool overcoat readily enough, but underneath it is one of those little black dresses, whose zip is, for some malevolent reason, stuck. She forces her right arm up her back, between her shoulder blades, pushing upwards with her left fingertips on her right elbow. She's pinching the zip and pulling down, but it just won't budge.

'You don't want me to help you with that?'

'No, it's all right.'

She gives up and simply drags the whole dress up over her head, but her hair is, of course, too voluminous, and gets caught on that naughty zip. For many long seconds she's standing there, spectacular, swearing fluently.

'You're *sure* you don't want a hand with that?'

'William, I can't see anything. It's making me nervous. Just help me get this off.'

I step behind her and enter the turmoil of her hair, a few strands of which have wound themselves around the recalcitrant zip. I tell her to keep still, take hold of the back of her dress on either side, and break it open, releasing the precious blonde strands unharmed. Deliria pulls the dress down over her shoulders and practically leaps out of it.

Regaining her composure, she turns those mineral-greens on me, and gives me that smile by which you could land an aircraft in the dead of night.

'Okay. Information time. Do you like my body?'

'You're probably one of the most stunning-looking women in the world. Yes, I like it a lot.'

'So men would find me sexually attractive?'

'Definitely. *Absolument.*'

'You don't think my bottom's too big?'

'No. No problems in that area.'

'Karl Lagerfeld likes women with no bottoms.'

'He's not exactly "most men". '

'No, I suppose not.' She puts her hand on my by-now-familiar physical response to her just being in the same room. 'My God, William. You're so *hard.*'

Oh, did I neglect to mention I've been naked for the last fifteen minutes or so?

She takes my left wrist in her right hand, brings it around the back of her, and slides it, with (did you guess?) my full cooperation, inside her panties. The flesh of her bum is unexpectedly cool. She gives me a firmly guided tour of each cheek, her thumb and fingers encircling my wrist.

'How does that make you feel, baby?'

'Any man fortunate enough to feel your bottom should consider his happiness complete,' I exclaim turgidly but with plenty of feeling.

'Do you? Consider your happiness complete?'

'Yes. You see how it curves out so much? With a guy it's much less.'

'And men would find that sexually attractive?'

'Different, hence attractive. Different to what their own bodies offer them.'

'And would men find it revolting to kiss?'

'Not at all.'

'Would you?'

'Just the opposite.'

'Do you want to?'

'Yes.'

She pulls down her panties, but being Deliria, she leaves them scrolled at the tops of her thighs. And I'm sure you can guess what I do next.

In the following two hours, there's a lot of 'why don't we try this?', 'why don't we try that?', and 'why don't you do this?' She even bursts into anecdote. 'This reminds me of the time … this reminds me of that film.' It's probably the most verbal 'sex' I've ever had, and as I told you before, I don't get off on phone sex. It's obvious to me that the function of language here is not to spice things up, but to distance Deliria, not so much from me as from what we are doing. It's safe to say she's pretty strong on *me*.

'I want you to be my sister soul for life, Will.'

Can't complain about that. With her strong hugs, real spine-crackers, she's very strong on me. It's the other thing she's not strong on. Oh, and kissing, she's not very strong on kissing either. Proximity suggests the experiment to her—my mouth is surprisingly penetrated and filled by her extended tongue, which is then withdrawn.

'No, I'm afraid it doesn't feel right.'

So some things don't feel right, but there are an equal number of things that feel fine. In a kind of bad-movie phrase, we are 'discovering each other's bodies'. When people say that, if they ever say it outside of bad movies, they don't mean discover, they just mean have sex. With us it means *discover*. My role seems to be to present her with, or be led by her into, sexual games in an ascending order of contact. These games are maximally theatrical. At one moment she's got me—get this—wearing a blindfold while licking whipped cream off her breasts. She's braless for the occasion but I don't get to see them. I only get to lick them. Some quite wacky things are, for her, completely acceptable. I mean, how many women do you know who want you to come on their back three times in a single night, then rub the stuff into their skin? Kissing romantically, on the other hand, is right out. As for making her come—unthinkable. So much so, that when I make a start in that direction she rockets off the bed, closing the episode.

'And would you say you were fond of me?' she takes up again. She's addressing the mirror; she's not looking at me. Her back is practically striped with my bodily fluids.

'Very much so.'

'And what about if I had a car accident? Do you think you would still like to do this to me if I were disfigured or brain-damaged?'

'Yes, I definitely would.'

'I see. And if for some reason I decided I didn't want to do it anymore, would that upset you?'

'It would.'

She turns around. 'Do you love me?'

'Yes.'

'Oh my God. Really?'

'Yes. I love you.'

'Since when?'

'Since the Immaculate fete.'

'Wow. So, for example, when we were walking along the beach that day, you were already in love with me.'

'Yes.'

'And pray, sir, why do you think you love me? Do you admire certain qualities, or is it a more primal desire?'

How do I love thee? Let me count the ways. Well first, I very much like your voice, the way it's not at all nasalised, rather unusual in an Australian. Second, I very much like coming over your body, as well as having strong fantasies about protecting you from danger. Okay?

'William?'

'What?'

'You won't do anything to me while I'm asleep, will you?'

'Jesus Christ. Of course not.'

'See you in the morning.'

'Goodnight.'

As morning heaves itself up for work, as magpies oscillate in the trees outside, as the thud-and-roll of the pornographic newspaper comes from the front verandah, I'm engaged in a religious contemplation of this amazing object, her face. I've been granted the opportunity to stare at her face without being rude. The major revelation is that she has *freckles*. Revealed by the night cleanser, these tiny brown spots blur into each other, their edges so weakly defined that the unfocused eye loses them. Also revealed, along the line of her jaw, are a couple of moles sprouting long hairs. I want details, details. I've never had the chance to just stare. Viewed from the side, the descent of her nose sports a small bump. A newly pierced earlobe is swollen, a crust of blood adhering to the sleeper.

She looks very English, but a clue to her nationality is gained from the cornflake-sized blotches of childhood sunburn on her shoulders. For a moment of soaring imagination, I'm transported back to Glenelg Beach, years ago, with Deliria walking in her child's confidence for hours on the beach, coming back screaming and crying, her blistered shoulders rising like bread.

I think I've reached the zenith. She's not going to grant me any more, is she? We'll continue, she virginal, me priapic. She'll entice, then repel, boarders. And through this will run an unbreakable courtesy, a *courtoisie*, a respect for unmarked boundaries, which at the moment seem to be kissing her and making her come. So onward, into a future of perpetual holding back, in which she'll give me increasingly sophisticated declarations of what increasingly resembles love. I'll subsist on this breathy diet, *un vrai troubadour*, while wondering if I can effect some change in her behaviour that will spring the locks. If I present her with an expensive gift? (Only an extension of what I've already done.) If I am *less* chivalrous?

I try to imagine her future spouse. Nightmarishly prosperous figures drift through my fancy, cheerfully raunching Deliria, while she pleads for Paganini.

She's bad news, man

The fanciful bio of Jaufre Rudel, a single paragraph, has him dying for love in the arms of the Princess of Tripoli, with whom he fell in love by listening to a physical description of her. (Remember, these guys were all about eighteen years old.) He journeyed to Tripoli by ship, was wrecked, and died twenty-four hours after reaching his objective. And if you believe all that, there's a nice used car I'd like to sell you.

What's quite eerie about old Jaufre is this one stanza, which I will roughly translate: 'I'm riding on my horse, I'm pursuing my goal, my goal recedes in front of me, the very act of forward progress makes my goal get further away.' That's a weird idea when you think about it.

In my tutorial I discuss this with Prosse, who is busy spilling food over himself. Shreds of unidentifiable nutrient cling to that helicopter-blade moustache.

'Surely he wants to attain his goal, though,' I point out. 'I don't think he's ambivalent about that.'

'The pursuit actually distancing him from her,' he chews, 'as if he were going backwards by going forwards. Very Anglo-Saxon idea, that, straight out of an Anglo-Saxon horror story. It's not like Provençal at all, it's much more complicated.'

'If he wants to attain his goal, he should stop pursuing. If he realises it's taking him backwards, he should stop.'

'He can't stop.'

When I arrived, Doug was busy kneeling at the foot of the bean trellis, transplanting the curled embryos of bean sprouts from a margarine container. He seemed to be having a good day. On a good day, he will attempt to mow the lawn one-handed; he will empty wood chips into the pot-plants; he will hose the cement. On a good day, he will manage a coherent conversation on a limited range of topics. On a bad day, he will stand at the gate pining for the junk mailer's arrival; he will escape on the tram without any money; he will destroy the telephone bill.

Later on, I have to revise my estimation of Doug's day. It's a bad one. Mid-afternoon, he roams the house holding a plastic bag of tomatoes. Very late at night, I'm woken up by the bounce of tomatoes over the kitchen floor. Doug is posed dramatically in the centre of the kitchen, as though for a classical sculpture titled *Hercules versus the Kitchen Tidy*. An assortment of rubbish covers the kitchen table. Doug, thoroughly absorbed, replaces the Kitchen Tidy next to the fridge and begins classifying the rubbish. It is not very dangerous, I tell myself. Just in case, I unplug the microwave and turn off the gas at the valve.

I pad through the house, noting Kev's six-pack of Cooper's Ale. I read a bit of Bernard de Ventadorn. He's just a versifier, really: competent, but on the downward slide of the tradition. Guillaume d'Aquitaine rides all over him. Ventadorn's babes are all basically the same: he's always cranking out stanzas about their beauty, virtue and chastity. The last two are pretty much synonyms. He's always going on about himself: his desire, his holy pursuit thereof. It's extremely boring. Guillaume d'Aquitaine, much more meaty, has at least one line about getting his hand up under the beloved's dress. With Ventadorn, you could never imagine meeting these women. They have no detail; you could never imagine there being anything wrong with them. After a while of his undifferentiating praise, you begin to suspect that if there were something wrong with them, he couldn't handle it. He could never admit it; he could never allow it to injure the purity of his love. Guillaume, on the other hand, would take in black teeth, bad breath, stretch marks, spare tyre and moustache at a glance, and concentrate on getting his hand up under her dress.

But what if she were *mentally unstable*? You can see where I'm going with this. It's not the first time I've wondered if there isn't something dark, dangerous and highly uncute behind Deliria's shoplifting, and now, her pranks too. On the morning after that 'zenith', I was met in the driveway by the sumo-cat. Did I mention the extravagance, the profligacy of its fur, which was always turning up in hairballs on the lounge-room floor, choking the vacuum cleaner? Well, my cleaning problem was solved, at any rate. She had shaved off its coat and whiskers with my disposable razor. It didn't seem to mind. She explained that she had wanted to see what it looked like. It looked like a walking plastic bag full of intestines. Couldn't she have waited until spring? Fearing its death by exposure, I dressed it up in one of the owners' woollen jumpers. I needn't have bothered: next day it was run over by a car. I still suspect its disorientation, when it staggered under the wheels, was due to the loss of its whiskers. I buried it in the back yard, choosing the softest ground, which happened to be on a slope. A thunderstorm followed. By the following morning, the body had been washed down the hill, into the creek, and the neighbour's little boys were discovered pulling out the teeth with a pair of pliers.

I see other things, too: this shoplifting business has got to stop. There's the danger, of course, but also I sense that in her inimitable, fun-filled, incidentally pleasurable way, she's using me. We never do anything that I want to do. Do we go on motorbike rides down to Second Valley? Do we go snorkelling, spearfishing, camping? I've just been spearfishing with Kev, in wetsuits because it's so cold in the water, and though I'm incompetent, it was the best fun I've had in ages. What do my days with Deliria consist of? Shoplifting from cosmetics stores, just duplicating what she's already got, followed by sensual death on the owners' bed. Yes, what we're doing, it's got to stop. The shoplifting, that is.

In the considerable freeing-up of time occasioned by Deliria's rehearsals, I do lots of things I can't really do when she's around:

clean the house, mow the lawn, bury the cat again. I study French and Thai. I get through a fair amount of a Thai filmscript. Another package arrives from the Thai-Australian Friendship Association: this one contains a car accident and judicial execution magazine titled *Police News*. I send off the appropriate return package, but there's nothing in Australia that comes anywhere near to the retch-producing full-colour close-ups and half-literate commentary of *Police News*.

After about a week, Deliria and I have the following telephone conversation:

'I picked up this fantastic pewter mug in this darling little shop on Unley Road.'

'When you say "picked up", you really mean "picked up". So how's your opera going?'

'Wonderful. Final countdown, dress rehearsal on Friday, opening night Saturday. You must come.'

'Definitely. So, do you know it off by heart, or do you sight-read it, or a bit of both?'

'Sight-read, of course. I don't actually like it that much.'

'Not Paganini, right?'

'It's not technically demanding. It's banal. Anyway, William, there's something we really have to sort out.'

'Ah.'

'What we're doing. It's got to stop.'

'Ah.'

'I'm in love.'

'Great! So, who is it?'

She's fallen in love with that Strength Through Joy poster, that stunningly Aryan product of nineteenth-century German immigration, Theseus. And guess what? They've had sex! Only joking. With virginal insensitivity, she narrates, over the phone, the whole course of her passion for him. She has liked him all year, but when rehearsals started, she saw him in the role of Inthusamit, the tenor warrior-hero. Desire was ignited by the following: the careless attraction of the robe slipping off his shoulder, and the stage directions, which demanded that he should kiss Amorn-vivat (played by 'a brainless nonentity'). But now she's reached an impasse, because he won't make the move. He always keeps talking about music. She'll try to direct the conversation towards, let's say, mid-range restaurants, and he'll politely complete a few exchanges on the topic before waxing lyrical on his true interests, e.g. David Oistrach's bow technique in the Violin Concerto in A minor, BWV 1041. So she wants me to help her. She wants me to help her to think of a way to make him make the move.

'Why don't you just be normal, for Christ's sake? Ask him out for coffee.'

As usual, the landscape is fully informed of my love's progress. A total eclipse shrouds the southern half of Australia, and we have an eleven a.m. sunset. Birds, tricked by the false dark, go back to their nests. Ululating pigeons arrange themselves for sleep; symphonic parrots fold their wings. Flies go to sleep; mosqui-toes get up for work. Bats come out and eat them. Dogs get wor-ried. Light-operated switches come on: the whole South Eastern Freeway lights up. Around the blackened sun, stars are visible. Everything in nature, and quite a few electronic devices, unite in telling me: it's *over*.

Kev sympathises. 'She's bad news, man. Stay away.'

Kev is so sane, so level. His girlfriend, so competent. His fore-arms, so thick. She's bad news. Kev is very practical. He is emo-tionally practical. I'm emotionally *im*practical. He looks only at the effect of two people on each other. He doesn't care about the woman's charm, intellect, talent for languages, appearance: none of this is essential to him. He cares about what the woman *does* to him. It's not how witty nor how free, nor yet how beautiful she be, but how much kind and true to Kev. On this point, he and Aure-lian Townshend are in agreement. Not quite as good with words as the late court poet, though, he comes out with the endearingly drab: 'You know, you gotta get on well together.' Which proceeds, however, from a solid understanding of the world that I don't have.

For the next couple of days I watch garbage programs on television: morning TV, midday TV, repeats of American car-chase shows. I even work up a liking for a B-grade Hollywood actor: I can imagine he'd be quite a nice guy to talk to; I could confide in him about Deliria, and he'd say, 'She's bad news, man.'

Down the hill at Flinders, the medievalists' continuous drinking session also provides relief. I develop an obsession with correcting people's spoken English: I am really in a bad way. The merest 'I would of' sends me into spasm. When I'm fairly drunk I make the ascent to Bellevue. On my work table is enshrined the frontispiece of Jaufre Rudel, where she's blotted her lipstick ten or twelve times. It's almost as if she's put it there specifically for me to use as a surrogate, which I'm afraid I do, unhealthily often, drunkenly pressing the pages to my mouth. Finally asleep, I have night terror. I wake up on the kitchen floor, surrounded by boxes of cat food that have toppled off the shelf. I wake up on the balcony, on the front lawn.

I'm not cut out for these feelings. Instead of wallowing in self-pity, I conduct an informal experiment with Kev's motorbike. How fast do I have to I get it up to before the sheer danger stops me from thinking about Deliria? I take this monstrous machine, one of the fastest production bikes in the world, down to Second Valley. I get it up to the state limit, 110 km/h. No, still relatively safe, still thinking about Deliria. Take it up to 180. No, still thinking about Deliria, although the South Australia Police are also on my mind. Yes, these Japanese motorcycles can certainly move along. At 250 on a straight road, the wind is trying to tear off my helmet; there is also a strong crosswind trying to push me into a hillside. I'm speed-reading the landscape. At 297 kilometres per hour, the bike's top speed, a hapless pigeon explodes onto the face of my helmet. I forget about Deliria.

To my surprise, I'm still alive; I haven't even crashed the bike. The pigeon, however … All that's left of him (or her) is some flay-marks of blood on Kev's shattered visor. Chastened, at 60 km/h, I reflect that life offers much. Consider the beauty of the sun, tilted over at the winter solstice, peeping over the fence at noon, a shy winter sun. Consider the wonderful washed-blue mornings Adelaide favours us with. Consider the recovery of Deliria's kitten: originally almost paraplegic with rickets, he now has sufficient power in his back legs to have captured and decapitated an adult blue-tongue lizard, which he deposits on the back doormat. I need something like him to take me out of the incredible staleness of myself, this monitoring of every feeling, which in turn engenders secondary feelings on top of it all. Let me bring the kitten some milk; let me involve myself in the rapid unrolling and rolling up of his specially bristled tongue.

Apart from the one fairly important omission, our soul-mateship is strangely unchanged. The sex was so decorative that its removal leaves us as structurally sound, or unsound, as ever. We continue to spend fifty percent of our income on lunch. The magnificent streamer of our talk continues to unroll in assorted locations. We arrange to meet at the foot of the lifts, at the Torrens footbridge, at the front of the Barr Smith, or in Rundle Mall. At any time, we might be satirising the Australian press, lampooning its owner, sending up the seriously sexual poses of store dummies, pitying people who wear bad clothes, or composing lists of deadly sins against taste. We listen to Paganini, Mozart, Bach. We read literary magazines. We criticise the poetry in the student weekly. In the Barr Smith's research wing, I show her how to use the journals. On the banks of the Torrens, she introduces me to Roquefort. At Glenelg, she manages to coax a coherent conversation out of Doug, on the subject of tomatoes. With a shy Kev, she discusses the ethics of shooting rabbits. With me, she discusses the latest hardline-feminist issues, the latest gay issues, the latest macrobiotic-diet issues, the latest atmospheric issues and the latest lifestyle issues. She also gives me a guided tour, not of her own body, but of the Music Department. So here is her revealed world, with its inevitable corollary, so much left unrevealed.

Theseus

The Elder Conservatorium of Music is the name that appears in concert handouts and enticements for overseas enrolees, but anyone who works there or studies there just calls it The Con. I thought it would be full of people bursting into song as they walked down the corridors, but instead, it's a typical Australian university department, with numbered doors, a common room, and billboards with students seeking or offering to share accommodation, or to do people's ironing for twenty bucks. 'Will mow lawns for twenty bucks.' 'Will do dishes: $20.' Some guy is offering to sell his CD collection for twenty bucks.

What makes it a bit different to, say, the French Department, is the glass-walled, not very well-soundproofed practice studios, or practice 'hutches' as Deliria calls them. In one of these, two oboe players bite their reeds between their lips and run up and down contrapuntal scales impressively fast, while in the next room a piano student plays a rendering of a harpsichord piece, from the court of Louis Quatorze, as I remember. The two pieces of music clash horribly, but the students have trained themselves to be selectively deaf: they just do not hear an instrument in the next practice hutch because that would interfere with their practice.

This revealed world of hers also contains posters of past performances by violinists with unpronounceable Eastern European names, a coffee machine puddled and slicked, next to it a coffee-donation box providing Deliria with a supply of tram fares, the standard ripped-vinyl couch, and a stack of posters for *Aphaphirom et Amornvivat,* or just *Apha* as they're starting to call it. Now usually I don't have much time for University Life: too many people running around shouting out things like *End Racism Now,* or

End Prostitution Within Marriage Now, and not enough people doing their essays. But I'll make an exception for Music.

Theseus walks out of one of the practice hutches. To say that Theseus is good-looking is like saying Leonardo da Vinci was good at maths. He is a physical genius; he just shames the rest of us blokes. His attributes are: Olympian shoulders, sculpted forearms, interesting facial planes, perfectly spaced blue eyes, a patrician nose, a fine jaw and gold hair. He is simply a catalogue of what the human male ideal is supposed to look like. And does he fuck it up by having a stupid voice? Can I confidently assert the superiority of my intellect over his? Does he make frequent grammatical errors? Does he say 'I would of', 'I seen', 'youse guys', and 'I says'? Is he boring? Does he talk interminably about doing up his car? Can I gleefully point out to Deliria his obvious homosexuality? Dear oh dear. I can't come up with a single reason why Deliria wouldn't want to sleep with him. He is a staggeringly handsome man, a couple of years younger than me, with an intellect well within the top ten percent. My feelings towards Theseus are amicable. This is what Deliria is attracted to, or in love with. Physical equality. Someone who isn't outclassed by her. I'm reminded of one of those sexual universals: people go for people who look about the same. There's a lesson for me somewhere here.

The occasion of this visit is the opening night of *Apha* at the Arts Theatre, the sort of second-rank joint I associate with school pantomimes, but it's only Music I and they can't afford to rent the Opera Theatre. I have a vast three hours to fill before they go on, which I spend with Guillaume d'Aquitaine and Jaufre Rudel, trying to write an essay for Prosse about the troubadour's receding goal. My goal recedes. My hairline recedes. Occasionally I foray into the backstage area, where not much is happening: musicians standing around in various stages of readiness, eating fish and chips out of a paper bag. Like most glamorous professions, music is probably ninety percent eating fish and chips out of a paper bag.

So Deliria and Theseus are to be an item. My main feeling on this topic is curiosity. Deliria getting a boyfriend is so hot in the tabloids that 'William and Deliria—Soul Mates for Life?' has achieved page-19 status. On the phone again, she's asked me about standard procedures. 'What should I do? You're a guy. You should know.' Well, Deliria, quite often, the man asks the woman to meet, just two people, for coffee in pleasant, neutral surroundings with some sort of time limit, e.g. he has to play football at seven o'clock. Less frequently, but increasingly often in these liberated times, the woman asks the man. Acceptance constitutes an undefined interest, probably sexual. They have a conversation. They exchange their world views. They manifest their personalities. They disclose themselves. Without actually verbalising their desires, they eventually *know*. Then something *happens*. Okay? Got it?

It's ten to eight in the packed foyer of the Arts, and I'm examining the cast photos and shots of the dress rehearsal. Disturbingly, Deliria's criminal behaviour has contributed to the props. There's that umbrella she stole from the Opera Theatre. Don't you think she's taking it that little bit too far? Consider the following sequence of events: Deliria steals a highly distinctive umbrella. Its owner, a lover of the musico-dramatic arts, with an inexplicable taste for boring seventeenth-century opera, comes to the Music I production. The umbrella is recognised. An open-and-shut case. And *so* Adelaide.

At the five-minute bell, a torrent of plastic wine cups goes into the bins. My ticket, confusedly recovered from one of the pockets of the Italian banker's suit (I still haven't discovered all of them), is given to an usher.

As it turns out, Deliria is in the orchestra pit and I can't even see her, though I can hear her well enough: any time the violin is doing something fiendishly difficult (double-stops, infinite sustain, impossibly fast arpeggios), it's her. Though I'm certainly not a musician, I now understand what she meant when she said the music was 'banal'. It's quite predictable, like a Vivaldi concerto written very rapidly for sales purposes. This composer, Verteuil, not unlike his modern counterparts, just has a bag of riffs that he sticks together in whatever order seems good enough. His music contains no surprises, no defeats of expectation, not a single cadence that you couldn't predict ten seconds before. However, it's not unlistenable. It's the kind of music that they would have had in lifts in department stores in the seventeenth century.

This brings us to Theseus, as Inthusamit. Tragically, he's miscast. Inthusamit is supposed to be a complete bastard, careless of other people's lives. Theseus plays him as some kind of wounded soul. Oh, may as well spit it out: he's terrible. He can't act his way out of a brown paper bag; he is unable to fit his personality around the character he's supposed to be playing. His voice, on the other hand, is a musical instrument of rare quality. He should be singing *Nessun Dorma* on Air New Zealand advertisements and making millions.

Generously invited to the cast party, I get to drink a large quantity of white wine while watching Deliria's attempts to interest Theseus. There's so much competition. Theseus is like the Sun, with his own little solar system of women and gay men orbiting around him. Deliria, also like the Sun, also with her own solar system, in which I try not to figure too prominently, is trying hard to get Theseus into her gravitational field. Will he prove too powerful even for her? Will she end up orbiting him just like the others? It's the *Clash of the Titans* here.

The landscape is again informed of my love. It's a nervous, charged, creaking landscape. Lizards sputter over the rocks like electric charges. On the hills above Flinders, the clinging rain is on the gum leaves, and we're given latent, stored showers as the wind heaves at a branch. Sheep stare at us. Rabbits flee. A potato-crisp packet is whirled and slammed against a tree trunk.

A cloud shadow homes in over Flinders, darkening it faculty by faculty, passing over the slabs of the Science buildings, over the duck-dotted lake. The wind combs the grass flat, baring its white lower stems; the narrow path is slick with mud.

Deliria is walking behind me, one hand tightly closed around my belt, frightened of sliding down the hill in those gripless shoes of hers. Twice she slips. I'm holding on to bunches of grass while she skids about. We come to an electrified fence, its top strand laced with orange tags, the barbed wire woven with sheep's fleece. She's just about to grab hold of the top strand when I stop her. Having just missed out on a couple of hundred volts, she tells me I am very knowledgeable. She stands by the fence, picking a scab of moss off a post and flicking it. Her pink raincoat is a lost shout against the scrub greens.

It's the first time she's been up at Bellevue since 'it's got to stop.' Back at the house, she tells me that after I left the cast party hopelessly drunk she made 'zilch' progress with Theseus. A conversation about Germany led not to close physical contact but to his assertion that he didn't think much of Australian women. That he didn't like their voices.

'What, is he deaf?' I almost shout. 'Your voice is lovely.'

After this failure, Deliria found herself agreeing to go to a disco, which she hated, just because Theseus might be going with them. He was dropped off at a taxi rank on the way there.

O rose, thou art sick. Indeed, she is reduced, she seems physically smaller.

Scene: Bellevue. The owners' house. Enter William and Deliria.

'What I need is some grandiose event that would focus his attention on me. Say, if I was in a car accident and he dragged me out.'

'Ah yes. The opportunity for heroism. That can be quite arousing.'

'The man who speaks from experience.'

'Yeah. But you can't exactly arrange a swarm of bees though, can you? No, I'm afraid you'll have to ask him out for coffee.'

'No, let's pursue this line for a moment. Just for fun. Now, if I were under threat of death …'

'Jesus.'

'If something arrived for me at the Arts. Anonymous threats. Danger. That would be just great. Ah yes, beautiful music student, anonymous threats, Theseus calming me down while I have hysterics.'

'Great for troop morale.'

'I should do it, William. Get some florist to send a wreath.'

From under the stage comes the voice of Kev: 'She's fuckin' insane.'

'Seriously. Can you imagine the visual impact of a wreath? And the words. Deepest sympathy for the loss of Deliria, something like that. Theseus would be all over me.'

'The people who would be all over you would be the police. The director would call them in for sure. And then you'll have to make a false statement to them because you won't be able to back out of it in front of your mates. Police go straight to the florist. "Tall girl? Very attractive?" "Yes, I remember her." You'd be up on a charge. And on top of that, you'd be kicked out of Music.'

'I don't think they'd call the police.'

Her destruction arranges itself about her with her willing participation. She consults the bus timetable, and looks up a Petal Station at Blackwood Shopping Town. She jams her feet into the wet shoes.

'Look. *I'll* do it. You'll get caught. I won't get caught.'

The roses in her cheeks

I'm good at this kind of thing. Oh, I'm aware that I'm doing it to impress her. I'm aware, all right. God, I'm so aware. While I'm fine-tuning the mechanism of the plan, she's complimenting me on my devastating intelligence, my quintessentially masculine attention to detail. We're discussing the note. What's needed is something very specific about her physical beauty, which will not seem incongruous attached to a wreath. I tell her we should compare her white skin to the lilies in the wreath. Now there's a nice time-honoured metaphor. No, she says. Too ghostly. Maybe *too* evocative. What about roses, I pursue. If we send roses instead of lilies, then something about the roses in her cheeks will underline her beauty, yet not seem too evocative. What about 'If only these were the roses in her cheeks'? William, you *poet* you.

Ten minutes later, I've packed her off to the Arts. Nothing can be allowed to suspiciously disturb her routine, although she's just kissed me in a way which is definitely not routine, and which would make Theseus extremely angry if he were going out with her. Wow, the exciting inner surface of her mouth, the marvellous clinking collision of teeth, the liquidity, the startling tongue. That should satisfy my erotic needs for the next couple of weeks.

It's a really blissful scene, with Deliria's kitten bouncing around the kitchen, birds challenging each other in the trees, and a resuscitated late-afternoon sun filtering through the picture window. On with the preparation. At the moment I'm writing a false address and telephone number that match up with the suburb of Noarlunga, miles away from the city, which is already a convincing explanation of why I'm not picking up the flowers myself and paying for them. I then think of a completely normal name. This proves not easy. What's a normal name these days? Myunt Shwe? Eventually, I settle on English descent: Paul Cosgrove. Anything else I might be asked? The address of the Arts Theatre I get from a telephone book. Time of delivery? Say, six o'clock. Look up a florist quite close to the Arts.

I'm inspired to a staggering competence. No detail escapes me. William takes charge. I will have to fake enough emotion to get the florist on my side, to get her to send the wreath without requiring any hard evidence like a credit card number, which I don't even have. Work up those tears, William.

'Petal Station.' Voice of a middle-aged woman.

'I wonder if you could help me. I wish to send a wreath of roses in sympathy.'

'I'm afraid we don't do roses in wreaths.'

The breathtaking stupidity of it. I can't even speak. Nearly fainting, I'm just replacing the receiver when the voice squawks up at me: 'We do bunches, though.'

'Could I have a very large bunch, then?'

'Certainly, sir. There's king-size at sixty-five dollars, or if you prefer large, it's fifty dollars.'

Well, *we* won't be paying for it. 'I'd like king-size, please.'

'King-size. Now, where would you like the flowers sent?'

I consult my notes. Get the tragedy in *before* the address, not after. 'Well, they're for an orchestra. One of their members has just passed away.' I quaver a bit. 'I'd like you to organise delivery to the Arts Theatre, that's in Angas Street, City, at six o'clock this evening.'

A respectful solemnity descends on her voice. 'Is there a contact person?'

Another slip-up. William, you fuckwit. 'Ah, the driver is to go around to the backstage area and ask for a Mr David Ng. That's pronounced *ngaw*.' The name is accepted. 'He will pay in cash for the flowers, and if there's a taxi he will fix up the driver too.' Neatly sidestepping the question of payment, I hope.

'Well, it's a bit unusual.' Her voice becomes very compassionate. Oh God, she is so kind. 'But I think it should be all right. Are you sure this person will be there?'

'Yes it's all been arranged.' I play this tricky game of anticipating the next question. 'Unfortunately, he is unable to pick up the flowers himself. He's physically handicapped.'

'I see. And is there any message you want to go with the flowers?'

Christ, I nearly missed the whole purpose of this. 'Oh yes. If you could take this down. "Deepest sympathy for the loss of Deliria. If only these were the roses in her cheeks."' Something about uttering those words: it sets me off, yes, I'm actually crying. My throat constricts with sobs. Tears drip.

'"If only these were the roses in her cheeks",' she repeats, flatly, just to confirm the wording. Christ, it's not even original. 'And what name?'

'Paul Cosgrove.'

'And your address, Mr Cosgrove?'

Read the address and telephone number off the sheet of paper. Hope she won't ring the false number to confirm. Don't thank her for bending the rules a bit: you're supposed to be overcome with grief. Replace the receiver. Put the paper into an ashtray, set fire to it, and scatter the ashes into the back lawn. The prank is going to work. I've done well, except that I've been a complete bastard as regards that kind woman, making a joke of her compassion. I care about the human consequences. I care all right, but I care more about the inside of Deliria's mouth. I'm sorry; that's just the way it is. It's terrible, isn't it?

Cast party no. 2, at the conductor's house, contrasts the highly civilised architecture of the renovated Federation home against a scene of student barbarity. Adelaide people aren't partied-out; in fact they're very much under-partied. With murderous intent, the show gets going at full speed as soon as possible: none of this sophisticated East Coast 1 am start. Everyone comes. We've got the whole cast, the crew, everyone's mates, everyone's mates' mates. We've got admirers, hangers-on, orbiters, Suns, satellites, asteroids. There's even a sextet of obvious schoolgirls, sparklingly orthodontal. The surface of the kitchen table is entirely obscured by six-packs, wine casks, and the clustered shoulders of bottles of beer, bottles of wine, bottles of Vodka Stolichnaya, Jim Beam, Mekong whisky, Green Ginger wine, Toros de España, Drambuie, Benedictine and Kahlua. There's a cooked fish the size of a dog. In the bathroom adjoining the kitchen is a bath full of ice. A layer of ice, a layer of bottles and cans, a layer of ice, another layer of bottles and cans. The Adelaide student party is well under way.

The prank has been inscrutable. Evidence? I haven't been beaten up yet. But whether the roses actually reached the Arts? Certainly no one's talking about it: they're too busy getting hammered.

The elegant muscular statement of Theseus moves through the crowded kitchen. As you would select your best shirt and tie for an important engagement, he selects the smoothest combination of movements to get across the room, except that, unlike you and me, he doesn't try. It's just in him, as in a tiger. Ever seen a clumsy tiger? He seems to touch no one, although I know he's brushing against backs and chests the same as I was.

So, how does one approach this god? With burnt offerings?

The face of Theseus looks upon mine. I'm Xenon-flashed. But, bafflingly, he's approachable; he's very easy to talk to. I have one advantage: I know from Deliria that musicians, if they're any good, generally don't want to talk about what they've just played or sung. So I just introduce the topic of the Australian wine industry, and its would-be competitors, the Chileans and South Africans. In two minutes he's introduced me to his mates.

'Baby, you made it.' Deliria sweeps through, fantastically over-dressed. Like a pedestrian hit by a sports car, I'm hurled out to the back patio where she tells me that, yes, the roses worked brilliantly.

'Oh, they arrived, all right. God, did they arrive. Pres, the conductor, came up to me. "I think you'd better come here for a moment." My God, there were so many. They must have taken up the whole back seat of the taxi. The note, it was weird. I thought I was going to laugh. And all the time they *don't know* and I *know*. Oh, it's so cruel but it's so hilarious. Then the taxi driver's getting nasty, he demands to see David Ng. Baby, where did you get that name, it's absolutely marvellous. He's going right through the theatre looking for him. "David Ng here? Anyone called David Ng?" And all the time with this great bunch of roses trailing all over the place, through everyone rehearsing, so that everyone gets a good look at them. Baby, I'm so proud of you, I could never have done it myself.'

'No cops, I hope.'

'No. That is, Pres said we should ring them but I bravely said don't bother.'

'And the point of this exercise? Theseus?'

'Didn't happen.'

I must like Theseus a lot. I must really want to be rid of her, to have her safely coupled. Listen to this: 'But a real gentleman, like Theseus, wouldn't want to take advantage of your distress.'

We return to the throng. The thread of this secret wrongdoing links us all night. I play the quiet male friend, stirred to noble yet contained anger by the sinister prank. Ah, the brave first violinist, a little scared, taking her mind off it by doing impossible Bach gigues. Is she projecting anguish? Not really. In fact, she looks as if she's trying to hold back strong emotion, which is the most difficult acting of all. What worries me is that I'm not a bad actor in real life either, and it makes me sick. I like these people. Theseus, Diz, Annie, Hennie, Joss, Ez, Prue. The invocation of names at a party. Just about everyone I've met is potentially a friend. All these Neddies and Freddies, Bizzies and Dizzies, the people who wear a bit of eye make-up when they go out, just to tease the yobs. They like me. I'm surrounded by people who enjoy talking about languages, even speaking them. Some of them are studying French, Italian, German. Theseus speaks German at home with his mum and dad. Beate speaks Italian at home. Prue speaks Thai at home.

I'll introduce you to Prue. Yes, Prue likes me. I like Prue. Love, entering unsoundly through the eyes, attempts to win me over. The agreeable handfuls of breasts, straining through the fluffy wool jumper, and the stomach like a springboard, certainly do their bit. Her hair is indian ink, like a loaded brush, dripping. A little sliver of epicanthic fold hoods the muscle of her eye. She's ethnic Thai. Her voice, however, is broad Aussie, as soft and soothing as a dentist's drill.

Prue wants to talk about *me*, of all things. 'So, what do you actually *do*?'

This terrifying question causes me to reflect that I should be in France. I should have been to France by now. I should have been to Bangkok. I haven't even been to Sydney.

'Well, I'm doing French honours. I basically write essays. Other than that I have lunch, amuse myself.'

'You must be pretty good.'

'I'm good at what I'm good at.' I suppose I can put up with the voice, after all. 'So what do you do then, Prue?'

'Uni plus part-time job. Work with disabled people.'

'Mentally or physically disabled?'

'Spinally injured.'

'Depressing?'

'No, actually it's great.'

J'en suis très admiratif. Someone actually interacting with the world in a meaningful way. And I bet she doesn't shoplift, either. She says that she gets penalty rates Saturdays and Sundays. I have exactly zero idea of what this means. Breathless in explanation lest I display my ignorance to anyone else, this visitor from a magical new world, i.e., the real one, says it means she gets one-and-a-half times as much money on Saturdays as during the week, and twice as much on Sundays and public holidays.

Where's Deliria? Enjoying her control over the world, no doubt, receiving hugs and offers of a lift home, enjoying the sympathy and support of her deceived friends.

'I don't suppose you heard what happened tonight?' Prue says.

'What, you mean that sinister prank?'

'Yeah. I tell you what, if we ever catch the person who did that ...'

'Yep. I can certainly understand that.'

'It's just a sick, sick individual. And it *has* to be someone from uni.'

'You've reached that conclusion, have you?'

'It just stinks of uni. And you must be absolutely spewing. I mean, you are her boyfriend, aren't you?'

'No. Just good friends, that's all.'

Any thrill I might have had, any of Deliria's thrill of destructive power held in reserve, any thrill of knowing that with two words, you can destroy that state of friendliness between you and replace it with open war, any of this bullshit cannot survive a two-minute encounter with a real woman. I *really like* Prue.

Deliria appears. Observing our sustained conversation, she comes out with an almost parental, 'How are you two getting on?'

'Where have you been hiding this interesting guy?' counters Prue.

Time has been sucked down a tube. It's three o'clock; I've had about twenty beers. The bath is completely empty, the kitchen table plundered of its booze. Prue is talking about her job, saying something about disabled men having frequent erections.

The god Theseus is sitting at the kitchen table, his smile directed at and received by a young chap of equal, yet complementary, beauty: i.e. he's black. He has drop earrings. A short Chinese dressing gown opens onto his shaved chest. He is extravagantly decorated, covered with silver crescents, scimitars, chains, bracelets, rings, a choker and a bronze arm-band. This is unusual all right: a non-straight-acting gay. He seems to be, indeed is, caressing Theseus's forearm, whose defined musculature lies carelessly, drunkenly over the table, beautifully veined.

I don't know, what would you give for Deliria's chances?

Night of the doll

I've just got another package from Thailand, which I'm examining, buzzing with a hangover. It's from a fourth-year Economics student, Terdsak. From the tabloid newspaper, there's the usual collation of business-related murders, 10,000-volt suicides, heart-rending child drownings, and grimly humorous road accidents. There's a video of a department-store fire with a Post-it note attached: 'Man jumping off roof.' There's linguistically interesting junk mail, masturbation instructions for women in their mid-thirties (*Ladies, did you know that masturbation can have significant benefits for your health?*), and the Thai driving test. Useful stuff. No language textbook would give me this. And when the hangover wears off, I'll certainly start memorising the vocabulary.

Terdsak's dad is a police lieutenant-general. Terdsak has never actually *said* his dad is corrupt, but it can be inferred. His salary would be about the size of my student allowance. His house is the size of the British Embassy. In its driveway are parked a Mercedes Benz 500 SEL, a BMW and a Land Rover. For his twenty-first birthday, Terdsak received a bottle of boutique red wine and a Porsche.

The Thai police are popular, he tells me. They never arrest anyone, except bad people. (He means sociopaths.) You've really got to have killed someone or smuggled heroin before you'll get anything more than a warning. Compare this with the South Australia Police, who will pull you up for simply walking around at night. I start typing out a reply.

Dear Sak

Re: South Australia Police

In Adelaide, uneasy pedestrians wait for the full cycle

of a 'Don't Walk' sign, in slashing rain, at twelve o'clock at night, with hailstones bouncing off their faces, just in case there should be a policeman lurking, waiting to give them an on-the-spot fine. The most orderly, sinless population in the world is continually nipped at the heels, booked for driving seven kilometres per hour over the speed limit, booked for doing an illegal U-turn on a magically clear road, booked for shooting a red light at four o'clock in the morning with a sick child in the back of the car. There just aren't enough criminals in Australia, Sak. The police don't have enough to do.

Yes, I reflect, sealing the envelope, the unquestioned, and unquestioning efficiency of the South Australia Police in enforcing such arbitrary constructions as traffic laws is matched only by their inefficiency in catching Deliria, who has by now got so much shoplifted clothing, she could stock a boutique.

Deliria emerges from the spare bedroom. She is in poor condition. Venus is not very well; the fair Aphrodite ails. She feels like a shrunken head, she says. I offer chrysanthemum tea as she walks up and down the kitchen in my dressing gown. Chrysanthemum tea turns out to be a bad idea: it causes upheavals in her stomach and she has to retire to the bathroom. After the puking session, we relocate to the balcony to catch the weakened winter sunlight. Between spasms of throwing up, she is gradually disposing of the owners' collection of matchbooks from American hotels, which she ignites, tossing the hissing flare over the balcony onto the back lawn. She was a bit messy at the cast party last night. Well wouldn't *you* want to get drunk if you'd just received a sympathy card for your own death?

After her clothes are dry and she's gone home, I meekly carry out the latest instalment of the campaign to interest Theseus. By now I'm thinking seriously about the police. Do I really think I can pull one over on the CIB? But what have we done that's actually illegal? Not paying for the roses. Now what would that come under? Obtaining under false pretences. I know there's a charge called 'wasting police time', so that would be two charges if they're called in. So, William, draw the line of dignity. You've already been pretty stupid with the roses, but you were clever enough to get out of it with your name untainted. You'll do another stupid thing because you agreed to it. And this will be the last thing you do to interest Theseus (who, let's face it, prefers boys) in Deliria.

Of course there's always the risk of Deliria just blowing the whole thing. She's always got to take it that little bit further. Would you believe that at the cast party she was talking to me in French about the roses, terrifyingly loud, with other people present, as if French were some special code that no one else had ever studied and no one could possibly understand. *Chéri, les fleurs sont arrivées.* Jesus Christ! It wouldn't take a native French speaker to work out what that meant. I think of the large number of other things I should be doing, things other than aiding Deliria in this useless quest. First, I should be ringing up Prue, whose phone number is in my wallet. (The old inequality: if you give a girl your phone number, it's nothing. If a girl gives you her phone number, it's everything.) Second, I should be assembling Terdsak's return package. I should be going to the Alliance Française, borrowing two videos on winemaking in Provençe, and watching them. I should be doing something about Montaigne's attitude to women. I should be getting a part-time job working with disabled people, getting penalty rates on Saturdays, Sundays and public holidays, saving up the money and going to France, and working as an *assistant* at a French high school. I should be completing these enjoyable processes. Instead, I do the following.

The stock on display in the Save the Children shop is a measure of what the affluent suburb considers rubbish: women's fashion just two years out of date, men's suit jackets with holes you can barely see, racks and racks of aviator sunglasses, 100%-wool overcoats, brand-new soap and talcum powder sets that grandmothers get for Christmas and never open and, crucially, a row of large dolls, from which I select one about a foot in length. Back at Bellevue I am confronted with a problem: how can I get one of the owners' white tea towels to look like the get-up of a classical violinist? I lose myself in the details of preparation, like some blissful terrorist assembling a bomb. I don't want to see outcomes, just details. The doll lies on the ironing board, its abundant plastic hair a stiff fan. No single feature makes me see her in the doll. But as I unfasten the blouse and the chest is exposed, the blouse catches in the shoulder's articulation, and won't come out: it's as if the doll were gripping it. *I don't want you taking off my clothes.* She must have known what I would be feeling as I stripped the doll. I don't know, would you say I was obsessed? I remove the skirt. I don't know about this strange excitement. I'm not going to kiss the doll or anything, but whoops, it's flipped off the ironing board and fallen on the stone floor. There's a sharp plastic crack. When I pick it up, I see a thin fracture has divided the throat. I'm certain a parallel voodoo accident has occurred. Has she fallen and broken her neck, through my clumsiness? This is crazy, I must admit, since her instructions were to pull the head off anyway. Standing back, I view my efforts at fashion design. What would Karl Lagerfeld make of this? The doll, standing on the catwalk of the ironing board, sports a knee-length black skirt and the customary white blouse. The pudgy limbs of the homunculus, and the enormous head, distort the adult proportions of the skirt and blouse. I'm not insane, I reason, it just looks that way. I cut the head off with a meat cleaver, put the head, body, small violin and glued newspaper-lettering note into a cardboard box, gift-wrap it and travel, inconspicuously I hope, into town on the 216. Hailing a taxi in Victoria Square, I offer the driver twenty dollars to deliver the unaccompanied parcel to Deliria at the Arts Theatre. A product of this innocent continent, he accepts.

Consider this Italian shirt, an ecstasy of polymer. It sings my shoulders. Suited, I appear affluent. The Angas Street footpath rings to the soles of my Ferrazzos. By pirating all my texts I've saved enough to actually buy this outfit. I'm approaching the pub now, the Royal Edward, whose high-ceilinged, brass-fitted rooms and rapturous art-nouveau balconies enjoy the favour of penniless students in German army greatcoats. I'm thrilled by a sense of my own competence in the sending of the doll parcel. Not many Australian guys would be able to pass themselves off as women. Oh, did I neglect to mention I cross-dressed for the occasion? With a wig, full make-up job (how much I've learned from Deliria!), tissue-stuffed bra and a black party dress, particularly in the dark, I was very convincing.

Like many successful wrongdoers, I have a tremendous urge to tell someone about it. I seem to have brought it off so well. *Don't even think about it, William.*

When I push open the timber door of the Hunt Room, it reveals the entire cast assembled on lounge chairs, unusually serious, faces locked. Deliria is seated, expressionless. Theseus is sitting about as far away from her as he could possibly get without being outside the pub. Prue sees me. The big-toothed grin gives confirmation that I haven't been discovered as the author of this measureless wrong. The conductor, Pres, is standing, addressing them, saying that he is sure the person who sent these parcels is in the room at this moment, and that if he or she is found out they will be expelled forthwith from the School of Music, probably even from the University, and turned over to the police. If any more parcels arrive, the School of Music will be on to the CIB in five minutes flat, and all matters thenceforward will be out of his hands. I back out softly, with gestures of 'not my business', and walk to the Gents, where I stare into the mirror. Noticing a chunk of lipstick on the corner of my mouth, I scrub furiously.

In the drinking and chatting session that follows, it would be convenient for me if people's conversation were limited entirely to details of the arrival of the package. Who picked it up? Did the taxi driver describe the person who sent it? Did Theseus fob

Deliria off with a hug again? What did people think of the note: did they think it was sinister or funny? However, people don't talk about things exclusively, not even if America's parking battleships off the coast. I'm talking to Theseus, and instead of proceeding straight to the description of the doll's arrival, the havoc it caused, the screaming and fainting, he treats me to an analysis and appreciation of the Royal Ed's architecture. Did I note the excellent bluestone exterior walls? I certainly did. And what about the interior decor, the wood fire burning high in the grate, the fire tongs and brass poker, so functionally decorative? Yes, they are marvellous. Does he actually like boys, I wonder? Or is it just that he doesn't particularly mind if a black guy strokes his arm?

Theseus just goes on and on, not mentioning the doll. Deliria now appears, accepting the consoling hug of some minor orchestral member, a girl with an indefinite jawline and one of those sprinkled-on complexions. The hug, it's easily observed, has at least as much desire in it as compassion. Deliria's sniffling bravely, holding back those tears. Jesus, what is it *for*?

Theseus and I are joined by Neddy, the black guy, who has the trademark 'gay' voice: the voice, incidentally, that most gays really dislike. You know what it sounds like. I don't like it much either, especially when he describes what they will do to the sender of the doll when they catch him (or her). Imagine the following description delivered in a mannered falsetto: 'First, hee-hee, we'll hold it down, pull down its pants and force some plastic hose up its bum. Then we'll put some barbed wire up the plastic hose, and take out the plastic hose so it's left with the barbed wire up its bum.'

Right, that is definitely the *last* parcel.

'Be brave, darl,' he continues as Deliria comes over to us. His black arm is startling on her neck: it rests there like a girder.

'Baby, there you are. Did you finish your marvellous essay? God, you've just got to read his essays. Baby, why don't you go and chat up Prue? Could be an opportunity for you.' She sticks out her wine-darkened, drug-blue tongue. Okay, fine. Chatting up Prue is fine.

Here's something you'll never see in a porno: a man and a woman excitedly holding hands. We do this between Prue's gear changes as we drive back to her place in her practical car, bought for 'a coupla grand' of her own money. You'll never see this, either: the way a woman's car is like a handbag, with packs of tissues on the dashboard, and bottles of mineral water rolling about on the floor every time she hits the brakes. You might see this, though: a man and a woman straining against their seatbelts, pashing at a red light.

When we get back to her place, it's on. There was never any question of it not being on. After zero preamble, we're in her bedroom, with her single mattress on the floor. She's dragging off her jumper, followed by the T-shirt underneath it. Her breasts jut through her liquid hair. She's giving me that *Yes-we're-doing-it* smile. I finally get rid of my shirt, snapping off a cuff button. Then there's a soft collision of faces and bodies, a meeting of skin temperatures, our lips' noisy exploration, the quickly discovered hard-on. Her small brown hand is busily exploring it, travelling over its outline, mapping it; then she's pulling off her jeans. They race down her thighs, and she chucks them at an armchair, not even looking. Still kissing, we stagger sideways, trip on the edge of the mattress, start to fall heavily on it, and by some instinct, whip our tongues out of each other's mouths before we bite them off. She reaches for a biscuit tin containing condoms, rips a sachet open, puts the condom in her mouth, crawls down the mattress and unrolls the condom over me.

She goes for the classic version, hooking her legs around my lumbar vertebrae and locking her feet together. They slip comically apart, so I reach around behind me and hold her ankles together with one hand. I'm not exactly looking at my watch here, but surprisingly quickly I can feel her contracting around me, like a throat swallowing really hard, and I'm getting there too. I stop holding back, and my entire body jolts in her arms, as if I'm being electrocuted. Then we subside into each other, gasping congratulations.

Later, I'm lying on the carpet, covered in knitted-wool jump-ers and German army greatcoats, fiddling with a small lamp. She's asleep, on that student's mattress, blankets lugged over her. Again, I have that opportunity to just stare, without being rude. Her shoulder, partly revealed, is that exact, striven-for brown, which she got by birth. The heavy, plentiful hair spills over the blankets, bucketloads of it. That's all we really know about people, isn't it: what they look like. I can be sure about Prue; I can be sure that her hair is black and that her nose has a bridge.

How it happened: if in the catalogue of human actions we talk about love, we want predictability, lack of conflict, two people who want the same thing. Above all, we don't want a lot of dia-logue, the woman breaking away giggling: 'I don't know why I'm doing this.' The man: 'Is it okay if we just … you know … touch each other?' We don't want it to be interesting, we don't want it to happen in an aircraft toilet at 60,000 feet. We don't want the inter-minable lead-in: 'She said no for a very long time, then she said yes.' 'In the end I granted myself to him, out of pity.' 'At first we were just good friends, but then, well …' There's almost no story with Prue, except the moment of ignition. I spilt half a glass of beer over her arm and started to wipe it off with this fairly expen-sive cravat I was affecting. The physical contact, the alcohol, the already-established liking. It's the non-courtliness that I like. This novel equality, her desires approximating mine, etc.

She's set the alarm for five. She's got this strange rigidity of responsibilities, the unnegotiable fact of those disabled guys with no one to get them up if she doesn't arrive. Almost immediately it goes off, and there's the scrape of her dressing, pulling on a pair of jeans in the dark, the denim loud against skin and toenails.

'You can crash out here,' she says. 'I trust you.'

As always—and you start to recognise it after you've slept with even just a few people, as I have (though I suppose it grows a bit familiar after you reach your century, or your grand)—it's fascinating to be granted access to the minor details of other lives. I've memorised Prue's kitchen. On the wall are sticky-taped posters of French Impressionists. Like me, she hasn't transcended sticky-tape. She hasn't begun the superior life offered by framed prints. What else does she get up to? Well, she's obviously a very practising first clarinet: sheet music in unfamiliar keys (E Flat, B Flat Minor) is spread over the kitchen table, systematically annotated (*Vivace here—NOT allegro moderato*) and speckled with tomato sauce. Two clarinets and a soprano sax are just lying there, out of their cases, on the ripped sofa. Really good classical musicians are so casual with their instruments. On the living room floor are scattered CDs of orchestral music: some pretty weird, experimental stuff like John Cage, but also jazzy George Gershwin, as well as the reassuringly standard Mozart, Beethoven, Bach. Concerto for Clarinet. The Duets for Clarinet and Piano. The Complete Clarinet Works for Chamber Orchestra. No food, though. What else? There's ordinary 'I'm not making a statement' clothes: jeans, white shirts, musician's get-up, T-shirts with no writing on them, inexpensive no-name trainers, four pairs of unpolished good shoes. The minimum possible cosmetics are just chucked anyhow on the dressing table. Some under-eye concealer, lid open, is cracked from disuse. I like this a lot: a surface disorder, but underlying it, a sense of purpose. And what's she doing now? Interacting with the world in a meaningful way, I bet.

On the way to Kev and Doug's, after a breakfast of pasta scraps, half a tomato and astonishingly bad instant coffee, I play that lover's game: I wonder what she's doing now? Let's see. It's 11.15 am and I'm on the tram. I wonder what Prue's doing? Would she be hoisting those disabled guys up on the hydraulic sling that she's told me about? Getting them into their cars and off to work? When I reach Kev and Doug's, a brief warm-and-fuzzy telephone call confirms that she's on her break. In the background is the clatter of the nursing facility: trolleys going past, buzzers craving attention. Most of the time we are giggling.

My second telephone call this morning is from Deliria, who excitedly narrates the Night of the Doll. While Doug is steadily classifying the rubbish on the kitchen table, she tells me of screams, horrors. It looked so frightening, they wouldn't even let her see it. There followed some speculations as to the prankster's sanity. Deliria then joined with enthusiasm in the planning of a ritual humiliation to be conducted backstage 'when they eventually catch him'. That's Deliria for you, she always wants to take it that little bit further, she's got to come up with all these marvellous suggestions for shaving his pubic hair and covering his genitals with toothpaste, followed by perhaps some light beating-up, all this to culminate in tarring and feathering the miscreant and chaining him naked to a Hail Bus Here sign on North Terrace.

And the point of this whole fiasco? Theseus? Guess what: nothing happened. Christ! All that effort on my part, and Deliria can't even get it together to … Oh Jesus. Well, as I said before, that's definitely the last parcel. It's not that I've become sensible or anything. It's just fear. And Prue. Fear and Prue. Yes, of all the factors that contribute to bring about the end of the parcels, my own good sense is the least significant.

Nothing

Prosse is continually doing unacademic, child-like things. During a peripatetic discussion of *Male Prostration and Female Uninvolvement in the Poetry of Guillaume d'Aquitaine*, a copy of which now lies on my desk back at Bellevue next to the latest edition of *Police News*, he cracks open a walnut picked up from the Humanities courtyard. Back in his office, the walnut contents are loudly masticated. A pile of pre-gathered but yet-to-be-cracked walnuts lies on top of a stack of back issues of *Linguistics Today*, as if a little boy's marble collection had got misplaced. How his students respect him I have no idea. If he weren't always in *Linguistics Today*, and if he didn't know the twelfth century backwards …

So, let's move to *Male Prostration and Female Uninvolvement* … or its alternative title, 'Guillaume d'Aquitaine and Relationships'. In those days, you didn't really have 'relationships', not the way we understand them. None of that stuff about taking care of each other's sexual needs, being a supportive partner, allowing each other sufficient personal space, awareness, consideration, teaching yourself to love the other person, serial monogamy as a viable way of being, serial monogamy as a life choice.

No, I'm afraid you just had love. And, shortly afterwards, death. This had a way of compressing the sexual timetable, I propose to Prosse. He agrees. How short their lives were, how crammed and intense, compared to the Warhol movie, the yawn, the boring epic of our lives. I'm twenty-two, and barring accidents or the end of the world, I'll still be around in 2065, impotent and senile. I can't wait. At twenty-two, Guillaume d'Aquitaine would enjoy perhaps five more years of life before typhoid, the flu, staphylococcus, or just a broken leg did him in. Can you imagine his concept of time? Of the length of relationships? Can you imagine Guillaume d'Aquitaine saying '*I don't think I'm ready for a relationship just yet*'?

I walk down the hill to Flinders; I walk up again. In the library are a lot of books. I find the ones about Provençal and read them, thereby constructing essays. Sometimes this is livened up by a violent incident, or rather, an incident which aspires to violence without quite getting there. A bus driver tells me he'll 'beat my fuckin' head in' if I jump on the moving footplate again. What's worse, I wonder, the jumping on the moving footplate or the verbal aggression? I discuss this with Kev. He tells me I can get the bus driver for uttering a threat if I can produce witnesses who'll back me up. The trouble is, he goes on, jumping on the moving footplate is a thousand-dollar fine.

We suffer from 'event poverty', to use one of Deliria's phrases. Nothing happens to you. To qualify that, things happen to *Deliria* because of the way she looks, but in general, if you're Fred Smith, you've got your job and your TV and whatever amusements you can afford. Daily life is nothing, here.

Bellevue Heights, almost incident-free, well illustrates Deliria's concept of 'event poverty'. Let's examine Bellevue Heights. We have a suburban grid, which we derived from a Roman city plan. This subdivision is measured into quarter-acre blocks. Houses of no aesthetic interest stand on each, occupying perhaps a sixth of the available land on each block. This is to furnish dwellers with a back yard and front lawn that are not used. What are they *for*? Are they for recreation? I never see anyone on the front lawn drinking beer. Wouldn't it be better if we were all crammed together with the side walls of the houses nearly touching and no back yard, and everyone played in the street? The way it's been set up, nothing happens to you. I don't mean it's always boring. Give me a good TV program and a mug of ginger tea, the *Collected Poems of Yeats* on a winter's night, or a long swim at Glenelg Beach on a summer's day. But these are not really *events*, just enjoyments. They don't happen to you. They don't mature you. ('So, what happened yesterday?' 'Oh, a good TV program happened.' 'A mug of ginger tea happened.')

I feel I'm not mature, because nothing has happened to me. I don't mean one big event, like the Vietnam War; I mean lots of little events that haven't happened. People I didn't meet. Places I didn't go to. All the times I just stayed home. The bizarre characters I've never had to deal with because I didn't meet them. The dangerous situations I've never had to extricate myself from because I was never in them. It adds up. After the age of twenty, life starts to become more and more quantitative. You start to become the sum of what you've done. How many people have you met, William, other than your family and people in your class at school? How many places have you been to, other than home, school, uni, church and the beach? How many things have you done, other than play sport, study for exams, have conversations, shoot rabbits and steal?

I'm starting to recognise myself to be Australian. It's the lingering youth, the incredible unsureness with which I navigate my adulthood, the stunning lack of progression between me at sixteen and me at twenty-two. At sixteen I was mature, studious; I had intelligent conversations with adults. At twenty-two I'm immature, studious; I'm sending headless dolls.

Deliria's the same: at eighteen, she looks somewhere in her mid-twenties, but she's not growing up. She's ageing but she's not growing up. Is it Adelaide that produces these people? We're incident-poor, event-starved, and we just don't grow up. Deliria 'knows a lot'; she's an A-grade (but non-practising) violinist; she can recite passages from Shakespeare; she has one of the most extensive vocabularies I've ever come across. There must be twenty thousand words that she actually uses in speech, compared to Prue's two thousand. Does she use words like *thus*? Yep. And *consequently, however, nevertheless, moreover, notwithstanding* and *whereby*. And, as I well know, the possession of a large vocabulary is linked to intelligence. She's *intelligent* all right. The trouble is, intelligence isn't enough. Does she know what penalty rates are? Does she know that conservatorium graduates are quite likely to end up working in office jobs in the Department of Education and Children's Services? Assuming she even finishes her degree. Does she know that she could end up teaching music to kids of mixed abilities, i.e. babysitting? She hasn't made the jump to adult life. I could say the same thing about myself. Prosse hasn't made the jump, either. Uni is full of people who haven't made the jump. Kev has made the jump, though. Prue has, too. Doug, presumably, once made the jump, but he's toddled back into the welcoming childhood of dementia: a couple of days ago I found a pair of his shoes in the freezer.

Adelaide, you will bring forth your children in pleasant surroundings; you will raise them to be innocents.

Coupla ground rules

Prue and I are having coffee in the South Australian Museum. This is what normally happens, isn't it? The man asks the woman to meet for coffee in pleasant, neutral surroundings (i.e. not at his place, redolent of socks; nor at her place, with bras slung over the backs of chairs). As advisable, there's some sort of time limit. She has to go to a clarinet masterclass at 3 pm given by 'some Rumanian wanker'. I likewise show myself to be a man of obligations: my presence is required at Flinders to supervise some Intro French students while they guess their way through 'a ridiculous multiple-choice grammar test'. We both hint at really full lives, bursting appointment books, 60-hour weeks. We've got lots of things on our plates. We can just about fit each other in. We establish that neither of us needs the other person to complete our lives. That little detail done with, we're straightforward. What does she think of Thai women? 'Barbie dolls.' Thai men? 'Bunch of wankers.' Thailand? 'Economic hub by accident.'

'Turn it around, Will.' First time she's used my name except on the phone.

'Okay. Let's see. Thailand: useful monarchy.'

'Thai society?'

'Status-ridden. Victorian England, a hundred years later.'

I would say this is the first time in the 20-year history of her life that someone has said to her: *Victorian England, a hundred years later*, rather than some platitude about Miss Universe, Tom Yum Kung or the Land of Smiles.

'Not exactly drawn to the homeland, then?' I continue.

'Not even with a winch and a tow-rope.'

She looks at me. I look back. About five seconds goes by. Try looking in someone's eyes for five seconds. Especially Prue's eyes: they're completely black. The iris and the pupil are the same colour.

'You must be pretty dedicated,' she says. 'You can read Thai. I mean *really* read it. I couldn't get past the alphabet.'

She puts her hand on top of mine: now there's a startling colour contrast for you.

We talk about clarinet technique. We explore the differences between woodwinds and brass, the pros and cons of sight-reading versus memorisation, and the subordination of individual style necessitated by orchestral music. We discuss the optimum age for beginning the violin, and what happens to second-rate violinists after the age of eleven. We talk about music in pretty much the same way as Kev and I talk about laminated steel, except that Kev and I don't stroke each other's forearms. Annoyingly soon, 3 pm comes around and the Rumanian wanker beckons.

Funny about Prue: there's not much of a story with her. She's very straightforward, she's engagée, she's no-bullshit, she's a consummate musician, she practises three hours a day, she takes care of these disabled guys, she's not a chick, she's not just a pretty face, she's not a bitch and she's not insane. She's had about six or seven boyfriends plus the usual number of one-night stands. Interestingly, she knows a lot about sex, but not in the way I'd expect.

'You don't get to know someone that well by having sex with them,' she's told me.

I wouldn't have thought of it; in fact, I would have thought almost the opposite, but it's one of those flashing insights—my whole brain knows it's true, instantly. You don't get to know someone that well by having sex with them. And while she clearly enjoys having sex with me, she has no real interest in the amazingly varied repertoire of sexual techniques as described in column three, page 19 of most women's magazines. No, she just hauls me on top of her, with those strong nurse's muscles of hers.

'Where did you get those muscles?' I say, and it starts.

'Coupla ground rules,' she says, after this nightly pairing has been going on for a week or so. We're seated at her kitchen table, which is now covered with a different manuscript, annotated with quite abusive notes about the composer, and tomato sauce stains.

'I'd want to know if you're having a relationship with Deliria. I mean, that'd be a pretty obvious thing that I'd want to know, okay? You don't have to answer that one right now.'

'Pretty basic stuff, though.'

'You look like you're gonna have a heart attack. No, no, no, I'm not coming down hard on you or anything. Deliria's your friend. You told me that. You were very clear about that. I already knew that. I just mean tell me things. You can tell me pretty much anything and I can handle it. It's when people don't tell each other things that it always ends up fucked up. Okay?'

'Okay. Thanks for, uh … backpedalling a bit.'

'Backpedalling's good.' She's got this sideways grin, the lips unusually thin for a Thai, sneaking up her right cheek. 'Backpedalling has its uses.'

So, am I having a relationship with Deliria? Pretty basic stuff, right?

The man invites the woman for coffee in pleasant, neutral surroundings, in this case a sort of retro-look place, with Baekelite radios, standard '50s lamps, General Electric fans, and tiny tables for two with chromium chairs. The man and the woman arrive scrupulously on time. The man and the woman order and consume coffee. The man tells the woman he's not ready for a relationship just yet. The woman (she's seen it coming a mile off) says yeah, she's not ready for a relationship just yet, either. That out of the way, they try to talk about something else: restaurant décor, Baekelite, US foreign policy. This doesn't work, so then they try to talk about how they will always respect each other, how they will always speak well of each other. They talk about how it's much better to just be friends, etc. They say stuff like *some things just aren't meant to work out*, and *some things just aren't gonna develop*. After these handy formulations, there's always the horrible question of who's going to leave the premises first. I've seen this coming a mile off, so I say, 'Let's just leave.' I dump ten bucks on the table and we just leave. And that's it. Prue's got an ignominious wait at a bus stop, while I trudge to the tram. I'm sorry, Prue. Some guys are just obsessed with Deliria.

Dinner

The owners' kitchen provides an insight into the late twentieth century. It is shelved with gadgetry, much of it redundant. So we've got the blender, which can also act as a grater, dicer, slicer and fruit-peel remover. There's also a grater, dicer, slicer and fruit-peel remover. And there's a battery of Swedish knives that, if they were sharpened and properly used, could perform all these functions. There's a microwave, with an accompanying convection oven, a gas oven, a toaster oven, a toaster, a sandwich maker, a corkscrew for every day of the week, an electric tin opener, a butterfly tin opener and a guaranteed-to-open-anything, computer-designed tin opener imported from the USA.

I'm preparing something resembling Tom Yum Kung. Without being able to find the exact herbs, I've at least got the huge Australian prawns (our prawns are just as big as yours, mate). I've got ginger, tamarind and limes. I've got some real mashed chillies from the Asian food ghetto in Gouger Street. It's nice to be involved in something completely material, something to take me out of the incredible staleness of myself. It's working, too.

Deliria's coming over tonight, staying over in fact. Nothing has resumed between us, though she requested some very explicit details about Prue, in that sexually clueless, interrogatory style she has.

So why is Deliria staying over? Don't laugh, okay, but without being vain, I think she really misses it. She does. It's just the schoolgirlish thrill of spending nights away from her parents. To her I represent some sort of adult independence. Again, don't laugh. The rituals of single living, cleaning the stove, buying food and cooking it, attacking the bathroom with the scrubber, doing minor repairs, paying the telephone bill: all these things are given a kind of glamour by her virtual non-participation in them at home. She doesn't do any housework. Her mother Louise, she confesses, *makes her bed.*

She arrives dressed entirely in clothes in whose theft I have participated. The beaded dress, each of those thousands of beads apparently sewn on by hand, would have cost, shall we say, two thousand dollars. The shoes: ah yes, the classic, can't-go-wrong black low heels. Two hundred dollars. The handbag: I don't know, four hundred? For someone with an income of about ten dollars a week, she certainly dresses well. So do I, as a matter of fact, the only difference being that I actually paid for this Thai-silk suit, which is so dressy that if I wore it in Hindley Street people would shout at me, if not spraypaint me. My sartorial practice has started to acquire her influence, just as the rugged Anglo-Saxon language began to acquire the polish of Norman French.

We eat a dip that smells like putrefied fish but tastes okay. It should really be picked up with whole boiled bamboo shoots, boiled squashes cut in half, and other marrows, but these were impossible to obtain. Bread will do. We tear hunks off a loaf of bread and go for it, enjoying the freedom from manners. There's something quite liberating about the way the dip slops over the bread and splashes over the table. She's got a big smear of it on her chin. She talks with authority about the developments in women's underwear over the last seven hundred years. The bra really started in the middle ages. Well yes, I knew that one. The bra. The corset. All this whalebone and starch, constricting and pushing up, simply to show men what they want, or what they think they want, or what women think they think they want. Meanwhile, this smear on her chin is flashing a semaphore code: it's a secret spy. It's telling me: 'No, what you really want is this. Beauty plus imperfection. *That's* what you want.' I have to agree with the smear. I want her very much. It's not perfect breasts, perfect face, perfect ass, perfect nose, perfect waist, perfect legs and perfect ankles that are essential to us. It's the smear. Look at it flashing away. How can she not know? It must be so heavy. Interrupting her melodious discourse by leaning over the table, whereupon the cuff of my silk suit trails into the dip, I steady her jaw with one hand, wipe the smear off her chin with a chunk of bread, and eat it. There is a gagging efflorescence of moisturiser.

'How naughty. How audacious.'

The food disappears. We move to the couch. I put on some romantic music, ask her if she would like to see my CD collection … No. Tell her what I really like to have is a nice, relaxing conversation with an attractive young lady, a nice dinner, a nice bottle of wine, a really nice … No. We have one of those conversations like a Gothic cathedral: spired, almost toppling, beautiful in its artifice and quite tiring to maintain.

'So, what about that film *The Boozer*?' she starts up. 'Wouldn't you say it was superbly realistic?'

I say something very undergraduate like, 'I hate realism.'

'Whoo! William, you'll have to back that one up.'

'Okay. What I mean is: if the point of the film is just to describe a bar, then I'd rather just go to the bar.'

'Oh yeah, I'd accept that.' And so it goes on.

Unwelcomely, the talk turns to Theseus. Well, there goes the mood. The season of *Apha*, as it's now universally known, is over, and Deliria, who was so dependent on it to provide her with opportunities for seeing Theseus, is faced with one of life's Red or Black choices: Will I cut the baby in half or will I give it to the other woman? Will I destroy Hiroshima or will I let the war continue until 1950? Will I ask Theseus out for coffee or will I give up this hopeless love forever?

'I'm going to do it. I'm going to ring him up.'

With that virginal cruelty, she does. She's using my phone to ring him up. Now I'm not territorial, but really. Worse, she turns on the loudspeaker. 'I stole his phone number from student records,' she explains. Well naturally. You wouldn't just ask him for it, would you?

Hey, now that *Apha*'s finished, what about coming out for coffee one of these days. Yeah? Great! So, when are we going to get together for coffee? Yeah? Great! Say, I notice that we've somehow failed to have coffee together. To what do we owe this staggering omission? What do you say? Yeah? Great!

I feel something's definitely wrong when Deliria, in a light Nordic accent, introduces herself as Anna Gunnarsdottir from the Cultural Affairs section of the Icelandic Consulate. She tells Theseus, whose excited, immediately recognisable voice comes through the loudspeaker, that his name has been chosen from among thousands for the right to enter a special competition on the topic of Icelandic geography. Four correct answers will win Theseus a trip to Reykjavik, plus five thousand dollars spending money. All he has to do is come to the consulate—here she gives the correct address—and ask for a man named Bengt Njalsson. Within one hour.

Fuck. When she rings someone up, she certainly *rings him up.*

'He'll be there in half an hour,' she says. This way she has of looking directly in your eyes, staring you down, smiling that double-rower. This way she has of walking over to you and putting her hand on the front of your pants, just knowing the hard-on is going to be there.

After about half an hour of our standard stuff, she suggests a game of simulated rape. Okay, fine. I can handle it if she can. The idea, she explains brightly, is to grab her, trip her over and get on top of her while she resists, all female resistance and all male aggression being completely ritualised. I'm standing in front of her, listening to the instructions, my clothes distributed around the lounge like a bomb casing after an explosion. She, as you might expect, is not entirely clothed, but not entirely nude either.

'So, are you ready?' she says.

Like any young lad who went to Help of Christians, I know how to sweep someone's leg. Deliria is precipitated, as gently as I

can manage, on the cushioning of her bum. It's just ridiculously
easy.

Her face changes in fear: it's just a flash, an emotional squelch.
She then masters herself, and in two seconds she's laughing. 'Wow,
that was so … unexpected. That's really skilful,' etc., as if perhaps
she didn't really know me, of all people, and that my going through
this ritualised aggression might somehow call up the demon in me.

'You okay?'

'Yes, of course, baby. I'm fine.'

'You sure?'

'That's very sweet of you, William. Yes, I'm fine.'

Scene: the couch. Deliria's lying there, her bra and panties like oil
slicks on a snowdrift. Her hair rains its blonde onto the pillow;
her mineral-greens hold me powerless, like Kryptonite.

'Do you want to get some cream, baby?'

The owners' fridge is blessed with a carton of Farmers Union
Light Thickened Cream. I return from the kitchen, tear off the
cover, kneel beside the couch, and pour a generous dollop over
her stomach. Then I begin to lick it off. Oh, the warmth of her
stomach under the cool cream, its flat plain; the way her hip bones
stick out just enough. It's so rich in incidentals, too: every now
and again I hear the trickle of her digestion, the powerful thump
of her arteries. Now there's an idea for a courtly love poem: 'To
Deliria's Arteries.'

She's got a different smile for once: not the awesome display of
the double-rower, but a mischievous, one-sided smile, as if she
were thinking up a particularly bizarre prank.

'You can put some on my breasts if you want.'

'Let me think about that for a moment.'

Then she gives me that beautiful smile, the smile towards
which all other smiles are but an attempt, the smile that could
signal other planets. I know her bra's not coming off, but really,
who else gets to do this?

I lay a stripe of cream over the top half of her breasts. I bring my face in very close to the stripe; it guides me in, as a lit-up runway guides a pilot landing. I hit the runway; my tongue travels along the stripe, gathering it up.

'How does that make you feel?' we both say, at exactly the same time.

I don't often see Deliria seriously startled, and that's twice today. Her eyes go wide. Then she recovers.

'Such *chiming*, William.'

'Anyone would think we knew each other very well.'

She gives one of her musical laughs. 'Okay. Escalation time. Where's that blindfold?'

I return from the bedroom with one of Deliria's hundreds of shoplifted scarves. She gets off the couch and knots it firmly behind my head.

'Now you *promise*, if you can see anything, you have to tell me.'

'I would, actually. But I can't see a thing.'

'Good.' I hear a rustle of fabric and a metallic click as she unfastens her bra. I hear the straps slide down her arms. I hear her moving back to the couch, and the light scrape of the cream container being picked up from the coffee table. Then I guess she's anointing her breasts.

'Come here, baby.'

I walk into her smell. She grips the back of my neck quite firmly, guiding me forward and down. My mouth collides with a cream-coated nipple. My lips enclose the beautiful circumference; my tongue is like a dolphin, eagerly nosing the centre, circling, flicking.

Deliria laughs tolerantly. 'You know you're *supposed* to just be licking off the cream, William.'

Towards this end, she applies another coating, guiding my head forward again.

'You can't see anything, can you?'

'No.'

This time, I'm supporting her breast with my hand. Oh, precious cargo! My mouth navigates the isle of her nipple; my tongue explores the interior peak, taking a winding path that curls its way up the side and arrives, at last, at the summit.

'William. Do you love me?'

'Yes, yes, I love you, Deliria.'

'Right. I've decided. I've finally decided, William. I'm going to give myself to you.'

She pulls off the blindfold. She's standing in front of me, her upper body revealed in all its magnificence, her lower half sheathed in panties.

Bedroom. In our absence the kitten has appropriated the bed. I sling him into the lounge room. An unusual silence is maintained between me and Deliria. We are monosyllabic and eloquent. There's a reverence, as in cathedrals. You just don't want to burst into chatter. *Wow, we're finally doing it. Wow, isn't this exciting.* No. We're on the bed. I'm kissing the familiar plane of skin-veiled bone behind her ear, kissing her chin, her neck, her cheekbones, her eyebrows. I'm weighing up the relative safety of unsafe sex with a virgin, with the clear and present danger of conception, and, I regret to say, I'm going to go with the …

'No.'

'What?'

'No, William. I just wanted to see what it would feel like, to be about to do it.'

'What?'

'I'm sorry. It was very awe-inspiring, though. Like a ceremony.'

'I don't believe it. I don't fucking believe it.'

'I'm sorry, William. I'm sorry.'

'Would you mind not doing it again?'

'I promise. I'm sorry.'

The hat

Boy, am I patient. Boy, do I persevere. After my one swerve in the direction of Prue, and Deliria's annoying detour towards the romantic ideal of Theseus, heartbreaking gay male, we're back doing what we do best: quotidian sensuality. Sensual death on the owners' bed has even replaced shoplifting. I could almost draw the rising graph of her involvement in me: it has its ups and downs but there's a net gain. Such a long way we've come, such a trail of horse's hooves along the beach. The chevalier William is again distracted from his Sunthorn Phu, his Sri Praj. Guillaume d'Aquitaine is sadly neglected, though I try to read a bit of Jaufre Rudel while Deliria's in the shower.

Of what does our relationship currently consist? Well, it's a bit unique. She's constantly reminding me of the 'uniqueness' of it.

'Isn't it great, William? We're so unordinary. We're so you-and-me-and-no-one-else. This could be the new *kind* of relationship. It could be the way human beings are evolving. Isn't it marvellous, Will? To be pioneers? To be on the cutting edge? To be unique?'

Yeah, sure. I could do with a lot less of the unique and a lot more of the ordinary. It's just that I can't get over her beauty. I can't. I can get over most things but I can't get over her beauty. It's a shame, isn't it? Years of feminism, years of learning to regard a woman as another human being, years of not calling a woman a girl, and after all this, I can't get over her beauty. Or her intelligence. Or her voice. Or her vocabulary. Or her love of Balzac. Or her knowledge of classical music. Or the way she mixes the milk with the instant coffee *before* pouring in the boiling water, rather than adding the milk last.

Oh, one other thing. Yesterday she said 'I love you', but, being

Deliria, she said she had just wanted to hear what it sounded like. And what did it sound like? Answer: 'Not telling.' Thanks a lot, bitch.

The most-massaged cock in Bellevue Heights takes a break to allow its owner, William, to accompany Deliria to a Music I dinner at Phuket Thai restaurant, the exact upper limit of our financial resources. Can I really afford ten dollars for garlic squid? Which is it to be, next semester's textbooks or the lemon-grass salad? Oh well, I can always pirate the textbooks. But anyway, I'm in a good mood: Theseus and Neddy told Deliria, 'You've got to bring that interesting guy along,' or so she tells me. Theseus arrives in his German army overcoat again (the trouble with a recognisable wardrobe: we know it's the only one he's got). Neddy's there, in an op-shop dinner jacket. Some other gay guy has a knitted-wool jumper from the Anti-Cancer Fund—the only possible way he could afford a knitted-wool jumper. In every way their clothes proclaim student poverty. I, on the other hand, in a Prestigio suit, look like a pimp, like I should be carrying a gun, like I should be selling gold wholesale or falling off my yacht. What ostentation, some might say, without seeing the adventure, the entertainment value, of wearing inappropriate clothes. Deliria, outdoing me by a long way, looks like she's just stepped off the cover of *Elle*. She looks like anything but what she actually is: simply a very successful shoplifter.

Thai waitresses blow about. They look more Cambodian, actually: they've got those really salient, purple gums. I talk to one of them in Thai about their newly installed Prime Minister (the usual corrupt Third-World bastard), and the current Australian Prime Minister (despite his obvious faults, not a corrupt Third-World bastard).

I'm aware that my stock with the music crowd has appreciated about a hundred percent. Australians, more than the English, have this touching reverence for anyone who's actually learned a foreign language, going hand in hand, in some cases, with an extreme distrust of those who speak ethnic languages in public.

'You know, you could get a job with a Thai-Australian company just like that,' says Theseus. His eyebrows are draw-bridged. I've never seen him look incredulous before. 'Exporting Australian wine to Thailand. Beating the Chileans and South Africans.'

Job. Company. Business. The world. Work. Maturity. Responsibility. Make the jump, William.

'That's just amazing, William,' contributes Deliria. 'I mean, I've heard some of those people who say they study Japanese. Most of them are just hideous. You're totally fluent.'

You might guess that it's far from unpleasant to be praised by Deliria in front of her peer group. Also far from unpleasant is a gentle pressure under the table cloth: yes, the magic acute angle of her knee is moving very slowly up and down against mine. Well, this is better than falling off the top of the Grenfell Centre. Are we approaching a coming of age? Could we be going public on this issue? At the moment she's definitely toying with my hand, lightly tugging then releasing the hairs on the back of my wrist. This latter body part is in full view on the table: it's practically spotlit. No one seems to find this out of the ordinary. What? A young woman toying with a man's wrist in a restaurant, when he's very presentable and she's drop-dead gorgeous? Isn't that just so normal, so to-be-expected? As if to underline this point, the life of the dinner table continues around us, without interruption. The usual incidents with Thai food occur: Theseus gags on a slice of lemon grass, Neddy has just burnt his mouth (too ambitious with those little green peppers, my friend), and the other guy is inexpertly stripping a prawn, squirting its brains over his jumper. The pairing of William and Deliria seems completely ordinary, acceptable, non-unusual, even, dare I say it, obvious. At this juncture, she brings her mouth very close to my ear, so that the light hairs on the external membrane, and even the underlying cartilage, feel her lips' movement.

'Oh, by the way, you know that Russian fur hat in Tremaine Rundle Mall? I want you to steal that for me.'

This relationship sucks, the voice of Kev shouts in my frontal lobes. I agree, or at least, my frontal lobes agree. Even though there's the dead giveaway of an erection, on which her palm and fingers rest knowingly (having toyed with my wrist hairs long enough), I'm aware that I've been attractive to other women, perhaps not as gorgeous as Deliria, but with far less complication. When, for example, did Prue ever ask me to steal a hat? All Prue did was tell me I'm great in bed, and, one day, when we're both ready for a relationship …

'No. Sorry.'

Deliria's hand immediately withdraws. 'Of course you realise what this means.'

'If it's going to be like this all the time …'

'Does it mean so little to you?'

None of these words are deadly force. Neither of us is looking the wrong way down the barrel of a twenty-two. If it were getting deadly, I'd be making references to the Icelandic Consulate. Christ, I've got so much ammunition on Deliria. She must know this. No, this is more like waving pistol crossbows at a thousand metres: a light show of force, rather than force itself. I know I'm going to steal the hat. She knows she's attached to me. We both know it's a bit fucked up.

'Just think,' she whispers, sexily enough, 'what it would mean never to touch my body again, never to have me hold your cock.'

'A woman of your brilliant skills should have no trouble in getting the hat.'

'I can't believe you've decided I'm not worth it.'

'Oh, you're worth it. But my policy has to remain one of non-compliance.'

We wind up the dinner, attending to our social obligations, fixing up the bill, giving the scrupulous but minimal tip, bidding our farewells, Theseus reminding me that he can put me in contact with people in the Australian wine industry, Neddy still sucking air into his burnt mouth, and the walk-on other guy disappearing.

We hail transport. The conversation proceeds to the next level of confrontation: not silence, but talking about shit like Baekelite, moisturiser and home renovation, as our taxi leaves the square mile of the city and potters down Anzac Highway.

The best time to do it is eight-thirty in the morning, she has often said. People aren't alert. People haven't even got up at eight-thirty. This, I perceive, is true. Yawning maintenance crews push industrial-sized vacuum cleaners. Cashiers are still fiddling with their time cards out in the staff entrance, in their puffy morning faces. No one seems to be lurking, ready to spring. I occupy myself primarily with the *how*, not the *why*. I'm not so hot on *why*. The Russian fur hat is located in a window display along with other animal products, made of minks and sables and foxes and seal cubs, all of which have surrendered their original forms to be transmuted into hats, gloves and coats. This is terrible. Did you know it takes eighteen minks to make a coat? Wouldn't you rather have eighteen minks running around your backyard, terminating blue-tongue lizards and generally partying it up? It strikes me that I haven't killed a single animal, if you except those mullet and arguably that hapless pigeon, since I met Deliria. The ennobling effects of love? Yeah, sure. How ennobling is stealing a hat? Not to mention the Arts Theatre affair. Concentrate on the *how*, William. Focus on task completion. Security. Contingency plans. Location of exits. What were those thick white poles, crammed with sensors, which flanked each doorway as I walked in? What is this unremovable plastic tag clipped to the hat? Jesus, this is dangerous. This could stop me taking up a career in Law. Looks like it'll have to be the fire exit or the 'Staff Only' exit, one of the two. I watch two huge security guards augment their weight problem by forcing cream buns into their mouths. How fast can they run? Does their radio have a police channel? Well, it's not just for listening to the Lotto results. The fire exit's a no-no: you have to shatter the glass, take out the key and unlock the door, which probably sets off the sprinklers as well. Visualise William having to pay for thousands of dollars' worth of damaged stock, when he can't even afford garlic squid. 'Staff Only' exit it is, then.

'So, *mon chevalier adorable*, how did you do it?' she asks, crowned with mink, her glinting, possibly oiled and certainly perfumed body standing at the picture window.

Here's the story. In the end, finding the 'Staff Only' exit guarded, ID Required Before Exit Allowed (what a fortress it was), I went to an unoccupied cash desk (labour is so expensive in Australia that no one can afford to hire a full complement of staff), leaned over, found the device they use to remove the plastic tags, got the tag off, diced it into a wastepaper basket, and walked boldly through the sensor poles with the hat tucked into the back of my pants and the Prestiegio jacket hanging down over it.

'How brilliant. How resourceful. I mean, who else would have thought of stealing the removal device as well? Can I see it?'

'The removal device?'

'Don't tell me you threw it away?'

'It was bolted to the desk.'

'William, you didn't *buy* this, did you?'

'Well …'

'You *did*.'

'Yes. Look, I'm sorry.'

'You *bought* it.'

'Yes.'

'You *bought* it. Oh, William, you shouldn't have. Jesus, William. I'm shocked. Baby, come here.'

Pingpong argument

Lunchtime of the same day, I'm down at Flinders. May as well put in an appearance. The contents of Terdsak's latest package are spread over the table in the language lab. Here we have a copy of the *Thai Nation*, whose beautiful Thai script looks so interesting to the unschooled Western eye that you are sure it must be communicating something of vital importance: some Buddhist truth, perhaps, or some clarion insight along the lines of 'All life is suffering,' or 'There is no happiness which is unmixed with ignorance.' When you can read it, however, it says that Mr Somsak Theeraparp, a chicken vendor on methamphetamines, held his son hostage for three hours yesterday, 'due to stress caused by credit-card debt,' holding to the boy's throat the meat cleaver used to prepare his breakfast. Fortunately, police were able to shoot Somsak. This is the newspaper; this is the style. Twenty important laws have just been passed, and they're getting a new constitution in through the back door. But the *Thai Nation*, apart from the reading practice it incidentally affords, is gutter. Let's move to the graphics, intended for breakfast viewing. Here we have a police officer holding up a severed head. Both of them look pretty serious.

So, French newspapers score big over their Thai counterparts, as regards most things that matter. But what can I do with French, apart from enjoy it and have it enrich my life? I suppose I could teach it; I could be like Prosse. Great option. What could I do with the Thai? A lot. For example, I could 'get a job with a Thai-Australian company just like that.' Make the jump, William. They don't need you in France; they need you in Thailand.

I compare myself to the Introductory Japanese students who are ploddingly repeating drill sentences along to tapes. Japanese is a bit like Medicine or Law: very few people who do it actually like it, or will ever be any good at it. God, listen to them. They are, as Deliria says, hideous. But they'll probably become Japanese-functional civil engineers, or seafood-marketing advisers. Unlike me, they know what they're doing, or they think they know what they're doing. I don't know what I'm doing.

So what do you actually do? Prue's terrifying question was about my future, not about how I spent my afternoons. Do I perfect my Thai, go to Southeast Asia where it's all happening, get a job in a Bangkok university, or do I go on more shoplifting errands for my worshipped object, my ever-receding goal?

Whose fault is this? A very un-Kev-like, or un-Prue-like question. *It doesn't matter whose fault it is. If it doesn't work, it doesn't work.* The two of them are a chorus of practicality.

It's my fault. I should have come down on her really hard at the first sign of shoplifting. I shouldn't have been so intrigued. No, it's her fault. She initiates everything; I just go along with it.

And how did it get to be such a *part* of things, anyway?

What would Prue do? Just suppose Prue and Deliria were mates. If Prue knew Deliria were shoplifting, wouldn't she sit her down and be really firm with her? Like this: 'Now you gotta be sensible, you're not a kid, you're eighteen. It's a crime now. It's not nicking things off shelves like a ten-year-old.' 'Yes, yes, I know it's bad. I really must stop. Thanks, Prue, you're a doll.'

I dump Terdsak's package in the French Department.

The landscape, ever-informed, is in turmoil. The wind is flinging clouds like plates, snarling the paddock grass, tormenting the tops of trees. I'm striding, sometimes slithering backwards and bellyflopping on the mud, back up the hill to Bellevue. My mission? To accomplish some symbolic act with all those French books she's given me, now that I've read them. I'll send them back to the shop via anonymous packages: my roses-and-doll skills should come in handy. I'll donate them to the poor Intro French students. I'll pay Deliria their value. I'll do something to morally distance me from the theft. Of this I am resolved. I will defy her; I will do something symbolising a refusal to be corrupted. Thus delivered from the burden of guilt, I will pursue a life of study and physical labour. I'll get a part-time job working with disabled people. I'll learn the value of money. I'll cease wearing Italian suits.

My resolution lasts right up the hill, through the corridors of shaking gums, past the infinitely repeating series of front lawns, past the waving and slashing TV aerials, and the gutters whirling with leaves.

She answers the door, in the Russian fur hat and a bedsheet. Actually, when you think about it, getting rid of the French books seems rather a useless gesture.

After we've spent about an hour in bed, she invites me into the kitchen for afternoon tea. The weather, you ask? A false calm pervades. Lazily unbuttoning a translucent raincoat, pouring the tea from an earthenware teapot (stolen) into two antique porcelain cups (stolen—different shop), she tells me she possesses two pairs of jeans stolen from Tremaine Rundle Mall branch, and that she is going to get a refund on them at Tremaine Westfield. Would I care to accompany her on this mission?

'Not really,' I say. 'In fact, would a simple "no" suffice?'

I wouldn't have to do anything, she says, just be with her while she gets the refund. Provide moral support.

'What about moral guidance?' I say. This elicits a laugh.

'Are you coming with me?' she asks.

'No,' I say. 'I've told you.'

This proceeds in a pingpong fashion for a good five minutes, the shots getting longer and longer, more elaborate, more daring, back and forth across the kitchen.

'Look,' she says, 'I really need you there with me, William, by my side, partners in crime. I need your quick reflexes, your famous physical decisiveness, your bravery.'

'Yeah,' I say, my voice dragging with irony, 'but will you really appreciate me for who I am, or is it just ...'

'Oh no,' she replies, 'it's not that at all.'

For the last few exchanges it hots up, it's getting dangerously real.

'What kind of man,' she demands, 'refuses a woman something when he's just had an orgasm?'

'That's right, bitch, always prefer manipulation to reasonable discussion.'

Then I'm afraid we begin to insult each other, using a range of swear words. The pain we inflict on each other is almost impossible to describe.

'Why don't you just leave? Just go back to your parents' house.' I imagine her permanent absence. Wow, I can do *essays*. I can go to the *language lab*.

'Do you really want me to go?'

'Madam,' I reply, sweeping off an imaginary plumed hat, 'I do.' I bend down, the tea service suddenly alive in my hands; the milk is leaping out of the jug. I go outside and throw it off the balcony, where it lands safely on a pile of lawn clippings, completely intact. Deliria, wearing the translucent raincoat and not much else, is already through the front door and out of the house, heading for the street.

'I'll never speak to you again,' she calls, turning the corner of the driveway. 'Never. Do you understand? Never.'

My next words, spoken out loud to myself, are, 'Oh my God. What have I done?' How, in extreme emotion, everyone resorts to the same clichés.

I locate my trousers, which are soaked in peanut oil. I put them on and run out of the house after her. Catching up with her pretty quick, I declare: 'This is a stupid waste. We don't have to do this. We can be okay, we can be really good. I'm sorry. I was just angry, that's all.' Thus concludes my argument: I was just angry, that's all. It's probably the least intelligent thing I've ever said to her.

After we've spent the usual amount of time in bed, we have the following discussion.

'No lifting, all right?' I say, fully dressed for a change. 'Just the refund.'

'Of course.'

'I'm not doing anything. Besides, I have to meet Prosse at five.' I tap my briefcase to bolster the meaning.

'Was your orgasm nice?'

'Yes. It was fine. Just remember.'

'I promise.'

Tremaine Westfield

If public transport at 11 am is like Death, at 3.30 pm it is like Life. As kids get let out from school, a surge of youth flushes through the bus. Girls in school uniforms, their knees sporting netball scars, shins daubed with Betadine, faces splattered with pimple cream, sort themselves into seats. Deliria's only a couple of years older than them, but, as in the Melbourne shoe shop, she could be twenty-five. People talk to her as though she's twenty-five. She's got that perfection, or, shall we say, completeness. Hers is the face that has reached the end of its development: all the subcutaneous fat is in the right place; all the bones are there. This is the peak. Nothing will modify except to 'mature', i.e. to lose elasticity, to coarsen, to put on weight. She will never be *more* beautiful; she'll be, in polite phrasing, *still* beautiful.

So, the woman who could be twenty-five reveals the plan, which in turn reveals her to be a very young eighteen. Apparently, you just get a credulous and helpful sales assistant and behave as if the jeans were yours. You just behave as if they're yours and people will believe they're yours. The two pairs of jeans suddenly flop onto my lap from Deliria's upended shopping bag. Christ, they look so unbought.

'They can't give you a refund,' I say. 'You can't produce a docket.'

'No, baby,' she ripostes, 'confidence is the key to the world, it's all just attitude and force of personality. If you just look and act appropriately, people will believe you.'

'Yeah, but they have to balance the docket against their stock count.'

'I've done it before, William. It works. Believe me, it works.'

'You've done it before?'

Entering the aircraft-hangar emptiness of Tremaine West-field, we play that game where you try to walk exactly in step, the perfectly matched lovers, like matched cuckoo-clocks. It doesn't work: the Tremaine shopping bag and the briefcase keep getting out of step. She's teasing me too: she keeps patting me on the bum, then dodging my return caress. Quite a show for the few who are here to witness it: a couple of ancient women like crumbling cliff faces, one or two old men still wearing hats in public and brown cardigans buttoned up to the sagging cables of their throats. They probably assume we're lovers. *I* probably assume we're lovers.

An old bloke holds up a shoe from a sales bin, stirring through to make up the pair. There's a slow, deliberate incompetence to his movements: you can see it's not real. There is no intention giving a motive force to his hands. He hasn't got any money. We haven't got any money either: all we've got is a thousand dollars' worth of clothes on our backs and two pairs of stolen jeans. I behave exactly like the old bloke: I look around the various sections, as if to get the info on what prices are doing these days. I'm just pricing this camera, so that when I have the money, I'll know how much it costs. Or I'll know how much money I need to have before I can afford it. Or I'll know that I can't afford it.

Department stores, Deliria tells me à propos, are full of things that no one can afford, and when they can afford them they wouldn't buy them from department stores anyway. I haven't noticed, actually; I don't spend as much time in department stores as Deliria. She goes on. Who would buy a personal computer from a department store when enormous discounts are available from specialist stores? But there they are anyway, on display. It's just so they can show you the price, to give you this consumer hunger, to expose you to the tragedy of your not being able to afford them. So you look for something that you can afford: overpriced moistur-iser, thigh cream that doesn't work, non-generic shampoo.

I see the escalators conveying the old ladies skywards. They are concentrating on holding the rubber handrail; their backs are curved and humped. Turn on the TV: everyone's young. Walk into a department store: everyone's old. I, too, though not beautiful, will be qualified by the years; to me will accrue the roomy Y-fronts, the sports trousers, the discount supermarket trousers, the cardigans, the warm and woolly, the sensible, the specially reduced. I, too, will grow to resent the way it's modelled by twenty-five-year-old men when no one under sixty wears it. I will wear my loosened flesh, without consolation. Montaigne says it pretty well: just about the only good thing about being old is that you can still get drunk.

Deliria is swinging the Tremaine bag. She's *swinging* that bag, not just allowing her arm to go back and forth as the necessary accompaniment to her walking, but every two paces the sharp polished-cardboard edges complete a ninety-degree arc. She has so much energy to spend, this girl, if no money.

Her mouth is shouting whispers. 'People will believe you. You just act like the jeans are yours and people will believe you. The same in theft as in life. In business, in love. Mechanisms, William, mechanisms.'

What about Prosse, I'm thinking. I'm confused about whether I can get a bus back to Flinders in time. I'm confused about how long it's going to take Deliria to accomplish this refund venture. I'm confused about Montaigne, who is good on age but lousy on women.

At the moment we're looking for the jeans counter. We're looking for someone who'll believe Deliria. This might be difficult: *I* don't believe her. I don't believe her when she says she's done it before, even though she supplies details: she plucked a pair of jeans from Tremaine Rundle Mall. She took them to Tremaine Tea Tree Plaza, where she obtained seventy dollars' refund. With the loot, she got her legs waxed and a pedicure. I just don't believe it. Of what significance is a sales docket if you don't have to produce it to get a refund? But the implication of this, that Deliria is *lying*... Actually, maybe a docket isn't necessary, what with Deliria's persuasive powers.

Tremaine Westfield. Jeans section. 3.45 pm. We clock a staff of two, wearing Tremaine uniforms with the black rectangular name-tag and white bas-relief lettering. *Hi, Jane. Hi, Coral.* Coral, a woman of some three-score years, stares at us. Her body has the rolling monumentality of the Adelaide Hills; her face is striated by years of dirty looks. Her specs hang from a chain. Coral, I would say, is not a happy woman. She probably *wouldn't* believe Deliria. Jane, on the other hand, is my age, with this sandy indeterminacy about her hair. Her make-up, incredibly badly applied, gives her head a transplanted look. She probably *would* believe Deliria.

'Hello,' Deliria opens, targeting Jane. 'I wonder if you could help me. I bought these jeans for my husband but he doesn't seem to like them. Would there be any possibility of a refund?'

Her delivery is convincing. As an actress in life, she's very good. It's almost as if she's flattering Jane with a confidence; it's as though she likes Jane and she really wants Jane to like her. The jeans are produced and laid on the cash desk. Jane examines the intact labels and price tag.

'Have you got the docket?' Ah! Cursèd detail.

'No, I'm sorry, I don't have a clue where it is. We've been extending and the house is a bit disorganised. Paint tins everywhere, you know the sort of thing.'

Sure she does. Jane probably shares a two-bedroom unit one-and-a-half hours away from work. I bet she dreams about extending, about redecoration, about having so many paint tins everywhere that she can't find the docket for the two pairs of jeans that she bought for her husband.

'Well, we don't normally do it without a docket, but.' Her hands are weaving. 'You know if it was just up to me.'

'If you could manage, it would be extremely helpful.'

'Where did you say you got them from?'

'Tremaine Rundle Mall branch.'

'Okay, hang on a sec, I might have to ask.'

A moment later, Coral is heaving towards us. 'No, madam, I'm afraid you must produce a docket.'

'Yes, I would love to produce a docket, it must be somewhere under the rubble. I know this is a terribly awkward situation for you. I hope we can arrange something.'

The indomitable Coral. The absence of docket is all. Beauty is powerless. Charm? Forget it.

'Well, I suppose we could have another look around at home, and come back tomorrow.'

Coral's shoulders rise in contempt. She stares monumentally. She doesn't feel the burden of reply. In fact, I think she's thinking: 'You stole those jeans. I've seen a million of you.'

'That bitch. That bitch,' Deliria is saying as we slink out of Tremaine and into the Central Mall.

I'm thinking, firstly, of Jane's tortured grammar, and how I could discuss it with Prosse. Her farewell to Deliria: 'If it would of been up to me, I would of given it to you.' Poor old Jane. 'If it had been up to me, I would have given it to you.' Secondly, I'm thinking of how I've never seen Deliria so obviously bested.

'I have to go back and see Prosse. You coming? There's supposed to be a wine and cheese with the Medievalists.'

'I want to go to CDXpress.'

'You said no lifting.'

'It'll only be for five minutes.'

'I don't want to hang around while you nick CDs.'

'Well, I see how my company is valued.'

'I'm not doing anything, you realise.'

'Of course. Five minutes.'

We're in CDXpress, supermarket of pop-music icons, with a new icon every six months. Silent, absorbed in choice, stupefied by the ambient music, customers graze at the racks and flip contentedly through the recordings. Between the cardboard cut-outs of a semi-nude, crucifix-laden Madonna and an ever-whitening Michael Jackson, both of whom can afford most things except musical taste, customers wonder if they can afford this CD when they can't even afford a pair of socks. In this browsing they are shepherded by a store manager, name-tagged *John*, and a couple of part-timers. Why don't *I* get a part-time job, it occurs to me.

Deliria is standing at the variety rack. This contains the unclassifiable stuff, the stuff that no one will buy except as, or maybe even as, a joke: One Hundred and One Bawdy Tales, Music from the Vienna Woods, The Speeches of Winston Churchill Vol. 2, Thunderbirds Are Go, The History of the Lute, Bouzouki Bonanza, Music for Plants, Music of the Killer Whales.

'Delightful.' With this comment she slips the Killer Whales CD out and tucks it into the front of the rack. Her hand is electrically blue-nailed, white; the buried veins are a dim blue.

Adelaide Spoon Players Ensemble, You Too Can Give Up Smoking, Peter Ponsil and his Tonsil, Berlitz Rumanian, Nicolò Paganini: 24 Capricci. Paganini? What's Paganini doing in this pile of shit?

'Must have it, must have it,' says Deliria of the Paganini, at least three copies of which she already possesses. It is placed at the front of the rack where it clacks against the Killer Whales. Does she know what she's doing? Her movements remind me, disturbingly, of Doug: going through the drawer of gas bills, pulling them out and flattening them on the kitchen table.

'Just five minutes, all right?' she repeats. 'Just five minutes.' She's exhausted the first rack and is combing the second. Her timed index finger hooks around the top right-hand corner of every CD. 'Must have it,' she repeats. The process halts, the desired recording is slid out and placed with its companions at the front, and the ludicrous titles clatter past again.

I surprise myself in one of the mirrors. Who is this mature-looking gent, in pinstriped trousers, white shirt and tie, and a black business jacket? He's someone with no money who is going to miss his tute. Deliria holds up for my inspection another variety CD, its cover showing drawings of farm animals. The farmer is an anthropomorphic pig, in overalls and straw hat, smoking a corn-cob pipe and carrying a bucket. 'Isn't this great?' she says. The CDs she has selected, flattened together at the front of the rack, are as thick as a telephone directory.

'Why don't you hold your bag open?'

'I just want to go.'

'We can go, when you hold the bag open.'

'Can't we just go?'

'Your bag's nice and big. Mine's too small.'

'I just want to go home.'

'It's easy. It's so easy. Come on, the bag.'

The briefcase yawns open in front of me. My notes for Prosse. A half-completed essay. *Anthologie de la Langue Provençale.* Deliria hoists the stack of CDs. Two of them slide out and break apart on the floor. The stack loses its symmetry, corners point angularly: all points of the compass are represented. The briefcase just won't swallow them. While she's jamming them in, I'm kicking the two fallen CDs under the rack, but she won't let her little ones go; she's diving under the rack after them, lying on her stomach, straining her arm for them. When she stands up, her raincoat is covered with adhering carpet particles. She's fiddling with the stuck-together CDs, trying to smooth and realign the confused edges, picking up the briefcase by the sides and shaking. The plastic cases are shuffling about, recalcitrant, not cooperating at all, their edges projecting like the teeth of a circular saw.

'Right! You!' The store manager is right behind us, face distorted with anger. Even his hair is angry, it's coiled and writhing and ready to bite. 'You!' he shouts in my face, ignoring Deliria. *Me?* In unerring stupidity, he grabs me. I'm caught in an overwhelming fast forward. John shouting, 'Into the room, into the fuckin' room.' I'm propelled between the two aisles and behind the cash counter.

Deliria, in whom this John displays complete disinterest, seeing nothing, is walking confidently after us, calling to the store manager, reminding him: 'Do you want me to come with you?' God, the normality of her voice, the calmness, the brightness. 'Do you want me to come with you?'

John hesitates, looking at me as though to ask for my opinion on this matter. 'Yeah, you may as well come too,' he agrees. I am shuffled past the two stunned part-timers. The sprinkled customers are frozen, as if iron filings have been magnetised. John's hand reaches out past me and wrenches a doorknob. A small office opens around me, and I am lit up by its fluorescent lights. Seconds later Deliria joins me. There is a furious scrabble of keys and a final click of the lock.

The escape

Immersion in the owners' bath warms and calms me. Shuddering at our stupidity, I towel myself dry and get dressed. You could be in a police station right now, William; instead you're sitting in the blessed ordinariness of Bellevue, with the array of power-tool calendars and the ever-strengthening kitten. Yes, that's right, we escaped. Or at least I did, and I think she probably did too. There is absolutely no triumph about this. We aren't clever. We're ordinary. I've had my own ordinariness held up to my face and shaken.

What happened was this: the office had a back door, that's all. John forgot the simple existence of a back door. That's what happens when you're angry. It didn't take us long to realise. She went one way down the fire exit; I went the other, trying the doors. That was the last I saw of her. Those fire doors heaved open for me, clanking open into the carpark. Nothing has ever been as beautiful as that carpark. I turned around: perhaps ten feet away from me was John, sprinting.

The pursuit dragged on for its hundreds and hundreds of metres, as two half-fit young men sloshed it out through puddles, throwing up sheets of water. It was so cold, I couldn't even feel my feet. Finally John, after bending over in the middle of the Westfield carpark to puke up what looked like his afternoon coffee, gave up and returned to CDXpress.

Now I'm back, but my blood is still thumping; the adrenaline hasn't quite leached out of me. The experience is just refusing to leave me. And I've missed my tute. I wonder what Prosse is going to say.

The stride of Deliria sounds on the wet glass of the driveway.

'Why variety CDs?', I want to ask her. 'And when are you going to stop?'

'My escape? My escape?' she jabbers. She's had her share of rain too. The translucent raincoat showers the carpet. Her hair is dark with water. She tells me she got one of the shop rear-entrances open and walked 'like a brazen hussy' through a jeweller's and into the Central Mall. I tell the story of John's pursuit.

'Were you afraid?'

'Scared shitless.'

'I've heard that fear can give men erections.'

'It's good that you're not flippant about it. I mean, it's good that you realise how serious that was.'

'William, it's all in a day's work. Really, those situations, you get used to them, you develop a professional detachment.'

'Did you see how angry that guy was?'

'If he hadn't seen you do it, he wouldn't have been angry.'

'God. Talk about rationalising.'

'You've had a very stressful day, William.'

There is a swish of tyres over water in the driveway. Two car doors slam. Two sets of heavy, confident footsteps come our way. Oh fuck. The briefcase.

'Cops.'

All items belonging to Deliria, including Deliria, suddenly gather themselves into a bundle in my arms. The raincoat, the suedes, her handbag, everything. I fling open the back door, hearing the chainsaw shriek of the kitten being flattened against the wall. I push Deliria out, shouting with my hands, pointing at the creek, the bridge. She can get through to the neighbour's property. She stands for a long moment in the middle of the back lawn, then turns. She is out of here, trailing the pink raincoat over the grass.

Well, this doorbell is not going to stop. It's calling my name. I know what I've got to do: I've got to keep the police inside the house as long as possible. I can't let them go exploring the back yard. I turn the door handle, noticing the manufacturer's name like never before, as a man being executed notices the details of the world he's about to leave.

The doorway frames two uniformed policemen, with regulation moustaches, and short back and sides. Their uniforms are a crisp definition. The younger one is holding my briefcase.

'Can I help you gentlemen?'

The blue police car pulls out into the evening. Six o'clock. I've managed to completely fuck up my life.

I answer the phone's shrill summons.

Heavy metal music provides the background as Kev drawls, 'Doug reckons there was a couple of cops come round looking for you.'

A knocking and scrabbling comes from the back door.

I dump the receiver. The opened door reveals Deliria, drenched, shaking, covered in bits of weed and geologically various muds. She's fallen in the creek. Shoeless, her feet are blue. Her teeth are going like castanets. Her lips, like blue lipstick, are so cold, she can't even form words.

A criminal record's not such a bad thing, Kev tells me. Lots of blokes on building sites have criminal records. No one's ever gonna know.

This marvellous practicality. I'm still flattened by the mere words, the conjunction of those two words, criminal … record … But Kev just waves it away, the knotty forearm handles all. 'It's gonna make bugger-all difference to your life,' he says. 'I mean, if you were studying Law you'd be fucked, you could never practise. Same if you wanted to join ASIO or something. But no one checks you out that thoroughly for most jobs. It's not a federal offence either. Only state. Outside of SA you're clean. I'd stay away from that bitch, though. She's fuckin' insane. She's bad news, man.'

Doug has no memory of the uniformed visitation. The tired

neurons just can't hold it together. He's sitting here at the dinner table with us right now, transferring his dinner to his pyjama top. For him, the police never arrived. His son is guiltless; the slate verandah never rang under the soles of the two officers. He is spared the shame.

Later, as Kev tactlessly watches a cop show about a crackdown on shoplifters, Doug sits bemusedly on the side of the bed, the hemiplegic arm forever poised at a forty-five-degree angle, fingers bunched into a fist, as if to deliver a hammer blow. I lose myself in the blessed, soothing routine of getting him ready for bed. Something more important than myself, something other than myself. 'So, you've got a criminal record have you? You think that's bad? I'll show you bad,' whistles the clogged trachea. Things could be worse, I tell myself, as I submerge the upper denture in the glass of water, and listen to the wild fizzing of the cleansing tablet. I could have a terminal disease. I could be missing half my brain. I could have emphysema. I could have osteoporosis. I could have Theseus's acting ability. Yes, William, consider the marvellous list of things that *aren't* wrong with you.

'I'm *there*, aren't I?' Doug's voice enquires. 'I'm *there*.' He is pointing to the armchair. Now this is Byzantine; this is really incomprehensible.

'You're *there*?'

'I'm *there*.'

'You're here. You're not there, you're here.'

'I'm there.'

'Yeah, okay. Whatever you say.' I lug the kilograms of blankets over him. 'You're there.'

Court

'The judge might be a problem for you,' says my counsel, Angela, with her business-suited glamour, her expensively waved hair, her agelessness, her double-rower. Miss South Australia 1985, shall we say. 'He really dislikes larceny.'

'Great.'

Angela's four-hundred-dollar fee is paid for by Doug, indirectly. Kev and I have power of attorney: we just withdraw money from his account whenever we need to. And boy, do I need to. I'm terrified that I'll be charged with wasting police time, or fucking the police around—something really heavy-duty. *You could be in a lot more trouble than you need to be if you don't tell us who she is.* You see, I refused to admit I knew Deliria. I told them a bullshit story about meeting a girl called Christine, in Tremaine Westfield, and then going shoplifting with a total stranger. Guess what: they didn't believe me.

I try to convey the story to Angela, without making the legal mistake of saying Deliria was involved. Tortuously I begin: I tell her that the police allege that there was a girl with me whom they allege I know very well, etc. Angela understands. She's competent. I'm *incompetent*.

Magically quickly, I'm sitting in Glenelg Magistrates Court, Angela next to me, in her beige please-'em-all outfit and matching satin shoes. Bet she didn't shoplift them. Relaxing a bit, with Angela's radiant professionalism to aid me, I can even enjoy the details of the courtroom: the magistrate's quite sloppy suit, the cardigans and supermarket trousers of almost all the male defendants, the legal language, and the really fast clicking of the word processor as the verbatim transcript is taken. Surprisingly, the atmosphere is not one of boredom, of having heard everything there is to hear of human weakness, but rather of friendliness and concern, particularly for the old people. Here's a decorated World War Two veteran, wounded in Libya, who has stolen a can of baked beans; an old woman on the aged pension, abandoned by her children, who has stolen a piece of cheese; yet another who has stolen a bottle of mineral water.

As my name is called, I get a pure chemical thrill. Angela's instructions whirl through my head. *Now then. This is what I want you to do. You're going to hear your name called, and that's going to be a bit frightening for you. It's always a bit frightening, but you're going to be a good soldier. And when you hear your name called you stand up near the desk over there and you don't say anything, I'll say everything. You're required to say 'guilty', and that's it.*

An elderly copper, the same one that's been reading out the charges all morning, gives a rambling though factually accurate account. At approximately four-thirty pm on the said date, the accused was at a shop called CDXpress in Westfield Marion where, with another person, he stole or attempted to steal ten compact discs to the value of eighty-nine-dollars fifty. At the part where I ran away leaving the briefcase, the magistrate chuckles: it's the funniest thing he's heard all morning. Even the court stenographer gives me a grin. Angela reads an exaggerated character reference: winner of the Banque Nationale du Sud-Pacifique award, brilliant academic record, young man of promise. Please don't fuck up his life. He's not a bad lad.

A heavy four-hundred-dollar fine, eight months to pay. Thank you, your Honour.

Angela and I say goodbye on the footpath. Formalities done with, legal services provided, handshakes out of the way, she gives me a no-bullshit look. She tells me I was lucky not to have been charged with dishonesty ('You *know* what we're talking about'), and that if I had, it could have got 'quite serious'.

Upside

Deliria proposes a 'Will's Not in Jail' lunch. I could do with a bit of a celebration, what with that police interview still ringing in my ears. So we raid Central Market, actually paying (Christ, have I learned my lesson), and come back to Bellevue with a feast resembling something out of Petronius. Kalamata olives, green olives stuffed with little bits of tomato, hummus, tabouli, about twenty different kinds of cheese, food I've never even heard of, like 'Piccalilli': whatever it is, I'm sure I'm going to find out. Basically, we've bought a highly representative sample of Australian migrant-influenced party snacks, plus two bottles of Semillon Sauvignon Blanc, favouring the Adelaide Hills and Clare Valley regions with our choice. The amount we've bought is so heavy, it threatens to burst the shopping bags as we trudge back from the bus stop.

Of course, with Deliria, there's no such thing as just 'having lunch'. She's always got to take it that little bit further. Now, for instance, she's reclining on the couch, her blouse unbuttoned, the black bra startling as always against her skin.

'Let's feed each other, baby.'

The Central Market produce lies in its disarray on the coffee table. I start with a seeded kalamata olive. My hand travels slowly over the white landscape of her upper body; two drips of purple juice fall from the olive, roll darkly off her throat, and keep going down the side of her neck. She opens wide. From where I'm kneeling I can see the entire roof of her mouth, even the ripples across her hard palate, even the grey amalgam of a filling. Oh, happy filling, to live inside Deliria's mouth! Then there's the unfamiliar warmth of the inside of her lips on my fingers as I place the olive inside.

Next comes a slab of Bismarck herring on a Jatz biscuit. This over-ambitious mouthful leaves a trail of pickling fluid over her stomach. I wipe it up with a broken-open bread roll.

She sits up and frankly removes the blouse. 'We wouldn't want this getting food on it, would we?'

The next item is a cheese-and-piccalilli open sandwich. With full intent, I drop several gobbets of the yellow relish onto the white slopes of her breasts.

'William, that's *so* naughty,' she says, through the sandwich.

My mouth dives on her breasts; my cheek scrapes her bra as I lick up the piccalilli. Its vinegar and mustard tang is mixed with deodorant and talcum powder. Mmm. An acquired taste, no doubt …

She gently pushes my head away. 'In a minute, baby, in a minute. Don't worry, you'll get there.'

I continue feeding Deliria olives, cheese and pumpernickel bread while she lies on the sofa with her blouse removed. I pop another olive into her mouth; I can feel her tongue moving against my fingers, in its moist, darting surprise. I've got an unbearable and absurdly visible hard-on. There must be a litre of blood down there. A couple of olives later, she begins to lick my stained fingertips, her tongue pushing through my fingers. Then she sucks two of my right-hand fingers into her mouth, where they jam against her teeth. I slide my free hand under her bra and she gives me a beautiful grin of permission, her teeth lightly clamped around the top joints of my fingers. I can feel her nipple denting into the palm of my hand. Then I lose my centre of gravity, and actually have to push on her breast so I don't fall on top of her and bang our heads together.

'Okay, William, let's do it. Let's really do it. I'm not kidding this time.'

She places her hand on the outline of my hard-on, where there's already a dark patch of fluid the size of a twenty-cent piece. 'Mmm,' she says approvingly. 'William, you're so reliable.'

She keeps her luminous hand on me, cupping me through the trousers.

'You're not going to pull out of this, are you?'

'No.'

'I don't want to wreck the mood, but you *are* a virgin, aren't you?'

'Yes.'

'Then I've got to get some stuff from the Chemmart.'

Once again, the landscape is informed of my love. Outside the Chemmart, the rainbow lorikeets are bright squirts of paint against the grey canvas of gum leaves; they are impossibly decorative, useless and beautiful, with their uproarious songs. On the 'No Parking' signs and surveillance cameras perch the loquacious magpies, tuxedoed, chewing on insects, piercing in their regards. Galahs tumble across the curved sky, pitching and rolling, coming to rest on electricity lines. The rosellas squawk in their tree-condos, quarrelling with the neighbours: the imported pigeons, the dull sparrows. Beyond the carpark stand the majestic hills, with their biscuity sandstone escarpments, grandly allowing the tiny human presence: the broadcast aerials, the dotted habitations, the coiling train lines. The sunlight skates down the foothills and across the back gardens of our brushed suburbs, where fossilised seashells call back through geological time. The stately clouds pull out of the gulf, past the stacked seaweed and the flopping waves, cruising across the city to park above the hilltops, where they unload their showers.

And so the world's ordinary contents, a few birds, the hills, and some clouds, are rendered new and unusual by love—they are magnetised, everything in nature swings and points north.

I'm back, with a bagful of gear (water-based lubricant, etc.). Deliria is watching a porno. You know the kind of crap? The ordinary, flabby guy; the ridiculous location (a laundromat); the woman's fake abandon, as if someone had made a recording of a cow giving birth, sped it up twenty times, and set it on endless repeat.

'It's not very realistic,' I comment.

'The man who speaks from experience.' She switches it off.

Oh, the smell of an aroused woman: the celebrated musk, like the smell that comes off a leopard's back. She's standing in the bedroom, unhooking her bra, urging off her panties.

You can tell when someone has no experience of kissing. They put too much into it. Deliria's tongue clambers into my mouth like a performing seal. She explores every crevice; she even discovers a decaying molar with a hole in it the size of a peppercorn. But hey, who's complaining?

We edge towards the bed, where the Chemmart bag contains its pain-reduction kit.

I can't believe what I'm seeing. Deliria, instantly knowing what to do, unscrews the lid of the lubricant, punches a hole through the soft aluminium hymen, takes my hand and squirts onto it a noisy load of the transparent jelly. The physical evidence of what we're about to do sits coolly on my fingers.

'Make me wet, baby.'

I look into those traffic-light greens. I have one of those zany, out-of-left-field thoughts: *I've seen that colour in a map.*

My middle and ring fingers push slowly into her hot liquidity. In the silent room, I hear the fleshy collision of our lips, the sucking, the clinking-together of teeth. There's so much to hear and feel. I've got my left arm around the back of her neck; there's a tiny difference in skin temperatures between my forearm and her nape.

'I think I'm ready.'

She opens her legs like a pair of scissors. There's the shocking intimacy of my putting myself inside her, the awed sharing of this knowledge. Then I can feel that I'm up against a pliable membrane. I look into her incredulous, encouraging eyes.

'Do it, William. It's not going to hurt.'

There's a soft tearing, a sliding apart, like a pair of curtains opening around me. I bury my face in the riotous immediacy of her hair. When she breathes, I can smell the olives, the Bismarck herring and the piccalilli, their odour rendered strangely beautiful. I kiss the lost valley above her collarbone. I kiss the hollow of her throat, the peach-down on her chin. Her lipstick is long gone, blended into my face. She doesn't close her eyes. As always, she's daring me to hold her gaze, that mineral-green gaze, like the Coral Sea photographed from space. *That's* where I've seen it before, I think as I pull out of her, my whole body going into spasm, and shoot a rope of white over her breasts.

'We've shared so much, William,' she says, stretched happily on the bed, her bra and panties in a heap on the floor where they are being clawed to pieces by the kitten. 'We've shared something I've never shared with anyone else.'

'It's great, isn't it?'

'And we've also shared something that you don't even suspect.'

'Talk about wrecking the mood. What?'

'Oh don't worry, it's not "Welcome to the World of AIDS" or anything.'

'I hardly assumed that.'

'Can you guess?'

'Oh, come on. Don't muck around.'

She drags the sheet over that sumptuous body of hers. So new, so unused. She peeks out from under its canopy. 'You've joined the elite.'

'What?'

'You've become a member of the Brotherhood of Cain. You're marked.'

'Yeah, all right. So what? I don't want to be a lawyer.'

'Don't you get it?' She gives me that smile, that all-conquering double-rower.

'You've been caught too, right?'

'Three times.'

Dear oh dear. Oh no. She's mad, you know she's mad. She's fuckin' insane. She's bad news, man. It's staring you in the face, William.

In the ensuing Q-and-A session she excitedly reveals the following. First time, it was a pair of stockings. Second time, a pair of earrings. Third time, a watch. How much did she get fined? First time, surprisingly little: thirty dollars. Obviously the magistrate didn't 'really dislike' larceny. Second time, considerably more: two hundred. Third time, considerably more: four hundred. Not bad going, though, when you consider how much she's actually got away with. By her calculations, it must be up to thirty-two thousand dollars by now.

Well, some women talk about sex. Some women talk about being caught shoplifting.

She also reveals another piece of information.

'That day with the police, I was out there in the creek. I thought, this guy does so much. He's willing to do so much. This guy's great. I knew it wouldn't even occur to you to cooperate with them. When I saw them interviewing you, I knew. I knew. I realised I could trust you with anything. My life, anything. My body. I trust you with my body. I find it very hard to trust people. I'm like that. I've never had sex. Before today, that is. I've never lent anyone money, either. It's this thing about trust. When I saw them talking to you, I realised I was trusting you with my life. And I was. Because the next time, if I went to court again, the next time, that would be it. A straight jail term. Next time, they said. And all this time I was with you, going on shoplifting expeditions, I had that consequence hanging over me. I can hardly believe it. Some of the risks.'

Too many revelations. She loves me. She's in love with me. She's always loved me, she supposes.

Kev, rung in as consultant, tells me that I've got to weigh up the pluses and the minuses, as we all have to do eventually. He also tells me that she's 'fuckin' insane' and 'bad news', but let that pass. Well, here goes. Let's weigh it all up. On the minus side we've got: well, she's a bit immature, she's got a few problems, she's been lying to me constantly ever since I met her, she's a compulsive shoplifter, she's got zero future in the public-service sector. On the plus side we've got: let's see, uh, she's witty, she's charming, she has a lovely voice, she dresses well, she has a taste for literature, she's not bad at languages, she is one of the most beautiful women in Australia if not the world, she can cook a bit.

That about wraps it up for the plus side.

Summer

Sumer is icumen in / Lhude sing cuccu. Green hills, undergo your yearly peroxide wash. Asphalt, begin your buckling and glutinous shifting under the feet. Cement, thou stunningly inappropriate building material, reflect the sun blindingly in our faces, till our necks, our white winter necks, go brick brown, and every throat is emblazoned with the Aussie sun triangle. Fashion, reflect this change in season: let flesh appear, let women display so much leg and arm and chest and stomach and back, and us poor blokes not allowed to stare—I wonder if the Islamics don't have a point. Lurid surfwear, assail our senses. Cycling shorts, make us ridiculous. Expensive T-shirts, mock our incomes. Bollé sunglasses, rip-offs and rip-offs of the rip-offs, come to dwell among us.

Sumer is icumen in, all right, and it bringeth many things. My honours degree for one, and the University Medal, to my surprise. Thanks Prosse! I suppose when I start applying for jobs I should tell them about the University Medal rather than the criminal record. Terdsak's packages, too, continue to arrive, slowed up by the Christmas rush. His letters and tapes contain the usual polite Thai requests for me to come over and see him in Bangkok, along the lines of our Western 'We must have lunch some time.' More importantly, he says his dad can set me up with a university job 'just like that'. Think about it: a police lieutenant-general getting a shoplifter a job at a university.

Sumer is icumen in, and it bringeth a noticeable decline in Doug. More and more frequently, he escapes on the tram without any money or ID. He is trying to locate the house in which he was brought up. Last time he got the right street, but due to some recent traffic-calming measures, he was confused by a roundabout. Alarmed local householders, unable to get any sense out of him, called the boys in blue, who delivered him to our front gate. Kev and I discuss what might have happened. The worst-possible scenario is that Doug would have been unable to direct the police car back to the Glenelg address. Time for some dog tags, Kev reckons.

Sumer is icumen in, and true to form, the pathetically fallacious weather is well up on the progress of my love. Things are hotting up. She's openly with me. 'We've gone public,' I tell her in the oven of the Glenelg tram.

Isn't it great to be ordinary? We've returned to the fold. The theatrical element in the sex is out. Playing with her hair and kissing her is in. Trepidation is gone. A daily electricity hums in my legs. We devote enormous amounts of time to fucking: in the pie-graph of the day it's a glutton's wedge. I sleep less; I'm satisfied. She's getting a lot better in bed. She's learning to surrender a bit. Nothing bad will happen; the demons will not appear.

What we now get up to between the sheets has really changed. It has become, in the clueless terminology of a women's magazine, 'relationship sex'.

We're woken by the brawling lorikeets, as the sun hauls itself up over the Mount Lofty Ranges, and the bedroom is day-bright at 6.30 am. We nestle into each other, conventionally enough, with her head pillowed against my upper arm. Her hand enquires downwards, encountering the trusty hard-on.

'We'd better do something about that,' she says, sitting up in bed, and in a single continuous movement, she pulls the quaint, Victorian-looking nightdress over her head and throws it at the wardrobe.

What follows is refreshingly normal. No blindfolds and Farmers Union Light Thickened Cream, no two-hour theatrical lead-up, and most importantly, none of that 'What am I going to let him do and what am I *not* going to let him do?' She climbs on top of me, the powerful columns of her thighs on either side of me, hair pouring down, breasts brushing my face in casual invitation; then she envelops me.

Mid-morning, she'll go out and shoplift or even *buy* a sex manual, returning at two o'clock in the afternoon armed with a diagram, asking, 'Have you ever tried it *this* way?' Even if I have, I'll say, 'No, never.' I follow her into the bedroom.

I'm taking the chivalry a bit too seriously. One night, *Le Chevalier* William and noted *Belle Dame Sans Merci* Deliria are walking down Rundle Street after a film. A carload of Calabrian boys drive past and shout something at Deliria, who, in the heat, is wearing a backless dress. It sounds like 'You Slut.' Or is it 'You Suck'? Whichever, the car, a hotted-up Holden Monaro with mag wheels, does a U-turn and comes back for another pass. In my hand is a nearly full can of Coke. With beautiful clarity, the necessary movements arrange themselves. My flexed arm, and the exemplary flattened parabola of my throw, are followed by a little meteor trail of soft drink and foam. I notice that the windshield is now a dense white spiderweb of cracked safety glass. I receive the inevitable beating-up. Deliria watches, horrified. I can't be doing this. I'm nearly twenty-three. Later, Kev takes an interest, amused at how I defended Deliria against the insults with a sort of Charge of the Light Brigade display of valour, particularly stupid considering that, as she was examining something in, or planning to steal something from, a shop window at the time, she did not hear the insult. He advises me not to go around frosting people's windscreens.

For some people, like Jaufre Rudel, goals are unachievable: they recede in front of you, the very act of pursuing them makes them get further and further away. Well, I disagree. Deliria's just moved in with me, complete with furniture. 'Why delay the inevitable?' she cracked. If that's not achieving your goal, then I don't know what is. I've overtaken poor Jaufre: his stallion's miles back.

Deliria has overcome a paranoia that the police are still looking for her at Bellevue, although she hasn't fully grasped our insignificance, our ordinariness; she hasn't fully grasped the minuteness of the interest we inspire in the police, compared to that aroused by people who steal cars, people who sell drugs, people who throw other people off bridges simply for replying to an insult.

I imagined her moving-in would simply be a formalisation of an arrangement that already existed in practice. I had forgotten Deliria's enormous ill-gotten material wealth. Thus, the spare room has become the Woolfian 'her' room, its original contents consigned to the garden shed. Let's have a look at this room. The owner's gastric-hued curtains have been replaced by white lace. Against one wall stands a desk of solid oak with dried flowers on it. I can be sure it's not stolen. How can you shoplift a desk? The drawers are full of calligraphy pens, graphic liners and fountain pens, which are stolen. What is it that she has about pens? A psychotherapist would be on to that one in a flash, but then he'd have to answer 'What is it that she has about cosmetics?' and also 'What is it that she has about books in foreign languages that she can't read yet?'

Against the opposite wall of her room is another item that isn't stolen: the wardrobe. Again, how can you shoplift a wardrobe? It's so crammed with clothes that the double doors belly out. Glued to a door is a poster for *Aphaphirom et Amornvivat*, which seems a while ago now. Her violin takes up residence ('don't worry—Skippy and I don't actually practise that much'), together with hundreds of volumes of sheet music in spectacular disorder: they spread and spread, eating up floorspace. When I notice some important stuff, Elder Conservatorium Second Year Entrance Practical Violin: Past Exams 1982-1992, hidden underneath a Grade III piano primer, I suggest we alphabetise the mess.

'Indeed, Will, why not bring order out of chaos?' she seems to agree. But we don't actually do anything about it. We just get used to walking over hundreds of volumes of sheet music.

On the archaeological layer above the sheet music are garbage bags of jewellery. Deliria doesn't have a jewel box. When you've got jewellery on that scale, it's garbage bags or nothing. There are books, too, in similar quantities. Deliria deals in cubic metres. Again, no bookshelf could hold them: it's got to be tea chests. A quick count and valuation suggests a purchase price of about ten thousand dollars—if she'd bought them. How many people do you know who have ten thousand dollars' worth of books?

Her reading matter displays a side of her that is new to me. Apart from what I'd expect (Jane Austen, the Brontës, the complete Arden Shakespeare, John Donne, Milton, Chaucer, Muriel Spark, Angela Carter), there's also Jackie Collins, Danielle Steel, Judith Krantz, Barbara Cartland, and a number of other trashy sex-and-shopping and adventure-romance writers. Now I would have thought that a woman who likes Angela Carter can't like Danielle Steel. While a woman who thinks *Nisi Dominus* is good music can actually prefer *Jesus Christ Superstar*, a woman who likes *Wise Children* can't like *Honour Thyself*. Can she?

Crowning all these riches is Deliria herself, stretched out naked and opulent on the sheet music, among the tea chests of books, among the garbage bags of jewellery. She comes out with the most staggering, most revealing Freudian slip I am ever likely to hear: 'I've often wanted to bring you into my womb—*Jesus!*—my room.' This is one time I'd give the good doctor his due.

Her moving-in also has a linguistic consequence: she refers to me differently in the presence of other people. It used to be just plain Will or William, now it's 'William, the guy I live with'. It does lend a more serious, permanent aspect to be so named. 'William, my boyfriend' doesn't cut it: it misses the intensity; the attachment is too lightly rendered. She doesn't use it. 'My partner' sounds like a couple of gays. So does 'my companion'. 'My lover' is too loaded—you can't pretend it's natural. 'My guy' I quite like. What about 'my husband'? That would be nice. Hey, why delay the inevitable?

What I'm enjoying, and can't get over, any more than I can get over Deliria's beauty, is this sense of finally reaching her. The completion, the closure. All the time, William, you thought your goal was getting further and further away, by the very nature of love, by your very efforts in that direction. You were thinking perhaps it *is* impossible after all; perhaps Kev's got a point, perhaps she is fucking insane, bad news, dangerous, a nightmare, a compulsive and habitual thief, and those are her good points. Perhaps someone more sensible, like Prue, would be more in your line. Prue, perhaps. Perhaps you should be looking at Prue. Perhaps you should be … and suddenly you tripped right over her. She's right there, she's there, you're there.

I can't imagine returning to Westfield Marion any time in the next five years, especially with Deliria. Imagine bumping into John. In fact I have bumped into him, in a way. I saw him pulled up at a red light in his panel van, those coils of hair still very angry. In a rush of pure chemical fear, I relived that whole car-park chase, but I was pleased to note, in and on his car, the instantly recognisable logos of scumbagdom: white rubber skeleton dangling from the rear-view mirror, dashboard covered with fluffy white synthetic material, leather-fringed tasselled steering wheel, and, dead giveaway, both panels of the van spray-painted with science-fiction light-porno fantasy scenes. I can just imagine him driving around Hindley Street at 3 am looking for a fight. Don't take this the wrong way: I know that I'm the bad guy in this story, and that John was wronged. It's just more fun that he's not, say, a sensitive young poet or a promising classical musician. The other point illustrated by this encounter is that, for a city of a million people, Adelaide is very small. I write to Terdsak and ask him: 'In Bangkok, what are the chances of seeing someone you know pulled up at a red light?' 'Zero,' he replies in his next package. You don't bump into people in a major city. Adelaide being a minor city, in every sense, you do bump into people, a fact that will be confirmed by anyone in Adelaide who has tried to have an extra-marital affair and go to a restaurant at the same time. I bumped into Deliria at the Immaculate fete. I often bump into Kev on Jetty Road. I often bump into Doug, who is usually shouting out things like 'home-grown tomatoes!' Once I even bumped into Doug on the tram, on his bi-monthly escape to find his boyhood home.

Bumping into people means we can't shop at Westfield Marion ever again, so today we take the bus to Central Market. It's very domestic, this business of going shopping and actually paying. We select mushrooms, Lebanese cucumbers and mandarins, and pay what they add up to. She's renounced shoplifting, out of respect for me. She can't endanger herself, she claims, because she knows I'll protect her, I'll put myself in danger for her sake. More likely, though, the sex-shoplifting equation is so exact, in Deliria, that lots of sex simply reduces the need to shoplift. She's just replaced one compulsion with another. Three times a day is nothing, for her. Ah, what a price to pay.

Central Market, for those of you who've never been there, is supposed to be an approximation of a European street market, but really it's completely Australian and sanitised. The chickens, to take an example, are sold without their claws and heads. The fish are sold recently dead rather than valiantly struggling. Stern laws enforce cleanliness. It's very pleasant, really: you walk along and the market smells sequentially as you pass the stalls: the face-crinkling smoked herring, the heavy fruit smells, the coffee surging into your nasal passages, the gastric cheese. At the moment I'm having a discussion at the coffee counter about whether Blue Mountain is really worth what you pay for it, when just ordinary Espresso seems perfectly okay, if not even superior …

But hold, who comes here? What did I say about Adelaide being a mini-city? The Olympian shoulders of Theseus negotiate the aisles. And the lime-shirted Neddy accompanies. Neddy and Theseus are shopping for vegetables: how refreshingly ordinary. Theseus shows a most untypical clumsiness when the plastic bag he pulls from the roller turns into an unending streamer of plastic bags that piles up, layer upon layer on the floor. Neddy compounds things by picking the wrong potato, the cornerstone, out of a pile. The resulting avalanche of potatoes partially eclipses Theseus.

'Let's go,' says Deliria.

'What?'

'You don't get it. We've got to go.'

'What?'

Her hand fastens on my wrist, and I'm dragged after her. I skid on a cabbage leaf, blending it into the cement floor.

'Can you stop pulling my arm?' I say, as my wrist clicks. She's still tugging.

'Please, just don't. Don't.' I can see the tears pooling up, ready to spill.

'Okay, okay. We'll go.'

I'm looking over my shoulder at the receding Neddy and Theseus, as they chase the rollicking potatoes down the aisle. I'm led out of Central past the smells, past the de-clawed and beheaded chickens, past the laid-out fish and ice, and the blue curls of tiger prawns. We come out into the summer night, spiralling back into the past, reliving past stupidity, having learned nothing. In the 216, Deliria sits with her forehead pressed against the backrest of the seat in front. Buses I have known. Chap. 2. The 216. Hail, Oh Bus! The passengers glance in interest at the rarity of a non-televised spectacle: public grief. Great, I think. Instantly labelled. Young couple with problems. I put to her the final, humiliating questions.

'This is about the roses and the doll, isn't it?'

'Yes.'

'You were caught, weren't you?'

'Yes.'

The pathetic fallacy is giving me the day off, which is lucky. What natural phenomenon would be appropriate to reflect the progress of our love? Global cataclysm?

She's always got to take it that little bit further. She's always got to be that little bit cleverer than she actually is. God, how many times did she say 'doll' or 'flowers' to me in French at those parties? That, in itself, would have been enough. But that wasn't it. (Oh, by the way, no one guessed about *my* involvement. Everyone thinks Deliria sent the parcels to herself. To everyone in Music I, she is the sole agent of her own destruction. I'm clean.) No, what gave her away was not what I'd expect, i.e., the vital snippet of information that she couldn't have known unless she had been in on it. ('How could you know that the doll was dressed as a violinist, Deliria, when you never saw it?') No, the truth is more simple and wrenching. Everyone knew it was her, nearly all the time. They were willing to forgive her once, twice even, because they loved her. The conductor's speech, at the Royal Ed ('I'm absolutely certain that the person who sent those parcels is in the room *at this moment*'), was addressed to Deliria.

How did they know?

Deliria wasn't shocked enough; she wasn't destroyed enough. She was unable to fit her personality around the emotion she was supposed to be playing. Remember her plans for tarring and feathering the miscreant and chaining him to a Hail Bus Here sign on North Terrace, after, or perhaps prior to, shaving his pubic hair? That started a few people thinking. You see, people in shock all want the same thing: sedation. Drugs. They don't want to get together with their mates and invent imaginative revenge scenarios.

Then someone, we'll never know who, submitted a written complaint to the Vice-Chancellor's office, and the venomous piece of paper wound its way slowly up the bureaucracy. Around the time that I appeared in court, Deliria was quietly expelled.

If it works it works, if it doesn't work it doesn't work. This, as applied to Love, as opposed to a car or a toaster, is the Kev philosophy of men and women. It is the doctrine of practicality, of the redundancy of love, in favour of compatibility, as if you were matching a table and chair. I can see it has some sense in it, but I don't fully subscribe to the doctrine of practicality. Maybe I haven't been burned enough. At any rate, I start asking myself some fairly practical questions about Deliria. Here's one that is on my mind often enough: what's going to happen to *me* if I stay with *her*? Let's make a projection based on the last eight months. Since I've been involved with Deliria, I've notched up a police record and a four-hundred-dollar fine, I've broken the law more times than I can remember, and I've had my balls kicked in by a group of guys. Based on the law of increasing involvement, I should be getting blown away by the police or the Calabrian Mafia some time in the middle of next year.

I'm losing my courtliness, I must say. Perhaps that's just in the nature of courtly love: it can't survive the collision with a real human being. The *joie* just isn't enough; it doesn't blind you enough. Sure, in a world where it was quite accepted that you'd be dead at twenty-eight, a beautiful face might go a long way towards excusing Deliria's behaviour. But I'm not Guillaume d'Aquitaine. I'm not going to be dead when I'm twenty-eight. I *am* wondering: what will she be like when she's forty? And I'm not talking about her body.

Videotrash, taking care of Doug

The packages from Terdsak arrive on a two-week cycle. This time there are a few Thai videos, a Steven Seagal movie dubbed into Thai (not too many language difficulties there, folks), *Police News*, *Murder 191*, and a linguistically interesting collection of junk mail. Terdsak has included items like boat tickets, election leaflets, and the promotional handouts you get when you go into a McDonalds. He's taken photographs of termite-extermination adverts that have been nailed up on telegraph poles. He's even put in a CD of a corrupt right-wing politician telling everyone how he's going to clean up corruption.

It provides an index of Thai society, as well as giving me the opportunity to learn the word for 'termites'. The corollary, which I had never thought of when I started this correspondence, is that it provides me with an index of Australian society that is available to few Australians. Take this horrifying magazine, *Murder 191*. Take murder as an index of society. Murder is murder, you might say, with some justification, but the difference between homicides in our respective cultures is that, broadly speaking, murders in Thailand are about love, business disputes or revenge. There is no random violence in Thailand. People don't kill people they don't know. They don't understand it. Once, when I referred to a drive-by shooting, Terdsak thought I was talking about a shooting gallery with an attached carpark.

Terdsak is also using his dad's influence to get me a job. Imagine, if you will, the Deputy Commissioner of South Australia Police ringing up the Vice-Chancellor of the University of Adelaide and saying that there is a certain young man whom it would be of benefit to the university to employ. And the Vice-Chancellor asking whether he would like the young man to start immediately, or whether it would it be okay if he started work commencing next academic year. That's Thailand for you. That's how it works; that's the part of the Asian economic miracle we don't want to know about. We want to know about low unemployment, tame unions.

So I'm likely to be awarded a job at a Southeast Asian university, through the medium of a corrupt police-general. You may laugh, or you may raise your virtuous eyebrows, but it's a job, and I've just found out that the job market in South Australia is as dead as a clubbed catfish. The poor little employment section of the *Adelaide Times* doesn't even fill the page. We might see a couple of executive appointments, a couple of accounting jobs, jobs in sales, very little white-collar clerical work, and a couple of jobs for specialised tradesmen (boilermakers, electricians and so on; people who can actually do things). Then we approach the bottom of the barrel. Casual work. Jobs selling DVD players, commission only: own car required (i.e. lots of travel and no transport allowance). Be your own boss! Pay your own salary! Pyramid sales. We see organisations like Naturometrics: companies in which you make your contract with deceit in order to be successful, or indeed, unsuccessful. More pitifully, there are jobs clearly aimed at exploiting people on old-age pensions. How does this sound: letterboxing catalogues at five dollars a thousand, when every letterbox is on a quarter-acre block?

Thus, I find myself almost immediately on the dole, standing uncertainly in a Glenelg Centrelink office, my linguistic skills coming in very handy: they help me fill in the form. I'm advised to apply for a job in the public service. With a recent shoplifting conviction?

Later, Kev and I are having a beer at the Grand Hotel.

'You thought about what you're gonna do?' In his hand is a stubbie of Cooper's Ale, beaded with condensation, its top and bottom just appearing over the edges of his palm. His hands are brutalised by work but you feel you can trust them. They are the kind of hands you'd like to have on the scruff of your neck if you were falling off a cliff.

'Well, I thought about getting a job in Southeast Asia. Thailand. Get a job at a university.'

'You'll have to pay for the airfare and everything, though. Have enough cash to set yourself up.'

I have absolutely no idea of how much I would need. The idea of, say, an apartment in Bangkok …

'You'd need a minimum of six grand,' Kev says.

This figure is incomprehensible to me: it's as if he has just said, 'You'd need a minimum of a million dollars.' I just see the figure six and all those zeroes coming after it. It's the zeroes that get me. If he had said 'sixty dollars', I could have comprehended that: it's an amount I've had in my pocket fairly often. Six hundred? Yes, I once had six hundred dollars in my account, before I met Deliria and started blowing it all on lunch. The amount Kev mentions is just one zero beyond my experience.

Deliria gets a job. Having told her parents she's taking a year off to gain experience of the world, she's got a job selling DVD players to people who can't afford them. She works commission only, with a nominal retainer. Although her job is 'own car required', she does it on public transport, and since the people who can't afford DVD players tend to live very far away from the centre of the city, the postcodes all sprout stunningly different digits, and there's a whole new set of buses to hail.

She's out at eight in the morning, and often she's not back until nine at night, when the sky is just a breath of blue over St. Vincent's Gulf. I do all the cooking. She's almost gibbering with fatigue by the time she gets home. Wouldn't it be so much nicer to be doing, just for example, Music II at the Con, with a first instrument violin, second instrument piano, a cosy English option, and those essays so indulgently accepted weeks after the deadline? How much more preferable to be getting a bit fuzzy at lunchtime in the Adelaide Uni bar, instead of having these heart-rending, manipulative conversations with the nouveau poor, travelling to their satellite-city postcodes.

Each dawn we are told of the imminent day by magpies, rosellas, willy-wagtails and mudeyes. Oh, the clockwork cheerfulness of these birds. Come on humans, they say. Get up, take part in this great society you've created for yourselves. I reflect that I would have unemotionally shot them all, before the civilising influence of Deliria's reciprocated love.

At this hour, Deliria in bed is a black-and-white photo. Colours do that, before the sun comes up: they lose their individuality. Anybody could be anybody. Brown, red, blonde, auburn—it's all the same. Deliria shifts: the mattress dips a bit. At six foot she's heavy.

I have a hot shower. She has a cold one. I eat, she doesn't. I shave, she doesn't. I submit the bathroom mirror to my full gaze. I shave the 'interesting' face, conducting a useless inspection of my hairline. The hair is valiantly maintaining a defence, but it's like Thailand invaded by Japan—it has to give way eventually. Ah well, there's still the young face, the good bones, the good eyes, the 'perfect eyebrows'. When you think about it, the hair isn't even you. It isn't tissue: it's just keratin, like your fingernails. That's the way to think about it.

Deliria puts on make-up, I don't. Her routine in the mornings begins with a splash of moisturiser, smoothed upwards so that the light facial hairs sweep up. It's supposed to give you an 'up' look. Then comes the patting-on of foundation (why does a perfect complexion require foundation?), and the Sistine-Chapel-ceiling smoothing-on of lipstick and eyeshadow. Eyeshadow for selling DVD players? Certainly. Physical envy, she says, is an important part of sales work. Most of her customers are single mothers with no cosmetics. As this physical envy most certainly extends to 'dress options', she tugs on her business suit. This item, stolen a few months ago in case she should ever need to do business, is a light cream two-piece linen suit, with knee-length skirt. The whole get-up is completely serious; it projects reliability. You can trust the wearer of this suit, it declares. Of course you can.

At breakfast, on the balcony, Deliria's kitten (Samuel, we've finally called him), his tail coiling and uncoiling, his back legs strong as a rabbit's now, springs around after birds—sometimes he kills them while we are watching. The back yard slopes down to the summer-dry creek, to the dead cat, now firmly buried and skeletal. There are the reeds where she hid, where she fell in love with me, she supposes.

Like the native birds' conversation, ours is semi-automatic, and begins early.

Deliria views my steak with mock horror. 'Do you realise that that was once a living, breathing animal, a cow? I mean, would you take the responsibility? Would you wield the axe?'

'Yeah, sure,' I munch determinedly. 'I just don't have the time.'

'Yes, but you distance yourself from it. You call it beef. How would you feel about calling it *cow*?'

'Fallacious argument. It's *cow* in lots of languages.'

I listen to the chortling straw in her orange juice. She's following a diet she found in one of those prescriptive women's magazines: only liquids in the morning. Orange and carrot juice, mashed bananas, mashed avocado, apple pulp.

'Bet you're back on solids in three days,' I say.

So this is us. We tease each other a little, not a lot. We relax a bit. We're not on show.

Hand in hand (the innocence of this love—we actually *hold hands*; we'll probably be holding hands in ten years), we ascend the street to Shepherd's Hill Road, there to await the 216. Hail, Oh Bus! The very traffic seems benign, the 'Walk' signs, the stones themselves ... Yes, I know it's only chemicals; I only 'feel' this way, and as far as the traffic, the 'Walk' signs and the stones are concerned, I might as well be in love with a model train set. I know. I just don't care at the moment.

The long commuter bus, jointed like a rubber concertina, arrives. We get on, our magnetised-stripe tickets zipping into the validator. I'm validated, Deliria's validated.

A tragic parting occurs at the tram-stop. Deliria won't be getting off for another hour or so, by which time she'll be in Gilles Plains or Parafield Gardens or Elizabeth or one of those suburbs where everyone is poor. I imagine (and I have to imagine this: I've never seen the way poor people live) that the television is relentlessly on. There's a pack of smokes on the table at nine o'clock in the morning. The single mum will be much too young, gazing at Deliria with that physical envy she unfailingly generates. There will follow a sad, manipulative conversation, always circling around the topic of purchasing a DVD player for a down-payment of twenty bucks and further payments which stretch out over years. *This will really change your life. You'll be able to rent DVDs.* And this is where the company, Videotrash, is truly diabolical. Deliria carries twenty bucks on her at all times. If the single mums don't have a credit card (and they never do), she's allowed to lend them the deposit if she thinks it will swing the deal.

Kev and I have a conversation with a GP, in which all those innocently named suburbs of Edwardstown, Mitchell Park, Ascot Park, Woodlands Park and Forestville reveal themselves to have been, all along, various levels of the nursing home hell, to which Doug is now being summoned. Kev and I resist, brothers locking ranks. We will take care of him at home. The GP admires our choice, but points out that we might not feel that way forever.

I recite verses of Guillaume d'Aquitaine and Sunthorn Phu, while getting Doug ready for the shower. His contused shin, the colour of raw steak, has to be taped up in a garbage bag. I hose the naked Doug while he sprawls on the shower chair, staring at the towel rail, scrotum hanging like a Christmas stocking. Today, he has only an intermittent idea of what's happening. At other times, he can be lucid, lucidly insisting that I put Pine-O-Kleen on his hair. Most of the morning is spent in this low comedy. Occasionally, however, he will refuse to be showered. In the time thus freed up, I draft letters of application to Thai universities, just in case Terdsak's dad can't muscle me in.

Eleven-thirty am. Click goes the TV, and on comes one of the daytime television programs that provide the informational intake and world view of Doug. It is accompanied by thousands of switchings-on in Edwardstown, Mitchell Park, Ascot Park, Woodlands Park and Forestville. In these wastelands, seventy-five percent of the population is over seventy-five. Meanwhile, in the poor belt, over a plastic woodgrain table, Deliria works her sales pitch. I think of the young mum, on her second pack of smokes, in a shapeless tracksuit, without even the will to wash her hair, and then I imagine the descent of Deliria like a goddess who has taken mortal form in order to sell DVD players to young mums on single parent benefit.

In the afternoons, with Doug, the emphasis shifts to 'companionship/supervision' rather than 'maintenance'. What this means is that I gabble a lot.

'So,' I gabble, 'one day, Kev and I, we went down to Victor Harbour and we climbed up Granite Island. It was great.'

He doesn't even nod. Apart from a slow heaving of his chest, he could be a piece of photo-realism.

I wonder what Deliria's doing now. In fact, I ask Doug: 'What do you think Deliria's doing now? Do you think she's sold any units yet?'

Zero response. It's like watching cement harden.

I consult the companionship/supervision list. 'So, do you feel like going shopping? What about if I drive you down to the Bay Village?' I callously consult Doug's medical file at a red light. Korsakoff's syndrome, I read. That's booze: cell damage and stuff. Brain lesions. Brain chemistry irreversibly altered. He may as well have been doing amphetamines and crystal meth for the last seventy years. His IQ is halved—he is now less intelligent than an adult chimpanzee. His perception of cause and effect is greatly reduced. Partly as a result, he is just aching to commit simple larceny. In the Bay Village, a display of mineral water attracts him and his one nimble arm. 'Do you want some mineral water?' I ask.

'Ye-es.'

'How much money you got?'

Doug is tilting dangerously towards the display. The once-magnificent upper body now shows a hint of kyphosis. Worse, he can't stop himself from hugging that mineral water to his chest.

'You're not going to cause any problems for yourself, are you, mate?'

'No.'

I don't steal the mineral water for him. I buy it.

What can the old teach us? If this were the twelfth century, plenty. They could tell you, for example, when it was likely to rain, because they could remember the pattern of the seasons for the last fifty years. They could warn you not to trust the Germans because they remembered there had been a war. When bloody black spots appeared on people, they would be able to tell you: *that's the plague—watch out.* In those days you wouldn't be able to read, of course, so you couldn't go and look it up. *60 Minutes* wouldn't do a special on it. You had to ask the old people.

What can the old teach us now? They can teach us that we will be old. They can narrate stories of archival value to those with an interest in, say, the Great Depression. People who can remember the Great Depression can relate things that were not filmed: wheelbarrow-loads of rabbit carcasses in the main streets of Adelaide, that sort of thing. Old people can give us a personal slant on what we've read about or seen on TV. That's about it. They're no longer important in the twelfth-century way. And we don't respect them because we don't have to; because the respect we're supposed to owe them was always, sadly, a function of what they could teach us. Can Doug teach us to set up a website? Can he tell us when the index is going to drop? Can he tell us whether XYZ is likely to be taken over by ABC? Can he tell us if we should be refinancing our houses at the attractive current rates, or waiting until they drop even further? No, he can only tell us the vitally important things: where all past years are, who cleft the devil's foot. We're not interested in that shit.

So, William. You've made the transition from academe to the real world—it's pretty real, taking care of Doug—and you're with Deliria, and nothing bad's happening. Cruel narrative has blessedly absented itself from our lives. Each day bears a family resemblance to the one before and the one after. There is none of this 'God, what's going to happen next?' The police make no appearance. We've reached a sort of Nirvana of eventlessness. This'll do me: the scent of Deliria in bed, the little notes she writes to herself. Yes, a woman's ordinary presence will do me fine, especially when it's this woman. And above all, there is Deliria's hesitant entry into responsible behaviour. She's capable of it. She achieves her sales targets. She never misses a day. She brings home legit dollars. She uses words like 'volume booking', and I have to look them up in a dictionary of Business English.

On one of these eventless days, having just got back from maintaining Doug, I robotically unload the letterbox into the rubbish bin. I dump all the bra catalogues, pizza-delivery flyers, leaflets for lawns mowed and ironing done. I dump the handout 'Is Your Home Really Safe?' (24-hour security service) as well as 'Awake!' (Jehovah's Witnesses) and 'How Serious Are You About Your Scotch?' Not that serious, mate. I then notice a letter on top of what I've dumped. What was a letter doing in the letterbox?

The sleek, Garuda-crested envelope sports Thai stamps, with the most recent image of King Bhumibol. It's not Terdsak's two-weekly package. Its contents could be summarised thus: the Bangkok University of Economics is pleased to offer me, subject to confirmation, the position of lecturer, academic year June to February. There are a lot of amounts of money, which look huge until I remember they're in Thai baht. When I do the conversions, however, it's still more money than recent graduates make in Australia. Plus a living allowance. I read the document five or six times. They go for the high style: 'Your profound knowledge and experience in this field' and 'remuneration' instead of 'salary'. Just Thai rhetoric: it's their standard acceptance letter.

The second item of major importance I find that afternoon is Deliria's cache.

I find it by chance. I'm trying to refuel the lawnmower and the petrol drum vaults out of my hands, swaggers on its rim, and crashes into a cardboard packing case behind the lawnmower, demolishing it, releasing to public view the awful contents. I view the sprawl of stolen goods, its terrible quantity and variety. It's as if a Roman legion has sacked a small-to-medium-sized town and stashed the loot in a tin shed in Bellevue Heights. Since giving up shoplifting, she has shoplifted fountain pens, calligraphy sets, classical CDs, French novels, fashion magazines, personal-growth books, party dresses, Zippo cigarette lighters, sarongs, and a set of 'Teach Yourself Italian' cassettes. In addition to these plural acquisitions, she has stolen a candlestick, a laptop computer, an antique pencil case, a brass vintage car horn, a pewter ashtray, a porcelain vase, a Mexican figurine, a Rolliflex camera, an image of Buddha, a Celtic crucifix, a carved-leather Indonesian shadow puppet, a Georgian vase, a crystal chalice, a hand-painted fox-hunting scene, and a German beer tankard. All those darling little shops on Unley Road. So, here we have a silver pencil case from 1752. George II, right? Guess what she keeps in it: coloured pencils. I heft the pencil case: it must weigh half a kilo.

What was she thinking?

So it continues, and has always been continuing. She has money. She's earning a commission on the DVD players, a substantial wedge of which enters her building society account on the tenth and twenty-fifth of each month. As an adjunct to this commendable industry, this stockpiling against future ills, she steals, whether it's a fountain pen or a postcard or a piece of cheese. One day she will go to a women's detention centre for four weeks. I know this because I've just rung the cops for an estimate, putting on the fifty-year-old voice of a stricken father: 'Officer, my daughter has been caught shoplifting three times.'

Dinner is a successful Lamb Korma, stretching my culinary skills to the max. The wine, a relatively expensive Cabernet Sauvignon, reduces fear, and after half a bottle of the stuff I'm ready to make a pass. As if this were a first date, I put my hand on top of hers. I then give her a business card, which she studies, keeping her eyes on it much longer than is necessary to read it.

'I've heard glowing reports of this woman,' I say. 'Glowing reports.'

She flexes it, and it bellies in and out, convex, concave. It says: 'Dr Sharon Warke. Psychotherapist.'

I play it light. 'You do have an awful lot of pens, baby. We should put on a garage sale. You know: "Calligraphy Lovers—A Dollar a Pen." Donate the proceeds to UNICEF. Raise world literacy.' For once, I'm gabbling, she's silent. The card flexes and winks.

Later, her head pillowed on my Korma-packed stomach, she tells me how she's going to give up shoplifting.

'I'm giving up shoplifting. I have to do it for you, William. I have to think of you. If I won't do it for myself, I have to do it for you.'

Alcoholics are exactly the same: the pledge freshly taken after each bender. Even after this declaration, it's still going to be a new pair of earrings every day, and her cosmetics collection expanding and diversifying in hundred-dollar increments. The magazines stuffed down the back of her skirt, these useless texts, read once or not even once, will just keep piling up in the bathroom, taking up space on the coffee table. And one day soon, I will be siphoning petrol into the lawnmower when, opening a previously unopened cupboard, I will be flattened by fifty kilograms of *Elle*.

I see a point where I may not be able to live with this. 'She' is fine; I can live with 'her'. I love 'her'. It's 'this' I don't like. Kev, low on rapture, high on practicality, says 'she' is 'this'; 'this' is 'her'. I don't know. Would you say there's something missing from his argument?

Somewhere in North Adelaide, sessions begin with Dr Sharon Warke. I don't enquire about their content, and Deliria tells me nothing, which is fine. I have to shut up, because I know these preoccupations with 'why' can become ends in themselves, not means, just ends; and the search for 'why' turns into the unrolling of a tender bamboo shoot—the layers come excitingly away as you discover a nice little bit of information, a clue, and you're picking away with your fingernail where you can't even see an edge, and then presto! Another layer lifts up, translucent, and you get nearer and nearer to the centre, the 'real' bamboo shoot. And when you arrive at the centre, which is nothing, and you're surrounded by all these yellow curls of shoot, which are Deliria, what are you going to do? Put them back together again?

Casino

The good news is, Deliria wants to come with me to Bangkok. The bad news is, you can't shoplift an air ticket. Deliria's skills and audacity mean that she can acquire a variety of goods without paying for them, but as yet, she can't score things like air tickets or houses. She tells me she's not so interested in simple theft any more. She can't be nicking things off shelves like a five-year-old. She's more interested in money these days. So, does her Videotrash job pay enough? Does the Pope have kids?

She wants to win the airfare at the casino. Her Videotrash management have been taking her there, giving her chip-hand-outs and teaching her effective win-systems.

'You've got to come to the casino,' she says, trailing her arm across the breakfast table, peeping over her soft triceps.

I reach for the shield of the newspaper, flapping through it in search of the tiny World News section. I can't find it. I can only find home-electronics advertisements, hair-loss clinic advertisements, casino advertisements.

'I've got this idea that is going to make us so much money.'

I finally locate the World News, a whole three paragraphs of the *Adelaide Times*, squeezed in between 'Water Rates Hike' and 'Obese Mum Sheds Kilos'. 'Prime Minister Damrongsak confirmed that …'

'Why would I want to go to the casino? It's rigged.' I've seen the advertisements: the copious breasts of hostesses floating past on the sides of trams, the cheery slogans.

'You can win. There are guys there who win.'

'Yeah, sure. Have you ever heard of a casino going broke because they had to pay out too much money?'

I'm Xenon-flashed. Comply, comply. All you have to do is comply.

'I mean, wouldn't you like to have enough money to just spend six months in Provençe, for example? Without working illegally?'

I stare at the newspaper. Fourteen-year-old Marisa Woodleigh, of Grange, was rescued from a storm drain.

Deliria recounts casino lore. She has a worrying belief in a man (he 'is really' a lecturer in Probability Theory at the University of Adelaide) who loiters around the Wheel of Fortune with a hand-held computer, documenting random outcomes. She also has a worrying belief in her Videotrash boss, Frank, who is such a successful gambler that he doesn't even need to work any more. She recites his wisdom as if it were the Sermon on the Mount.

'You don't bet on every turn of the wheel. Learn to hold back sometimes. Discipline, my dear Will. Discipline.'

'Yeah, sure. Discipline.'

Another nugget is delivered, glistening with half-learned jargon. With all wheel-based games (roulette, the Wheel of Fortune), there's something about the number three that 'interrupts' the 'natural succession of outcomes'. Whenever the number three comes up you hold your bets for a while, go and have a cup of coffee or something, catch up on the latest political developments in Southeast Asia. When you come back, make safe bets. Ten dollars on red, for instance. Nearly a fifty-percent chance of doubling your money. Only losers bet on their birthdays, their lucky numbers, their addresses, their employee codes. Only losers think they can win at thirty-five to one.

Armed with these guidelines, instead of anything like logic or experience, she, or even I, could make a lot of money on wheel-based games.

The conversation speeds up. 'There's something about a casino that no other meeting place can duplicate. It attracts the widest spectrum of society.'

'So does the beach,' I counter instantly.

'But a casino is the hallmark of a great city,' she thrusts.

I parry: 'No it's not. In fact, the opposite is true. No great cities have casinos.' I thrust: 'Would you call Las Vegas a great city?'

She parries: 'Lots of people go to Las Vegas.' She engages: 'And it's really the only interesting thing about Adelaide. It's the only thing Adelaide's really got that pulls in visitors from interstate and overseas.'

'The beach,' I block. 'Name one big city that's got a decent beach.'

'Sydney.'

I throw down my sword. 'Yeah, all right. Miami. Cape Town.'

'Los Angeles.' She gives me that famous double-rower.

'Da Nang,' I contribute.

'William, how knowledgeable.'

Of course I don't mind going. First, I've never been to a casino. Second, it's probably healthy for me to meet some blokes from the real world, blokes whose main activity is not thinking about Jaufre Rudel. So, she knows I'm going, I know I'm going, but each time my will bends to hers, we have to have this well-conducted swordfight, with blunted foils and plenty of courtly rules. All part of the *joie*, folks.

She gives me a sketch of the casino businessmen crowd: the dark-grey suits, the well-chosen ties, the uniform of wealth. She tells me why they would want an eighteen-year-old woman around them. This should be interesting: why indeed would a bunch of heterosexual thirty-year-old men with lots of money want a beautiful, gorgeously wrapped and penniless eighteen-year-old girl around them? The answer, however, is not the obvious one.

'They want me around them because I'm suitable to be around them. I'm of the same magnitude. I'm not dwarfed. They've got wealth. I've got beauty. You know: Birth, Fame, Wealth, Beauty, Talent. The five cardinal virtues. The hot quintet. Beauty and Wealth hang out together.'

'Same league.'
'Same league.'

We go there startlingly well-dressed. I'm wearing a black wool suit, its price tag a thousand dollars. *If people saw you in a thousand-dollar suit, it would never cross their minds that you were simply a very successful shoplifter.* The vivid green tie is in a Windsor knot; Deliria showed me I was still knotting it in a Help of Christians' knot, a schoolboy's knot. The Windsor knot packs a lot more authority. Ah, the effect of good clothes on the mood. Ask Deliria. She wears a black crushed-velvet skirt and sequinned top. Her legs, those two magic metres, are packaged in their black silk, butterflies perfectly aligned on her ankles. On her waist flexes the meshed steel of a belt. Sadly, scraps of lint adhere to the skirt, the result of me washing her stuff with the towels. Together we begin to pick off the lint, while assessing the merits and weak points of an art video that she 'actually bought'.

We outshine all other passengers on the 216, a feat so easily accomplished, in fact, that it leads to a disturbing question: why, it might be asked, are two such expensively dressed young people not driving a car? You could actually buy a secondhand car for what this get-up didn't cost. Let's just say that we left the BMW at home because we might be doing a bit of drinking. We drink responsibly. We're also afraid of random breath-testing. Why, then, don't we get a cab?

Let's just hope no one asks us any questions.

Entering the marbled foyer of the Adelaide Casino, we progress with linked arms past the job-smiles of the front of house personnel. So, do you get many other leisured rich in here? We turn heads, we redirect conversations. 'Look at *them*,' I overhear. It's pretty silly, I agree, this pretence. I've got about twenty bucks. Deliria's got about five.

From James Bond movies and Casablanca, I'm expecting dinner jackets, smoking jackets, evening wear, exposed cleavages, women with very expensive coiffure casting lingering looks, thin black cigarettes, dark calculating figures half-hidden behind columns, blackjack commentary in French, one or two spies, people with tiny two-shot Derringers strapped to the insides of their wrists, people with throwing knives concealed in their socks. Failing this, if it's not as glamorous as a James Bond movie, then I'd expect a more watered-down, believable, 'real' version: blackjack commentary in mispronounced French, for example; non-smoking signs in several languages.

Everyone is poor. In a clobbering defeat of expectation, the crowd seems to be drawn exclusively from the low- or non-income-earning bracket. The croupiers would certainly earn more. Hunched and intent, his forehead grooved in concentration, a man in drawstring supermarket trousers contemplates the minimum on blackjack. He looks like he should be stretched out in the South Parklands with a flagon of port; he looks like he should be standing up in front of a magistrate, strongly denying that he stole a tin of sardines.

Around the Wheel of Fortune, a woman's throat hangs like a paper bag; the backs of her hands show an impasto of liver spots. Colour is leached from her hair to reveal its mere fragile keratin: the pale blues, greys and whites of old underpants. She holds fewer than ten chips, of the lowest value; she is betting every three spins of the wheel, her careful bets tidied away by the croupier.

Not everyone's poor, or old, though: it just looks that way at first. After a few minutes, a couple of decent suits are, in fact, visible around the roulette table, while examples of expensive casual clothing can be seen at the bar. Fruit drinks with umbrellas are held. Costly behaviours are indulged.

The most well-dressed and attractive people in the room are the croupiers. They look like Coke commercials: they are radiant, young and free. They are all precision, sliding the clinking chips towards the clients, bestowing a job-smile, chopping those banknotes down the chute with the plastic note-chopper, the movements repeated so often they are no longer even thought. Their speech recalls the reassuring friendliness of a TV anchorman announcing a road accident: it contains just the right degree of concern for the tragedies unfolding in front of them. What do they feel, seeing this continually? How can they watch people behaving stupidly, night after night, and respect them?

The idea of chips is clever, I reflect. You wouldn't have the same emotional attachment to a plastic disc as you would to a fifty-dollar note. You wouldn't be able to get rid of a thousand dollars as quickly.

So, what would these heartbreakingly small mounds of chips equate to? Is that a day's work? Two days' work? A week's? Or not even work, but old-age pensions and the dole?

The non-enjoyment is thick, gesture is dulled and slowed: everyone's rolling with the punches. Another fruit drink with its attendant umbrella. Another fifty-dollar note transmuted into discs. Another careful bet raked away.

'This is crap,' I say.

'You're not giving it a chance.'

'I find it a bit mournful, to be honest.'

'You won't find it mournful if we walk out of here with a hundred dollars. It can be done.'

A hundred bucks: now that would be quadrupling our capital.

We encounter the Wheel of Fortune, two-dollar and five-dollar versions. We stand at the two-dollar, shouldering downmarket gamblers. Here, you find people who are not even dressed up, people who can't dress up because they haven't got any clothes. I note the frayed ancient trousers, the shiny knees, the papery fabrics, the twenty-year-old bodyshirts, the tent-like house dresses, the jumpers with cigarette burns, the tracksuit pants, the zippable plastic cardigans, the brown plastic sandals worn with light-blue socks.

'It's ridiculous,' comments Deliria. 'No one here has any class whatsoever.'

Is the logical step, departure, taken? Guess.

She wiggles further in towards the betting table, through those cardiganed, tracksuited shoulders. Next to her is an Italian kid, very young, his jaw still emerging from adolescent fat. He's just won a hundred bucks. Good on him. With it, he might be able to buy a decent jumper.

Deliria congratulates him. He stumbles his thanks: he is shy. Or it's the Xenon flash of beauty close up. The ratchet of the two-dollar wheel shrieks again, while male and female croupiers perform their smiles. When the ratchet stops, the Italian kid has won another hundred bucks. His CBD of chip-skyscrapers is graced by another office tower. Nice one. I like the back of his hand as it enfolds his chips. It's a Kev hand, a big trustworthy work hand, a picking-up-pipes hand, tanned even over the olive. On its broad, brown surface alights the white moth of Deliria's hand.

'Can you spare a couple of chips?'

Leaving Deliria to chat up the Italian kid, I consume a ridiculous cocktail with too much ice and not enough alcohol. After ten minutes Deliria arrives. The Italian kid, she tells me, has no class whatsoever, and she's lost the two chips. When is Frank going to turn up? What's happened to Frank?

'I think I'd like to go, actually.'

'You haven't given it a chance. It's so early. Nothing is happening. These places never get going until about eleven.'

'I just want to go somewhere I *like*.'

'Just give it a chance. You're not one to wimp out, Will.'

'I'm *not* wimping out.' Jesus, I'm raising my voice. 'Do you have any idea of how ridiculous you looked over there? Dressed like a million bucks asking for two chips.'

'Shh. Everyone's looking at us.' Then she must realise something. She makes some clicking noises, chiding herself I think, tongue loud against palate. She steps back from the fight we're very obviously about to have. 'Okay, you're right. It was a mistake.'

'Deliria.' The name is spoken behind me, in a light German accent.

'Frank, baby. Frank, this is William.' I complete my turn. I'm Xenon-flashed (male version). This guy could model suits for Daniel Hechter.

'William,' the perfect teeth smile. 'Yes, she's told us heaps about you.'

Frank's colloquial Australian meets the pronunciation of a German film star.

'Lads might not be on their way,' he continues to the room generally. 'Just got pulled up by a radar.'

'Vlad the Lad, Marcus the Carcass,' Deliria subtitles. 'The sales team.'

What do people talk about when they don't know each other that well? They go for the common ground. Between me and Frank, the common ground is this terrifyingly thin isthmus: ironing. I can see that, like me, he's in the habit of ironing his own shirts: there's a crease across the collar. Perhaps, I suggest, if he does the reverse side of the collar first, as I do, he might obtain a crease-free result. He ponders this, thumb and forefinger framing the sculpted jaw. 'I'll try it,' he announces. That about wraps it up for the common ground.

Frank receives a mobile telephone call. 'It appears our lads have been done.' He begins to curse the South Australia Police, focusing on their attention to speed limits. Deliria's looking at me encouragingly. Go on, William. Say something interesting.

'The trouble with the South Australia Police,' I open, 'is that they think they have to enforce the law. They don't really have the concept of a non-enforced law here. In many countries around the world you can go any speed. If this were Thailand, for example, you could go a hundred and forty down Anzac Highway as long as you didn't have an accident.'

I have Frank's full attention. 'A hundred and *forty*?' Deliria bestows a double-rower.

'Adelaide roads are built for speed,' I continue. 'Wide, well-sur-
faced, not that many curves. Dual carriageways, quite often. You
look at, say, Marion Road. No one in Thailand would even think
of going down Marion Road at less than a hundred and ten.'

Frank gives vent to much reverent swearing in his light accent.
I've hit the spot: he is a petrol-head. I feed his addiction with stories of a land where no one gives way to pedestrians, where police
can be bribed with lunch money, and where everyone drives to
work at a hundred and forty.

Common ground finally established, Frank does his bit at
firming it up. 'Training was superfluous,' he says of Deliria. 'It's
just *in* her.'

Well, I'm not going to discuss the ethics of the single-mum
target group with a man who's just bought me an expensive drink.

Keno? Two-up? Blackjack? Roulette? Or what about Wheel of
Fortune, upgrading ourselves to the five-dollar version? Frank,
in an Armani form-fitting jacket which offhandedly displays his
athlete's shoulders (oh no, not *another* Theseus), flings down a
handful of hundreds, not even counting. A collective intake of
breath is heard: some of these people haven't even seen a hundred-dollar note before. The notes are transmuted into chips.

'I think I'll just watch,' I disclaim, but really I just can't bear the
thought of smoothing out a scrunched five-dollar bill on the felt,
enduring the knowing expressions of the croupiers.

Deliria doesn't come up against the low-denomination problem: Frank slides her a couple of chips with a casualness that suggests he's done it before. She places her tidy bet at five to one. The
wheel is spun. Its colours merge into white, the numbered nails
repeatedly thwack the leather stop, these impacts blending into a
single tearing note, then separating as the wheel slows. Where's
that Italian kid, I wonder. Cleaned out? Sensibly gone home with
a bankable hundred dollars? The wheel stops. Deliria has pulled
it in at five to one. She's sitting on fifty bucks. Again, the ratchet
tears the air over the sprawl of bets. This time Deliria has made

a safe bet—even numbers—but with everything she's won. The wheel continues almost frictionless, as if it could go on for weeks. Every wheel is different, she has said to me, with her small but growing stock of casino superstition: every wheel has a personality. Now, spokes of colour appear out of the white blur, infrequently at first, then more and more often, until quite suddenly we can see them all, and numerals circle into visibility. It's going to be a red. It's going to be a red. The little racing car of the jackpot logo passes slowly through the ratchet, eliciting a sharp inhalation, then a long, slow letting-out of breath, as it swings out on its wide orbit, not to return again on this spin.

The wheel stops on zero. The female croupier gives a nurse's smile, and rakes up every last chip on the table.

Slammed by the loss, we hang around the bar. After all, only losers bet on every turn of the wheel. We manage a few crap conversations, the kind that die after six or seven exchanges. Topic: clientele. 'Look at that guy.' Topic: decor. 'Nice sense of space, don't you think?' Topic: alcohol. 'Yeah, Jack Daniels is really good if you're dancing,' I say. I have never even tasted Jack Daniels, I just heard someone say that once. If you could hear yourself on tape, William. During these painful routines we are joined by a friend of Frank's; you could usefully describe him as the Unknown Businessman.

There's one thing Deliria has taught me that I think is pretty useful: the technique of instantly sizing up someone's income, based on the value of clothes worn. See the Unknown Businessman's suit: it's bespoke tailoring. Though he boasts a forty-four-inch waist, it doesn't slop over the front of his trousers like the unfortunate guts of blokes you see in the street. That's two grand. Most businessmen have six suits, so that's $12,000 just on suits. The percentage of income spent on clothes is ten percent, so that's a minimum income of $120,000 a year. Unless, of course, he is simply a very successful shoplifter.

So what's Deliria doing? At the moment, she's behaving like a pamphlet titled, 'Do you Have a Gambling Problem?'

'I could have *had* that hundred dollars,' she says to Frank, exhibiting the textbook behaviour pattern. She hits Frank up for a couple of chips. In five minutes she's lost it all. I buy a double Jack Daniels and throw it back in one.

At least Frank is behaving sensibly: he's getting us out of the casino. With his blinding smile, he announces that we can all go to the Nikkei and 'just hang' at the Unknown Businessman's suite. A warning bell tinkles: I have to be up at six, or face the consequences of Doug grappling with the shower by himself. I explain this to Deliria, breathing the whisky over her face.

'But you've never seen a suite at the Nikkei,' she replies. 'Wouldn't you like to further your experiences?'

In a few minutes, we're wrapped in the smell of the leather upholstery in the Unknown Businessman's car, moving down the abandoned streets to the Nikkei. The vehicle ascends into the carpark, circling repeatedly. Half the building is carpark. We get out on 8A. Nice to see you, 8A. The Unknown Businessman (let's call him Dave) enters a lift with Frank, obediently followed by William and Deliria. The lift, containing a couple of extras from a Korean tour group, soars. The polished but unreflective metal of the lift doors refuses to show me anyone's face. The lift slows queasily. I should not have drunk that Jack Daniels. The retarded simulation of an American voice announces: 'Thirty-eth floor.' The doors slide apart. Deliria, Frank and Dave issue through them. I manage to step on one of the Korean tourists' duty-free shopping bags. In drunken apology, I bend down to pick it up, and hit my forehead on the cutting edge of his telescopic camera lens. The lift doors start closing with smooth inevitability. I'm hurled forwards with ridiculous purpose. The doors clamp around my body, then spring apart, generating yelps of concern from the tourists. Ejected from the lift, I see myself in a mirror wall.

Ever cut yourself on the forehead? I'm fascinated by the perfect semicircle of this cut, the way it's been punched into the skin, the way the blood flows smoothly and quickly downwards from the edges, like rain sliding down a window. I look like I've just been given a backyard lobotomy.

At the end of the corridor, Dave produces the key. A competent snick of the lock is followed by the trio's disappearance into the room. Deliria calls to me to hurry up. I move unsteadily along the corridor, passing the soothing Impressionist prints. Behind Dave's door I can hear bland mood music, the kind of vacuous shit that is welcomed in Pacific Rim countries. Deliria would hate it.

I have a strong and very untimely urge to throw up. I run back to the lift and press the button, but it's hopeless. In the fire exit I deliver myself of a stomachful of puke. Disgracefully emptied, I turn to the fire exit door. It seems to have … it's got no handle on this side. Jesus, it's a *fire exit* door, William. It's one way. Suddenly, I'm sprinting down the staircase, swinging on the banister at the turns. There must be a kilometre of stairs. I emerge at street level, re-enter the hotel foyer and crawl up the lift with another Korean tour group, stopping at every floor.

Dave's suite is what you would expect from hotel rooms that you've seen in films: the wall featuring three landscape reproductions with the artists' names in big letters, the real wood of the writing desk, the intimidating sound system with controls few people really understand. In this lavish anonymity, Deliria is sitting next to Dave on the couch, on the coffee table in front of them a tray chess-gamed with small bottles of just about everything. On another couch, Frank reveals an alcoholic streak: he's made a large dent in a bottle of gin.

'And do you always stay here on your visits?' Deliria asks Dave, with a smile that she really shouldn't be giving him.

Dave starts rambling in the affirmative, lurching into a paceless anecdote. In the Nikkei wine bar, there is a special glass engraved with his name. They will keep it for six years. He says this about eight times.

I manage a few more pretend conversations with Frank. Topic: Central Market. 'It's one of the few places you can get decent caviar.'

Deliria wants to get Dave's special wine glass sent up. She is on the phone to room service. 'Oh hello, Karen, baby, I wonder if you would mind ...'

Frank and I are 'just hanging' on the couch. 'What happened to your forehead?' he asks, noticing for the first time.

Dave's night is accelerating, Deliria-style. 'I can't drink red wine on top of scotch,' he slurs, even as the engraved glass and uncorked bottle have been placed in front of him. Deliria pours. 'Maybe just half a glass,' he acquiesces, as the level of red wine climbs to the rim.

'To the success of your business trip, then.'

Dave drinks obediently, half-emptying the glass, which is instantly refilled. Deliria drinks water.

Deliria takes Dave out onto the balcony 'to observe the stars'. The bottle of wine is perched on the ledge, just crying to be elbowed off. To escape this, and to avoid another mutually embarrassing conversation with Frank, I retire to the bathroom, where, after giving my cut forehead a pat with a wet flannel, I just sit on the toilet seat. From this vantage point, I see yet further evidence of Dave's wealth: a single large bottle of Horos de Cuir. If he spends that much just on the act of shaving, however drunk he might be tonight, he'll be sober in the morning, and a lot richer than me. Exit the bathroom.

While Deliria and Dave have been observing the stars, Dave's bespoke-tailored arm has encircled Deliria's waist. It's not revolting, not really: I think Deliria's just being polite. But I wonder when she'll start to swing away a bit, not so urgently as to suggest disgust. (Rule no. 1: Deliria—'Never humiliate a wealthy businessman in his own hotel suite.') I look to Frank for a solution, but he's gone, taking the gin bottle, leaving nothing but the impression of his body on the couch, and a butt in an ashtray. Well then, exit Frank.

Deliria comes up with a solution to the problem that doesn't involve humiliating Dave. She topples the wine bottle off the thirtieth floor.

Something is happening to Dave's shape. Strength goes out of it like a sigh; his fearsome weight drags him down, and he slumps to a kneel, his face resting between two columns of the balcony. Still conscious, he tries to recover himself by pushing against the concrete: he succeeds only in toppling backwards. The sound of his upper body hitting the ground is unexpectedly loud, like that of a bale of wet laundry hitting a pavement.

'Let's go, Will.'

'Is he okay?'

'Let's just go.'

I take a closer look at Dave. His right leg is extended. His buttocks, and most of his hundred-and-forty-plus kilos, rest on his left leg, which is bent double. Soon, no blood will circulate in that leg.

'We can't leave him like that. His leg'll go necrotic.'

'William, what are you doing?'

I'm wrestling with Dave. I'm behind him, the wall of the balcony scraping my back. I've got my arms around his body; my hands meet and join across his considerable chest. Dave, in the full bloatedness of his prosperity, is not helping me very much. I do a stand-and-turn, get him off the balcony, and lay him out on the floor of the suite. He'll be all right. In the morning, he'll still have both legs. As an afterthought, I take off his jacket and rearrange him on his side with pillows, in case he pukes while unconscious and drowns in his own vomit, as he fucking well deserves to.

At three am, Victoria Square displays its merciful indifference. The fountain is still there, floodlit. Nothing has been disturbed by our stupidity. The birds will wake up in the morning the same;

there will still be dogs barking and junk mail. Deliria will still go to Videotrash; the young mums will still be poor, still reading crap newspapers and smoking twenty cigarettes at breakfast.

Sleep-deprived, with the tinkling alarm bell now a clanging hangover, I review the events of last night while shepherding Doug through Bay Village. How do you feel about it, Will? Amused? Alarmed? Amused and alarmed? Very angry? Are these events simply what you can expect when you're with a woman who is something that other men crave? If she were just ordinary, like Kev's girlfriend, or even just good-looking, like Prue, none of this would be happening. *This* would include such gems as The Italian Kid and the Unknown Businessman. (I can just imagine the latter gentleman picking himself up, very creased, purple-faced, with a hangover rivalling my own.) So, is this normal? Is this 'what happens'? Or is this shit?

Most of us look okay, and to some extent this determines what happens to us. If you look like Kev's girlfriend, you'll get a steady job and your life may be incident-free. If you look like Prue, you'll probably end up with a presentable boyfriend, someone who looks roughly of the same magnitude. If you are genetically incomplete, your life will be fucked. Whereas if you look like Deliria, your life is going to be off the scale, full of incident, sparks, variety, disturbance, clamour, broken hearts strewing the pavement. This is normal.

My goal recedes

Kev and I sit watching a crap video: black cops beating up white suspects. On the table are the traditional strewn handfuls of Krunchy Krisps, a full ashtray, a depleted pack of smokes and five or six crumpled beer cans.

We talk about unrealistic fictionalisations of cops, before moving on to one of Kev's favourites: unrealistic movie depictions of snipers. Did I mention this before? You've seen them, so Hollywood-serious, squinting down the lens of a telescopic sight, closing one eye, thus tightening the muscles of their faces, which in real life would ruin their aim. Kev reckons all movie snipers should do six months' training with the Australian Army Reserve. I couldn't agree more, mate.

So this is what we're doing: drinking, smoking and watching TV, talking about such ludicrous items as movie snipers, when Deliria telephones to inform me that she is at the Glenelg Police Station.

So, it's finally happened to her. All those clever evasions through handy fire exits in department stores conclude in this: all that time she put in, learning how to dodge videocameras, learning how to inhale the coveted item into her handbag, learning how to store small valuable objects in the fingers of a glove—all that work results in this. All the cleverness, the skills, the insane bravado; all the talking to people, making friends with people as she stole from them; all her genius for the five-minute friendship—all is wasted; the world she has created for herself in the corners of boutiques and change rooms is nothing, and her discoveries, nothing. And my own strength, or my fixity, in keeping her clear of the police, is nothing.

And what was it this time? A collection of Lithuanian postage stamps?

I start Kev's motorbike. How do we describe the starting-up of motorcycle engines? Some people say they roar into life. This one, naturally obeying the pathetic fallacy, whimpers. Something's wrong with the petrol feed. The bike limps down the street, then suddenly, whatever was blocking the feed line is shaken loose, the machine suddenly accelerates, and I'm going a lot faster than I should be.

Ever ridden a Japanese racing bike while drunk? Don't try it. I manage to mount the footpath at a merry eighty K's. In front of me are two plastic rubbish bins that are not where they should be. Actually, I'm not where I should be. The rubbish bins dive to either side of the bike. The front wheel busily locates potholes and roots of street trees, drains, someone's lawn sprinkler, council saplings, a couple of bricks and a pile of newspapers. A terrified cat zips under a parked car. The front wheel bursts open a plastic garbage bin. Scraps of food splatter the visor of the motorcycle helmet. Going over a hefty tree root, I pancake my balls on the petrol tank. A metal pole comes up. God, that's all you need to complete your life: a metal pole. I stick on the brakes, and the whole rear of the bike flips sideways, dodging the pole. I flounce back onto the road and get back under the speed limit.

What has she done?

Wait a minute: why am I even in a hurry? I have this illusion that by getting there quickly I can solve the problem; just by trying, I can force that swarm of bees back into the hive; just by trying I can unsting her, she won't have to go through this. She can be back there among the barbecues and the blackened chops and the exploded sausages, young, unformed, undamaged, running under the sprinkler on summer's bleached back lawn, speckled with couch-grass blades, her hips like a pencil, innocent of any crime, wearing beach shorts with plastic animals sewn on them.

I see her fleeing past me, pursued by a cloud of bees that are her own demons, all the sins that she has committed, and have been committed on her, wanting to catch her up and demand recommission. I'm running after her over the lawn, trying to save her life again; with a simple hoot of an ambulance she'll be fine, she'll be right, mate; but she's running away from me, leading the cloud of bees, and I fall behind, watching the grown woman recede down the clipped nature strips.

Face it, William, you can't do anything. There comes a time when you've just got to stop trying.

Then, in a brief yet intense encounter, the median barrier of Anzac Highway chews through the knees of my trousers, and snaps off Kev's rearview mirror.

When people escape the consequences of their actions, they think it's great: they chortle the details, they really let you know how clever they are. They treat you to a detailed narration of how the threat, arrowing in at them like one of Kev's crossbow bolts, was deflected like a mosquito, just waved away by their own expertise. Such narrations would include the rear-exit escape from CDXpress, and in the more distant past, the escape from the Melbourne shoe shop, elegant as anything, as crisp as the step of *allegro* heels on a morning pavement.

When they are caught, on the other hand, when they are interviewed by the police with a tape recorder, when they are released on five thousand dollars' unconditional bail, clams could not be more reticent.

I interrogate her in Doug's kitchen. Doug watches intently enough, as a dog might.

'What did you do?'

She jerks her head from side to side. Well, this is really productive.

Now that the alcohol has started to leach out of me, and I'm less numb, my right knee has really started to hurt. I have one of those zany, inappropriate thoughts: what if Deliria is of no future consequence to me, but my knee feels like this for the rest of my life?

'You can't make it go away by not telling.'

'I have to exercise a woman's privilege.'

'Did you get caught shoplifting something?'

'No.'

'What was it this time?'

'It's not that.'

'What is it?'

She is pulling strings of twisted-together cotton from the kitchen tablecloth, rolling them into balls between her thumb and fingers, and flicking them under the dining room table, where they sit.

Oh Christ. I finally get it. 'Is this about last night?'

She pulls at the tablecloth. I put to her again the final, humiliating questions.

'This is about last night, isn't it?'

'Yes.'

A bottle of wine later, she begins to talk. The Unknown Businessman, Dave, offered her two thousand dollars while I was in the toilet. Then he passed out, brain-dead from alcohol. While I was arranging his near-corpse, she removed the money from his jacket pocket. After all, he was going to give it to her anyway. When he woke up (she surmises), he found himself short of a brick of fifties, and called the CIB.

'I don't believe it. I don't fucking believe it.'

'He was going to give it to me.'

'Jesus. He wouldn't have missed a hundred, but for two thousand of course he'd call the CIB.'

'He said he was going to give it to me.'

'You're insane. He knew Frank.'

'He *said.* He was going to give it to me.'

'The cops. I mean, look at your record. Who were they going to believe?'

Time for damage control. What can we do? Get drunk.

Fairly soon, we have emptied three bottles of wine. So, I wonder what Frank's doing now. Frank, with the elegant male-model look, making thousands a week out of desolate young mums.

'He doesn't win at the casino,' I realise drunkenly. 'He just rips off single mums.'

'He does win at the casino.'

'Maybe. Not as often as he claims.'

'He's a sick guy anyway.'

We have one of our dear old conversations, climbing in artifice. We imagine Frank, soon to be arrested, the back seat of his car awash with credit cards stolen from old women in nursing homes (his latest scam, we fantasise), doing a runner for New South Wales in his BMW, leaving behind Videotrash, the sales team, the lucrative young mums, the casino, and the thwacking ratchet of the Wheel of Fortune. It's a beautiful conversation.

'I think the cops are going to try to get you for larceny or something,' I say.

Deliria's shoulders go into spasm and she starts crying, the mucus pouring from her nose. She wipes off the stuff on the back of her hand, like a child.

I continue, inexpertly toiling away. 'But a good lawyer, like Angela, will hammer the fact that he offered you the money. "Middle-aged businessman thinks he can throw money around and entrap beautiful young girls": that's newspaper headlines, in Australia. And also, she'll convince the court that you didn't do any *more* than what you did. You didn't plan it, for example. That wine bottle. You wouldn't have done that if you'd planned it. And what about that night-staff girl? Why would you draw attention to yourself like that, if you were going to rob him?' I conclude my presentation with a confident plug. 'Angela's *very* competent.'

She grins for the first time today. 'The man who speaks from experience.'

'Yeah, thanks.'

We are suspended like a jewel of rainwater on a barbed wire fence after a thunderstorm, gathering our weight for the earthward plunge. We will go back to Angela and associates, and pay thousands of dollars for their expertise. There will follow months of dread, months of fear put off, as time flows glacially towards the court appearance. And then what? A reduced sentence? Case dismissed? I don't know. I can't help her anymore. Angela can help her. I can only love her; I can't help her.

Angela

I can't be fucked taking public transport to a legal appointment, so I steal Doug's car and drive Deliria into town to see Angela. A lot's been going on over the last twenty-four hours. I must admit, I really took charge. Deliria, as panicky as the Emperor Vitellius, was preoccupied with trifles: that her parents had finally found out about her secret life, that Kev had told her she was 'fuckin' insane' to her face, and that I was going to abandon her and do a runner to Thailand (well, to be honest, I had thought about it for five seconds). But as soon as I looked up 'larceny' on the Internet, I told her she had to write down everything, from the moment the Unknown Businessman rolled up at the casino, until the moment the police let her go. So Deliria has written down this lengthy account, with several different stolen calligraphy pens, on practically a whole ream of A4 paper, which she now clutches in one of my document cases. She's going to read it to Angela *ASAP*, i.e. as soon as I can find a carpark.

You see, it's quite possible the police can't make the charges stick. It's quite possible Deliria hasn't broken the law.

Angela, with her efficient-looking, hundred-dollar haircut, takes one look at Deliria and gives me a small, confidential smile that says, '*Yes. I can see exactly why you refused to cooperate with the police.*' We're welcomed into the calm, professional suite and Deliria begins to comment on the beautifully restored colonial bluestone mansion, and on the mix-and-match copper fireplace, as if they mattered. Angela politely goes along with this delay tactic for a few exchanges (she must have been through this a thousand times), before saying, 'Well, shall we begin?'

'I'm sorry. I'm just a bit nervous.'

'Yes, I perfectly understand that. It's quite natural to be nervous.'

'Is it all right if I have my future husband with me?'

This way she has of dropping enormities on you …

'Certainly. That's quite in order.'

Then, after she's done all this nesting business in Angela's office, fiddling with a desk calendar and picking up an 'adorable little photo' of Angela's niece, Deliria starts reading her story.

When she gets to the part where Dave started fondling her bottom while I was in the toilet, and where Frank took that as his cue to leave the building, I feel a pure chemical rage in my stomach. On mature reflection, however, I'm glad I didn't see those events, because if I had, I would almost certainly have kicked Dave's teeth in, and then I'd have been charged with aggravated assault and probably have had to pay for twenty grand's worth of dental work.

Deliria talks faster than a DJ on speed. Angela's doing that women's listening thing: nodding, direct eye contact, saying 'yes' and 'mm-hmm', 'you poor thing', supportive aphorisms, the whole lot. A brilliant listener, never interrupting.

'And then I sort of pushed his hand off, and then he did it again, and then I pushed his hand off again, and I almost slapped him but you don't go humiliating a wealthy businessman in his own hotel suite, do you, it could be so dangerous. So he sort of settled for putting his arm around my waist, which was really, really unpleasant, and then I thought, God, I hope Will comes out of the toilet, I *so* don't like the way this is going, and then Will finally came out of the toilet, and then I pushed the wine bottle off the balcony like a signal to Will, you know? Help, it's going wrong, it's going really seriously wrong. And all I wanted to do was to get out of that hotel room, I was *so* over this wealthy businessman thing that I said to Will, "Let's go", twice. But then Will starts picking this guy up, because he's collapsed on the balcony, I'm not sure exactly about this part but you can get that from Will, and then Will had taken off the guy's jacket and I saw this billfold fall out on the floor and I thought, *Excuse* me, but you *promised* to give me that money, you *promised*. You actually *said*: "I like you. I'm going to give you two thousand dollars." His exact words. He said that *five times.*'

'He *said* that. That's important. Please continue. Tell me everything, Deliria.'

'Okay. So, while Will was settling this guy, I counted out exactly forty fifty-dollar notes and put them in my handbag. And there was also quite a lot left, too. That billfold was absolutely nine months' pregnant with cash. Then finally we left. And then the police thing happened.'

Deliria then launches into another pretty detailed narrative about the police interview, and Angela's being very supportive. Then Deliria starts crying, telling how the police threatened her with five years in Adelaide Women's Prison, and had laughed openly when she suggested that Dave had offered her the money. Again, I feel that pure chemical rage. Try assaulting a police officer, William. See where that gets you.

'They always do that,' says Angela gently, as Deliria completely breaks down, completely giving herself over in this voluptuous surrender to grief. 'They *always* do that. Oh, you poor thing.'

Finally, after this tremendous download of information, and a few cups of Chinese tea all round, Angela comes up with an action plan.

'Now then. This is what we're going to do,' says Angela. 'Although I know you want to focus on the sexual assault, and you may even wish to proceed with that later, first we need to focus on the police matter. There's lots of good news. First and foremost, larceny's five things, and the police have to prove all five of them. The police aren't legal experts, which most people don't know, and the boys and girls in blue often get things wrong. That's why people like me have a job. So you "took" and you "carried", as we say. However, this … person … said several times that he was going to *give* you that money, and I believe you one hundred percent, and I can also make the court believe it. When he *said* he was going to give you that money, that's called "consent". So that was, in fact, *your* two thousand dollars, as you rightly believed. Particularly in view of the fact that you removed the exact amount and not any more than that, in spite of the billfold containing approximately five thousand dollars, as you said. So you've got an excellent prospect of beating the larceny charge. For this reason, I'm going to advise you to enter a plea of "not guilty". We've still got some evidence to get hold of, for instance, this "Dave" character … Men like that, it's never the first time for them, so we can almost certainly look forward to obtaining a history of "accosting or importuning for immoral purposes", as it's called.'

'It's disgusting, isn't it?'

'Yes. It's totally disgusting. And illegal, too. So if you *wanted* to go after him, and you *might* be able to … and *I'd* want to … But let's just put that aside for a while and focus on getting you clear of this problem, which you might agree is slightly more serious. Okay? Once we get his history, it's in the bag, as they say.'

Deliria gives Angela the double-rower. 'I'm *so* glad I got that all out into the open.'

'You were well-advised to come here,' says Angela, giving me a nod. 'Well-advised.'

'He's great, isn't he?' says Deliria. 'Did you know he speaks Thai fluently?'

'Marvellous,' says Angela. 'I'm not at all surprised. Okay then, well there's a little bit of witness prep that we'll have to do, a little bit closer to the actual date. William, for instance, you'll almost certainly be needed to confirm Deliria's account, and there might be one or two people from the Nikkei that it might be useful to talk to, but basically, Deliria, you're going to be okay.'

'Thank you *so much* for your help. Isn't she great, William?'

'Yeah, Angela's great, isn't she?' I then look into those strong espresso eyes, just for a moment. 'You've helped us a lot.'

'Good evidence, good detail.'

'Good lawyer.'

Angela gives a significant laugh. 'Thank you. Oh, by the way, this part might interest you, William.'

'What's that?'

'The judge.'

'Oh no.'

'No, no, no, it's not what you think. He *really really really* dislikes police incompetence.'

'Excellent.'

So we leave the 'wonderful bluestone mansion that could actually have been owned by Captain Charles Sturt or someone', and proceed out along the tree-lined pavement in elegant Hutt Street (nothing has ever been as beautiful as that pavement), and I burst out laughing as I find I've scored a parking ticket.

Envoi

Deliria's case didn't even get to court. As predicted, the Unknown Businessman had a history as long as your arm, and the efficient Angela needed to do about fifteen minutes of persuading before the cops dropped the charges. Then, after a six-grand loan from her mum and dad, Deliria no longer had to win her airfare at the casino. Christ, how simple things can be, if you simplify them.

Bangkok. City of Angels, radiant city, royal capital of the nine noble gems. City of traffic, of valleys of car roofs. Unbalanced city, city of vast inequalities. Untidy, beautiful, golden, disorganised. A bit like Deliria … When the sun strikes the hammered-gold roof of Lat Phrao temple in the morning, and there's a blinding light, but there are still bits of guttering falling off, knocking passers-by on the head, I think, 'Yep. That's her.'

And the weather, you ask? The pathetic fallacy is still functioning merrily, providing its continual commentary on our love. Today: 38 degrees. Ninety-percent humidity. No storm warnings. Forecast: many more sweaty nights to come.

We're both working, too, and it's great. Government policy here is *Work or Die*, and it's amazing how inventive it makes you. Deliria has obtained an excellent, highly remunerative position as a pole-dancer (only joking: she's teaching rich kids classical music); I'm teaching English at the Bangkok Uni of Economics. Thanks, Terdsak's dad (whom I've finally met: a jovial chap, only corrupt in order to pay for his fleet of mistresses, nothing sinister).

The shoplifting's stopped. Pretending that we were going to buy wonderful hand-carved ornaments made by disabled people, I took Deliria to Klong Prem Correctional Facility, Women's

Section, where they help each other deliver babies without medical assistance, inject each other with heroin bought from the guards, and, incidentally, make wonderful hand-carved ornaments. Guess what? She didn't steal a thing. She's even started visiting women prisoners in for life. Talk about unpredictable …

Once, I saved Deliria's life from a swarm of bees. And there was that stuff with Angela, when I thought it was the end of everything, and it wasn't. Maybe I've got a bit of physical bravery. Maybe I've got a bit of *savoir-faire*.

But what about this: wouldn't I have lost my sanity in Adelaide without Deliria? I don't know what you think, mate, but I reckon I could have been one of those blokes you read about in a small column of the *Adelaide Times* who tops himself with a shotgun in a garage for no apparent reason. Or perhaps a less gory version: a Prosse, an academic with shelves of texts you couldn't even sell on the Internet. Don't you think Deliria saved me too?

Anyway, I've finally written three courtly love paragraphs for the twenty-first century. I hope you like them. She does.

Deliria's eyes are chrysoprase, like the Coral Sea photographed from space. Sometimes her beauty hits me like a gentle slap, a slap a leopard might give you when it's merely playing around, as when she grins at me over the breakfast table. At other times, when she's just walking down the street causing traffic accidents, it's a hammer-blow, like a jolting realisation of the existence of God.

Her gaze is scorching, like the Australian sun at 3 pm on the hottest day in history. A sun that melts windscreen wipers; a sun that buckles railway lines, derailing commuter trains; a sun that demands rescue helicopters be lined up on hospital rooftops.

And I can meet that gaze forever now. She is my sun. She gives life; she is the source. Every atom, every mountain, every valley, every sea has its origin in her. She is my living fire, my galaxy, my swirling universe, containing all. She is my Virgin, my redemption, my salvation. My Deliria, glorious and flawed. She's The One, O fellow chevaliers who journey through the dark forest of the passions, all trails leading you backwards: she's The One.

Chris Heffernan grew up in Adelaide. Initially he wrote poetry, becoming involved with the Friendly Street group of poets and being published in Australian literary journals. In the early 1990s he moved to Thailand, where he immersed himself in Thai culture and worked for many years in the field of education. In 2007 he returned to Australia with a bi-cultural family in tow. He spent the next several years on the academic staff at the University of Adelaide and writing *Deliria*, his first novel. He was back in Thailand writing his second novel—set in Bangkok and Sydney—when he passed away unexpectedly in 2014, aged just fifty-two.